THE WHEN-WITCH AND THE WOLF

A SHIFTER'S CLAIM NOVEL
BOOK FOUR

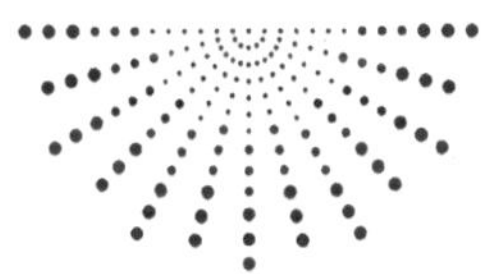

L.B. GILBERT

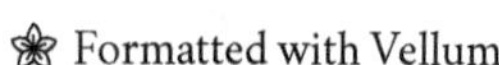 Formatted with Vellum

TITLES BY L.B. GILBERT

The Elementals Saga
Discordia, A Free Elementals Story
Fire
Air
Water
Earth

A Shifter's Claim
Kin Selection
Eat You Up
Tooth and Nail
The When Witch and the Wolf

Charmed Legacy Cursed Angel Watchtowers
Forsaken

Seven Families
To Hell and Back
Don't Touch

Writing As Lucy Leroux

The Singular Obsession Series
Making Her His
Confiscating Charlie, A Singular Obsession Novelette
Calen's Captive
Stolen Angel
The Roman's Woman
Save Me, A Singular Obsession Novella
Take Me, A Singular Obsession Prequel Novella

Trick's Trap
Peyton's Price

The Spellbound Regency Series
The Hex, A Free Spellbound Regency Short
Cursed
Black Widow
Haunted

The Rogues and Rescuers Series
Codename Romeo
The Mercenary Next Door
Knight Takes Queen
The Millionaire's Mechanic
The Billionaire Boss and the Barista

INTRODUCTION

Third in the Columbia Basic pack, wolf shifter Derrick is number one in romance and passion. Determined to find a mate as dominant and fiery as himself, Derrick won't settle for just anyone.

When Derrick and his pack start receiving mysterious text messages indicating impending doom, they realize it's up to them to protect the innocent people who are in danger. With the stakes rising, Derrick is hellbent on uncovering the truth, starting with his new neighbor. Despite her beauty and mystery, there's more she's hiding.

Time-traveling witch, Meghan, has waited forever to meet Derrick, her fated mate through time and space. Finally, he's in her house and in her arms. She'll do anything to keep him there. But she's prey to an evil she can't quite name--and it will stop at nothing to destroy her. Together, the wolf and witch set out to find a future together--despite the odds stacked against them. Can Derrick keep his witch in his own time without losing her to a world where he can't follow?

PROLOGUE

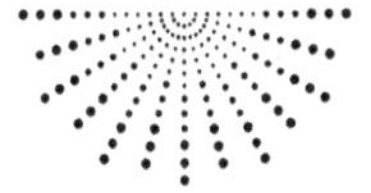

Twenty years ago.

You *are Derrick f'ing Sheridan, and you do not believe in ghosts.*

The stern warning didn't work. Derrick could feel a cold sweat dampening his thick cotton sweatshirt, and for a second he contemplated running. But he didn't. He was a werewolf after all. His uncle was the chief for crying out loud. So, he would *not* run.

Then his sensitive hearing caught *that* noise again, and he tensed despite himself.

It was definitely a shout, but one that cut off abruptly, like someone slamming the remote's off button because the TV came on at full blast.

You can't run.

The plaintive voice sounded female. Derrick might not be as big or as strong as some wolves, but he was no coward. If somebody needed help, then he had to stand his ground.

Derrick waited for the noise to come again, claws out as he

strained his ears, but all he heard were the normal night sounds of the woods.

It must have been the wind, he told himself. Derrick had been camping at higher elevations with his family. He knew how the wind could sound like a person shrieking when it blew between the rocks a certain way.

There was something about this clearing that made the wind do the same thing. That was what his cousin Connell said and why Derrick hadn't turned down the dare from the Jessup brothers to sleep out here all night.

But now sneaking out of his house to spend the night in the Haunted Hollow felt like a stupid idea. It was cold and dark, and he wasn't even allowed to shift because it was against the rules.

"We'll know if you cheat," Levi Jessup had said, poking him in the chest. As if being in wolf form meant they didn't get scared. His claws wouldn't do anything to a ghost, which he guessed was sort of the point of the no-shifting rule.

I should have just broken Levi's finger. Next time either of the Jessups poked him like that, he was going to do it, even if it meant getting lectured by his alpha again about controlling his impulses.

Thinking about his uncle pumped him up a little, enough that he stayed where he was. It was starting to get a little less dark, the sky between the trees going dark blue instead of black. It was still cold as a witch's tit.

Hunkering down against a pine's trunk, he pulled up the collar of his jacket and settled down to wait. He'd made it this far. If he could hold out just a little longer, dawn would be here, and Levi and Gus could eat it.

He sat there, wishing he'd brought a book. The terms of the bet didn't allow him a flashlight, but there was a bit of moonlight and he had good night vision. But he hadn't brought a book, which was why he was sitting on the ground focusing on every little noise the woods were making around him.

"Con—"

Derrick jumped up so fast he scraped the back of his jacket on the rough bark.

Shit. He couldn't tell himself that was the wind. It hadn't been as loud as the shriek—more of a ragged whisper. Also, it had been a man's voice this time. A weak and utterly creeptastic one.

His breath was coming in pants now. *I will not run.*

Then Derrick caught a flicker out of the corner of his eye. He was desperately trying to convince himself it was a trick of the moonlight when a ghostly white face popped in and out of existence thirty yards away.

Yelping, he pivoted and ran pell-mell up the hill. He'd just made it over the ridge when he tripped on a big tree root. Flailing, he lost his balance, rolling down the steep incline and landing at the bottom with leg bent awkwardly beneath.

Howling despite himself, Derrick blinked back tears. That snap hadn't been a tree branch. He'd broken his leg. he swore in agonizing pain, using a word that would get him grounded if his mother heard it.

He twisted to look back, but the ghost wasn't there watching him.

That was enough for him to get a grip. Breathing slow and steady, he managed to make his racing heart slow, but once the adrenaline faded he was shivering and unable to block out the pain.

Stripping down wasn't easy, especially when he had to work his jeans down over his broken leg. It hurt like a son of a bitch. It hurt even more to rip his new jeans open with his claws, because he knew his mom was going to tan his hide.

Once he was naked, he took a shaky breath and rolled over onto his stomach. He shifted with a grunt of pain. Derrick couldn't run on three legs, but he could limp out of here. It was better than hopping on one foot.

Lips set in a grim line, he started up the ridge, trying to pick the easiest path. But his progress was slow and painful.

A shower of stone rained down on him. Startled, he looked up, baring his teeth and growling.

"Derrick," Connell exclaimed. His cousin scrambled down the ridge, concern stamped on his face. "What the hell happened?"

Whining, he lifted his muzzle and gestured with his head toward his broken leg. Connell let out a swear of his own and finished hustling down. Blessed with above-average werewolf strength—being the chief's son had perks—Connell picked him up, muttering the whole time about jerks.

Derrick was pretty sure he was talking about Levi, but he let out a whimper of protest regardless.

"I'd ask how this happened, but you should wait to shift," his cousin advised.

Weres almost always healed more easily as wolves, and at this age Derrick was lighter in his animal form. That wasn't always a given, but their muscles were pretty dense either way.

Connell didn't have a problem with his weight, but the ridge heading to the house was unstable. He stumbled once, sending a jolt of pain through Derrick's whole body.

"Sorry," Connell apologized as they topped the ridge. "But you're lucky. I was out for the night and then someone came by and decided to try and break my window."

Derrick hmphed, the sound close enough to *"What?"* for his cousin to understand.

"I was sound asleep, and someone threw a pebble at my window. Two or three actually, hard enough to mark them. But when I looked, they had taken off. I thought it might be you. That you wanted company, so I came out to check. But I guess it was Molly. Or maybe it was Lisa," he said, naming two of his female admirers.

It was gross how many girls made total fools of themselves over Connell, something his cool cousin took in stride, never embarrassing the girls who chased him even when they did annoying shit like this. But it *was* lucky for Derrick one of the worshipping hordes had gone and woke him up, otherwise he'd be limping all the way home.

Connell got him to the clinic, and he shifted back to two legs so he could get fitted for a cast.

The multi-story building functioned as a small hospital, but wolves had a long memory and most remembered this as a shack where they had come for rudimentary care. A three-story modern medical building now stood in the shack's place.

"I can lie, you know," Connell said, giving him a crooked grin when the doctor was done. "A half-hour longer and you would have made it all night and won the bet."

"That is practically all night," he agreed. "I'm going to call it a win."

"Well, I'm not going to contradict you. So, what happened? Did something spook you?"

"No. It was nothing like that," he lied. "I was just jogging around for warmth and stepped on loose rock. It slid out from under me, and I lost my balance, landing wrong."

Connell sighed in commiseration. "Bad luck."

"Yeah," he agreed. A tiny niggle of guilt made his chest tighten, but he couldn't admit to his older cousin that he actually saw the ghost out there.

My imagination got away from me. That's all.

CHAPTER ONE

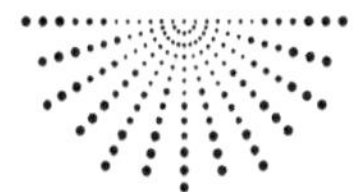

Derrick's phone buzzed for the third time in as many minutes. Neck cording in annoyance, he threw open the door to Jeannie's Deli, standing in the threshold as he fished the slim device out of his pocket. He narrowed his eyes at the nonsense on the screen—a string of numbers. Dismissing the text, he growled, startling a man who was exiting.

"Sorry," he called behind himself after a quick sniff confirmed the human wasn't pack.

The stranger ignored him, walking away very quickly with his ham sandwich clutched to his chest. Derrick didn't blame him. His growl didn't sound remotely human and for good reason.

Irritated, he dismissed the message and ducked inside so he wouldn't let out the air-conditioned coolness that was so precious at this time of the year.

Werewolves were cold tolerant, but the reverse wasn't true. Come August, even Lake Veris, his hometown situated high in the Rockies, became insufferably hot. *It's almost enough to make a guy shave all his fur off.*

"You gotta watch that growling, Derrick," Jeannie muttered in a nearly subvocal reprimand as he reached the counter.

She wiggled her eyebrows significantly at the mixed crowd scattered across half a dozen tables. Only half of the faces were familiar. And unlike every other time he'd been in here, the werewolves were in the minority.

"When did this place get so popular?" he asked suspiciously.

"Since the summer people started reviewing us on Yelp," Jeannie told him pointedly, but her disapproval lasted only as long as it took her to pick up her order pad.

"The usual?" she asked, always appreciative of a wolf with an appetite.

"Please," he said, giving her his most winsome grin.

Blushing despite the thirty years she had on him, she scribbled out his order and clipped it to the wheel suspended over the passthrough window. George, Jeannie's son, took one look at the order, two triple roast beef sandwiches with light garlic mayo and tomato, and stuck his head out of the window to wave.

"Thanks, G," he signed. "Put some extra aioli on those babies."

"No problem," George signed back. "How was the meeting?"

"*Boring,*" he replied with a shrug.

"Don't jinx it. I like it when things are quiet," Jeannie said, adding her two cents after having caught enough of the conversation to make out what they were signing. "Better throw some salt over your shoulder."

"And mess up your floors?" He smiled for about two seconds—the amount of time it took him to get another text. It was the same string of numbers, but this time they were followed by an entire screen of fire emojis.

Screw this.

Jaw clenched, he deleted the message, blocking the number for good measure. Not that it would do any good. He'd blocked this ass at least five times already. Whoever was sending the texts just changed the sending number and kept messaging.

If this lasted much longer, *he* was going to have to change phone numbers. The idea pissed him off, picturing the headache involved.

This wouldn't be a big deal for most wolves, but his position meant he had to be available to everyone at all times.

Derrick was fourth in the Colorado Basin pack, right behind the chief's kids, Connell and Mara. But with Mara off on an extended honeymoon and Connell's tendency to drop everything so he could take off with his Elemental mate to save the world, Derrick was tied to the home front for the foreseeable future.

The younger members of the pack would take the change of phone number in stride, but werewolves lived a long time. Some of the older members of the pack were alive before the invention of the telephone and continued to eschew technology today.

It had taken some paw-twisting, but the old guard had been given cellphones of their own and instructed on their use. But many didn't use them or the pre-programmed numbers in them. These elders would dial him direct on their rotary phones from memory and would no doubt howl in complaint over having to memorize a new number.

And to think that's the most excitement I can look forward to this summer. Tamping down his irritation, he leaned against the counter and scrolled the news, wondering if he was going to die of boredom.

It was an important job, overseeing the security of the entire pack. But things had been dead quiet, and Derrick was this close to doing something drastic. It was either seed the lake with those pods that funky water fae had left behind to see what hatched...or look up one of his ex-girlfriends.

No, even I'm not that desperate, Derrick told himself. *Mystery pod-hatching it is.*

Sighing, he scanned the crowd for other packmates when his eyes snagged on a small figure in a familiar navy-blue hoodie.

Derrick frowned. The small human female had moved into their territory in the spring. She'd crossed his path a few times that first month, but he hadn't seen her since.

Actually, I've never seen her. Not her face. She had been wearing that ridiculously oversized sweatshirt with the hood. It hid her face more effectively than a cowl.

The extensive covering hadn't been suspicious back in April when there had still been a cold bite in the air, but now? He was tempted to strip off his tank top and go topless to keep cool. Meanwhile, this girl was bundled up like winter was coming, Night King and all.

Derrick made it a point to know all the town's permanent residents, Supernatural *and* human, but he was starting to realize this girl had slipped through his net. He didn't even know where she lived.

He was going to have to rectify that.

But all thoughts of investigating the newcomer flew out of his head the second he saw Edgar McGill shuffling across the parking lot.

Derrick grabbed the two sandwiches Jeannie had just set on the counter and waved a quick goodbye. A short sprint and he was next to Edgar's beat-up black SUV before the man could open the driver's side door.

"Hey, Edgar."

The older wolf looked up, the lines around his mouth and eyes carved more deeply, his usual sun-browned skin now parchment grey. Derrick suppressed a wince. He hadn't seen Leeland's father for a few months, only in passing as they drove past one another.

The last time they had spoken was at the funeral.

"We were hoping to see you at the meeting," he began. Once upon a time, Edgar McGill had been one of Douglas Maitland's most trusted advisors, but ever since Leeland had died his father had become a recluse, rarely leaving his neat two-story Colonial across town.

At least it used to be neat. The last time Derrick had passed by the house the yard had been unkempt—the lawn overgrown with weeds and filled with random bits of trash. One of the garbage cans had been lying on its side in the driveway, the rubbish inside spilling out.

The sudden deterioration had concerned him enough to stop driving. He'd pulled a crushed meat wrapper out from under the wheel of the truck parked haphazardly in the driveway. Edgar must've been aware he had knocked over the waste bin, but he hadn't cared enough to clean it up.

Derrick had picked up the mess, collecting it in the bins before setting them for collection. He'd knocked at the door, but Edgar hadn't answered.

Thanks to his enhanced sense of smell, he'd known the older wolf had been home, but when the door had stayed resolutely closed, he'd left. The grieving father needed a little more time.

His elder looked smaller and faded, almost like a photograph of himself that had been aged by too much sunlight. Derrick's mind dredged up memories of fishing with Edgar and Leeland on the lake or hiking up in the higher elevations.

The formerly hale and hearty man had aged ten years, maybe more. His vibrant red hair was pale and colorless, the grey much more prominent. His skin shared that grey pallor. It also looked so much thinner. The blue veins under the surface were also distressingly visible, giving his skin a new fragility.

Edgar didn't respond to him.

"Can I buy you lunch?" he asked, trying again. He held out the second sandwich hopefully.

His outstretched hand was ignored so long Derrick thought his offering would be ignored, but Edgar accepted the sandwich, mumbling a gruff "thank you."

"We can go inside to eat it," he added, his thumb jerking back to the diner. "I bet Jeannie would love to see you."

Edgar and George's mom had gone to school together, and he'd seen them talking at almost every community event, so he knew they were friends.

But the older wolf shook his head. "Got someplace to be," he rasped.

"Are you sure?" Derrick leaned, reaching out to put his hand on his arm, but Edgar jerked back, raising his hands in a broken gesture.

"I can't." Edgar turned away, blinking. "It's too much. I can't see you and not think of him."

"I know." Derrick's throat was threatening to close up. "But you can't shut yourself away. There are so many people who care about you, who *need* you."

The accepted wisdom among Weres was that there was no smell

for emotional pain and suffering, but Derrick knew that for the lie it was. Edgar's entire body chemistry had transformed this past year, his grief a cologne that clung to him.

Edgar moved closer to his vehicle. His flat and nearly lifeless eyes touched his briefly. "Douglas has been by. No need to worry about me. I'm getting out of town for a while. Need a change of scenery."

"Where to?"

It was damn nosy, but it would have been weirder if he hadn't asked. Pack meant being in each other's business.

Edgar lifted a listless shoulder. "To see my sister."

Derrick racked his brain, trying to remember where Marcie lived. Somewhere in Oregon. "Do you need me to water your plants? It would be no trouble."

But Edgar was shaking his head, getting inside the car. "Got it covered," he said before closing the door. He wouldn't even look at Derrick as he turned the engine on.

Backing off, he let Edgar go with a resigned wave. Hopefully, Edgar's sister would be able to get him to reengage with the world. It would be too easy for the old wolf to lose himself in his grief. Dangerous too.

He didn't think Edgar had the potential to run rogue, but he could pull away, his beast going off into the wild for long stretches until one day he didn't return. His wolf might hunt at first, but he'd stop soon enough.

Then he'd just let himself slip away.

Eventually, they'd find his remains in the woods. It was the way they lost many of the elders when their mates and loved ones were gone. But the pack was stable and had been for a long time. A wolf like Edgar had dozens of ties in a pack like this. Plus, Douglas was a possessive chief. He didn't let any of his people go without a fight.

God willing, Edgar still had a lot of good years ahead of him. Derrick made a mental note to call Marcie's place in a couple of days to see how he was getting on. The database the pack maintained was diligently kept up to date—one of the chief's rules. Her contact information would be there.

While he was at it, he'd find out the new human's name and where she lived. One of his pack mates would have input that information once it was clear she was staying more than a few weeks. The chances of her being a threat were about as likely as her sprouting wings and flying, but crossing every T was part of his job as pack enforcer *pro tem.*

It wasn't like he had anything better to do.

CHAPTER TWO

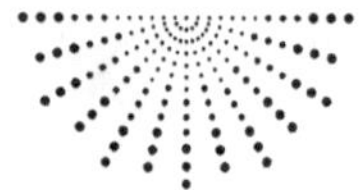

Derrick scowled at Amalia, the current tech geek on call for the pack.

"What do you mean you don't have a record for her?" he growled.

Amalia was a submissive. Normally he would watch his tone with a pack submissive, but Amy was one of the three pack techs. She was part of the team that kept their phones and laptops updated and secure. Amy also doubled as Douglas's secretary, which meant she dealt with dominant wolves all damn day.

Whether it was a local wolf who had to see the chief in person or an irate alpha calling to report a problem he or she couldn't deal with on their own—Amy had seen it all. So she was singularly unimpressed by his bark now, especially since she was well aware no bite would follow.

"I know who you are talking about," she said, cutting him off when he repeated the girl's description for the third time. "But I don't have a name or an address. Just a note that the 'girl in the blue hoodie' rented a cabin on the far side of the lake."

He scowled. "How is it possible we don't have more information?"

At the very least the database should have had the girl's name. The pack owned all of the lakeside property. Renting out those cabins to tourists was one of their money-making ventures. Many stayed occupied throughout winter for humans who came out for cross-country skiing or snowshoeing with their cubs.

They were usually pretty good about keeping tabs on the non-pack population in town. True, humans weren't as closely monitored as the Supernaturals in the area, but they were still observed, just in case.

It wasn't difficult. Like the lake area, most of the property in town was controlled by the pack in some way shape or form. Humans didn't have many opportunities to buy houses in the area by design.

As for other Supernaturals, they were few and far between. Most were aware that this was wolf territory and gave it a wide berth. The few exceptions were those with close ties to pack members, like the gnome who was old friends with Garry, an elder wolf, or Logan, the Elemental Connell had mated. Elementals were a class of witch so powerful even other witches avoided them.

That they had failed to do the basic due diligence on anyone—even a human—was a staggering oversight.

Amy frowned, squinting at her computer screen. "You said the girl was here in the spring and is back again now. Maybe she just rented a vacation cabin twice."

She tapped on the screen, bringing up the rental records.

"Except she hasn't." Her concern deepened. "We don't have any solo renters—everyone is in a family or friend group."

Amy looked back up at him. "Could she be here with other people without our being aware of it?"

"Doesn't mesh with what we know." Every time he'd seen her, she had been alone. Most human females didn't enjoy solitude. Especially young ones like the small stranger.

In his experience, human women in new surroundings sought out friends fairly quickly. And one of the pack's females would have gone out of her way to befriend her if that were the case. It was the sort of thing they did with mysterious newcomers if only to check them out. That and wolves were curious, some would say downright nosy, creatures.

"Okay, it's a little weird no one knows where she lives," Amy admitted, tapping her keyboard absently without pressing down one of the keys. "But I think I know why. The first note about her came from a shopkeeper in April. She'd probably been around a few weeks before that…"

"Which coincides with the time Mara and I went to Europe," he finished with a grimace. He leaned on Amy's desk and scrubbed his face with a hand.

Mara Maitland, the chief's daughter had gone off with Jack Buchanan, a former special forces turned mercenary and security consultant. The pair had been investigating the activity of the Denon, a corporation capturing and illegally experimenting on their kind.

Things had gone to hell fast when Mara had gone missing, kidnapped by the same group. But the chief's daughter had turned the tables on the bad guys. Derrick had helped her and Jack liberate an entire castle full of captured shifters.

"Once you got back, things were a little crazy with Jack and Mara's wedding plans, and the town was hosting all those rescued shifters who needed a bit more time to recover. It's not an excuse, but it explains how she fell through the cracks." Amy tapped a note. "I'm making a note to call a few of the shopkeepers to make sure they try and pump the girl for more information the next time she comes in."

"Don't bother," he said, standing up. "I'm going to go out to the lake to check out all the cabins at the far end."

There weren't many out there. Most of the vacation properties were clustered on one side near the dock and general store.

"I'm afraid that's going to have to wait," a deep voice interrupted.

Derrick's head snapped up as the chief appeared at the threshold of the office.

Douglas Maitland was wearing his usual jeans and button-down shirt with the cuffs rolled up past the elbows. He stood an inch and a half shorter than Derrick, with the same lean but densely muscular build as his son Connell. His hair was a few shades darker—closer to Derrick's, save for the touches of grey at the temples that made him look like a distinguished diplomat or CEO.

But those who saw the classically patrician facade and expected a cool sophisticate were either blind or in for a rude surprise. Douglas's power pulsed under his skin, the force of his dominance like a black hole, a well of gravity so powerful it pulled everyone in around him.

This was why he was the Canus Primus—the leader of all the North American wolf packs. Only his children came close to his strength and level of dominance. By comparison, Derrick was a distant fourth, but that still put him high up in the Colorado Basin hierarchy.

Technically, Derrick was strong enough to lead his own pack. He could have founded his own or taken over a satellite pack in need of new leadership in a different part of their territory.

But so far, he hadn't felt a need to move on. He liked living in the thick of things near his closest relatives. Douglas was his uncle by marriage, and Mara and Connell were his cousins. His parents were away on an extended cruise around the world with some of their friends, but they still made this town their home.

"What seems to be the problem?" he asked. Derrick could tell by the chief's expression that there was one.

Wordlessly, Douglas held up his smartphone. There on the screen was the same message he'd gotten. But it wasn't identical. Douglas's message had a photo attached—a screenshot from a map application. A pin had been dropped in a sea of green.

"Half a dozen pack members have received this text. The number is blocked. The other pack techs can't trace it."

Derrick took the phone from his superior, swearing under his breath. "I thought I was the only one getting this spam."

Except if Douglas was getting the texts as well, then it wasn't as simple as that. Derrick could count the people who had his phone number with his fingers. It was him, his kids, and a handful of elders scattered across the territory. Even most of the pack alphas went through Amy.

And looking at the pin, the light dawned on him. Those numbers he'd dismissed as random gibberish were latitude and longitude, coordinates for the location marked on the pin. Douglas's text also had quite a few fire emojis. More than his.

The chief took the phone back. "Someone wants to bring this spot in the woods to our attention. I want you to drive up there and check it out. Take a second wolf if you feel the need."

He lifted a dark brow. "Backup for a wild goose chase?"

"That's why it's an option. If it were anyone else, I'd insist they not go alone, but it's you."

Derrick accepted the confidence in him with a simple nod. The chief knew his people and their abilities. If the weird texts were some sort of trap, Derrick was more than capable of evading it.

He also had the skills to make whatever enemy might be hiding out there ready to spring a trap on a too-trusting wolf have some serious regrets.

"I'll take care of it now."

Douglas nodded and turned to Amy.

"Talk to the other techs about the source of the calls. If they still can't trace the sender, bring in Cassandra to help. I want to get to the bottom of this now."

Both he and Amy straightened and nodded. Deciding not to waste any more time, Derrick bid them goodbye, promising to update them once he got to the location marked by the pin.

Wild goose chase or not, he had a mystery to solve now.

CHAPTER THREE

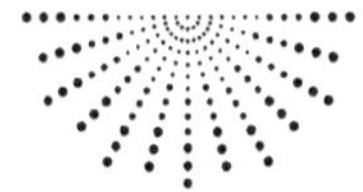

Derrick's curious and optimistic attitude nosedived roughly an hour later—right around the time he had to abandon his truck at the side of the road. The spot on the map was deep in the woods, nearly twenty miles from the highway.

There were few trails and no access for vehicles. The location marked by the pin was only accessible on foot.

It wasn't the distance that bothered him. Wolves enjoyed a good hard run. No, it was the idea that he was dancing to someone else's tune that got under his skin.

Speaking of...

Derrick locked his vehicle and walked into the woods. Confirming he was alone, he stripped, stashing his clothes and phone in a small cross-body bag. The bag was custom-made, designed to fit him in both forms.

Normally, he would have left his stuff back in his truck, but he needed his phone. He'd promised to check in with the chief as soon as he confirmed nothing was happening at the location they were being herded to.

Like a sheep or a lemming, he groused mentally.

Well, if present their practical joker *was* going to learn a hard lesson. Wolves weren't docile animals. They were predators, and they didn't take kindly to being led around by the nose.

He shifted with a pleasant shudder, transitioning to four feet for his run. Derrick could run pretty fast in either form, with the endurance of a shifter in his prime. But his senses were sharper as a wolf, particularly his sense of smell. If he was heading into a trap, he wanted every advantage.

Shaking out his fur, he pressed his paws into the ground and began to run. The forest flew past him in a blur of green and brown. Soon enough his second nature took over, his love of speed and pleasure at being a wolf in the wild like a bass-filled song pulsing through his body.

But despite his wolf's joy in the run, Derrick kept his wits around him, making note of all the scents and sounds even as he passed, a silent missile streaking through the woods.

The landscape grew rugged. He slowed down a few miles from his destination, taking greater care to scan the area for hidden enemies. But aside from the odd bird or squirrel he smelled and saw no one.

That doesn't mean I'm alone. Derrick understood there were spells that could cloak a person's scent and heat, the markers a wolf would use to track a body. But he knew from his conversations with Logan that none could make someone invisible. At best a spell could "encourage" a person to turn their attention elsewhere.

At his insistence Logan had cast that spell on herself, teaching him and several other alpha wolves how to recognize the signs of that kind of enchantment. It had taken his stubborn brain a while to penetrate the spell, especially when cast by a master of magic of Logan's caliber.

"The trick is to spot the slide," she explained.

And that was exactly what it was like—the mind would just slip over a spot in the surroundings in an unnatural manner. Most people wouldn't notice the way their brain just skipped over a certain area, but he'd practiced over and over until he was confident he could penetrate any version of that spell.

Which was why he was certain there weren't any villains hiding in the shadows under the trees. Suppressing a growl, he decided he was close enough to the location to stop running. Moving with the same slow and deliberate movements he used to stalk prey, he entered the small clearing marked by the pin prepared for battle.

And found a big fat nothing.

Derrick padded around the clearing to be sure, but there was no threat. *A fucking wild goose chase*, just as he'd thought. Except there was no juicy fowl for him to snack on at the end of this farce.

Irritated—and now hungry to boot—he decided to wait a bit to see if a threat would materialize. A half-hour tops.

He made it a few minutes before he gave up. Snorting in indignation he turned tail, getting ready to run back to his truck when he remembered his report to the chief. Taking a last look around, he shifted, unzipping his pack to take out his phone.

A tiny mewl froze him in his tracks. Listening intently, his predator's brain did the math, pinpointing the location of the noise.

Shifting back to wolf form, he walked a few hundred yards east. He dropped to his haunches at the edge of the clearing where a jumble of rocks stretched just beyond the tree line.

Letting his nose guide him, he peered between the gaps in the stones.

The small, narrow space created by the pile of stones and boulders was little more than a hand's breadth wide, but it was big enough to shelter the two creatures inside.

He stared in disbelief as two sets of luminescent eyes blinked up at him. Another tiny mewl sounded—weaker than before.

The beasts were shifters. Tiny baby shifter cats. And they were in trouble.

CHAPTER FOUR

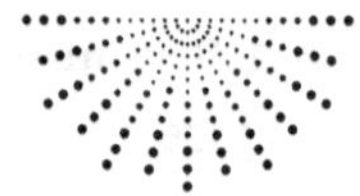

Swearing a blue streak, Derrick snapped back to his two-legged form, grabbing the top rock of the shelter and tossing it aside to expose the opening to the light of day.

It was a huge mistake.

Inside the space between the boulders, the baby cats cowered. *Idiot,* Derrick berated himself. If he wasn't careful, he could scar the jaguar cubs for life, or worse—scare them to death.

And such a thing might be possible. The poor babes were in terrible shape. Bedraggled and battered, the tiny beasts were starving. He could count each rib under their matted and mud-streaked fur.

Derrick put up his hands. "Oh, hey. Sorry little ones," he apologized, pitching his voice to eliminate as much of the innate growl as possible. "I mean no harm. I'm here to help you…"

His voice trailed off, the realization strangling him. "I was sent here to help," he finished in a whisper.

Derrick racked his brain, trying to remember how long he'd been ignoring the texts directing him here. *Hell.* He couldn't remember.

Bile rose in his throat. What if he'd continued to ignore the texts? Or if the chief hadn't made him come out here?

Then another weak cry interrupted his self-recrimination,

reminding him that he had a far more important task to do. Beating himself up could come later.

It took long, agonizing minutes to get the little beasts calm enough to listen to him. Even then the male took a swipe at him with a tiny claw when he reached for the female.

It was a brother and a sister, with the protective male being older and bigger. Their scent was too similar despite the sex difference. He wouldn't be able to pinpoint their exact age until they shifted to human, but he knew better than expect that they'd show him that more vulnerable form anytime soon.

Winning their trust was going to be a long and hard battle, but he needed some of it now. He had to convince them to come with him. Derrick didn't like how the small female looked. She was barely moving, her sounds frighteningly weak.

Heart squeezing tight in his chest, he addressed the male. "All right, you have to listen to me. Your sister is in bad shape. You need food and water and a warm place to sleep."

This part of the woods was at too high an elevation. Even in summer, the night in this neck of the woods would be cold. They weren't completely exposed to the elements in their little shelter, but it wouldn't have provided enough protection. They would have still felt the bite of the cold. It would have sapped their strength, something they couldn't afford in their weakened state.

The male's worry for his sister worked in Derrick's favor. The small boy stepped forward, his little claws sheathed. Derrick went to pick him up, but the cat butted his hand away, nudging them toward his sister.

"There, there," he crooned. Cradling the smaller trembling kitten to his chest, he soothed her as best he could.

Picking up the second cat cub, he reassured them they were safe in a soft voice. He was painfully aware the actual words were poor and inadequate. But that didn't matter. At this point, the only thing that they heard and understood was his tone.

What was more important was that they felt his strength and dominance. The fact that these were cats didn't matter—they were predatory shifters. Their beasts recognized his dominance and his strength and would lean on him for protection.

Had they been healthy and strong, he might have had a hard time getting them to respond without fear, but they were in a bad way. The cubs were beyond caring that he was a big bad wolf to their cat.

"It's going to be okay," he promised. But Derrick was worried. He had to get them to Kiera or one of the other pack medics now.

Adjusting his hold on them so they were both cradled in one arm, he unzipped his pack. Wrapping the cubs in his shirt, he set them on the floor so he could tug on his pants. After adding socks and sneakers, he decided against shifting and carrying the cubs in the unzipped pack. It wouldn't sit right on his back. And the poor things needed to feel his heat. They could do that through the cotton of his shirt, but not as well if he added the layer of waterproof nylon of his bag.

Which was fine. He couldn't run as fast on two legs, but the speed of the wolf might prove too much of a shock for the cubs in their current state. That and running as a human would allow him to speak to the cubs the entire way.

So that was what he did. Running at a rate where he could still control the smoothness of his pace, Derrick made good time back to his truck. Bundling the cubs inside he positioned them on the seat so both cubs would be touching his thigh as he drove.

He waited until he had the truck back on the road to call the chief's office. "Amy, send an alert to the clinic. Get medics on standby. Two juvenile *Panthera onca* patients are incoming."

He proceeded to describe their condition in terse words, using clinical descriptions and cutting off any questions about how two leopard cubs had come to be alone in the middle of his pack's lands.

Derrick stuck to the facts and ended the call after making sure the medics had all the details he knew. Reassuring the cubs was more important than satisfying Amy's curiosity.

They didn't need to hear him telling his people about how they'd been abandoned and left to die in their territory.

CHAPTER FIVE

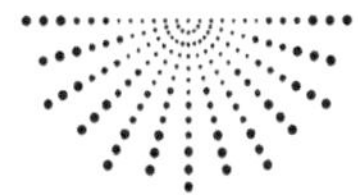

Douglas was waiting outside of the clinic exam room where Kiera, the pack medic, had set up their diagnostic equipment.

"You're sure?" he asked, his face dark with anger and concern.

Derrick nodded. "Theirs was the only scent. No signs of an adult, leopard or human."

He looked at the cubs, pitching his voice low enough that even their sensitive ears wouldn't catch his words. "They must have been dumped in the thickest part of the woods on purpose. Even shifter cubs wouldn't have been able to get more than a dozen miles on their own. Given their size and current condition that's as far as they could have gone."

His jaw stiffened so much it almost hurt to speak. "There are no roads—no real trails out there. Only rocks and trees. There's a small stream a couple of hundred yards from the spot. I could hear it, but I doubt the person who abandoned them had intended for them to drink. The kid probably found it on his own, making camp at the closest shelter to it. He also hunted for him and his sister."

There had been small bones—rodent-sized ones—near their shelter. Also, some leftover bug bits. The kid had most likely scavenged whatever he could, but cubs that size would have had little training, if any, in how to hunt.

The kills had been made in desperation, the cub's survival instincts kicking in to save him and his baby sister.

The female cub was on the edge. She was showing signs of severe malnutrition, more so than her brother. The baby girl hadn't been able to choke down the raw rodents like her brother.

They could still lose her.

"I want to go back out and hunt down the piece of shit who left them there."

"No." Douglas shook his head. "I'll send out a team to scour the area. We'll track down the bastard who did this. But the cubs need you here. Your voice and scent mean safety. You can't disappear on them now."

The words penetrated through the red rage that had been riding him the entire drive back. "Of course," he agreed gruffly. "You're right."

They hit pause on the conversation as a few nurses came in, wheeling in more equipment from the pediatric suite.

He bit back a growl as they fussed around the kids, blocking his view of the cubs. "That fucker who texted their location has to be the one behind it."

"Possibly," Douglas said.

"It's more than possible, but I don't get why the hell this individual left them out there. If someone wanted us to save them, he or she could have dropped them off somewhere in town. It's empty enough in the middle of the night. The kids would have been better off, and we would have found them that much sooner."

It made no sense.

Douglas agreed. "I've been looking over the text I received and the ones sent to your phone."

Derrick didn't ask how his messages had been examined. His phone was monitored by the pack techs, a safety measure they had initiated a few years back when the pack had run into trouble with Weres losing their wolf form.

That problem had been resolved when Logan and Connell unearthed a traitor in their pack, but not before one of their cubs had briefly gone missing. Sammy was safe and sound now—also a dragon shifter instead of a wolf, but that was a story for another day.

That painful time had taught them a lesson about staying in constant communication. Now all the senior pack members carried a pack-issued smartphone. Consequently, Derrick had given up the expectation of privacy years ago.

If there were any messages he didn't want the pack techs to see— to a lady friend for example—he used one of the special encrypted messaging apps he'd installed for that purpose. Amy had promised that the phone didn't have key-logger software installed. That was close enough to privacy for him.

"The urgency of the messages built until their nature was almost frantic, as if the sender was genuinely concerned for the cubs." Douglas's mouth compressed. "If the sender was the one who abandoned them, that worry makes no sense."

"It is bizarre," he agreed. "But whoever did this is obviously sick in the head. We can't expect sense from this asshole."

The chief made a rumbling sound in the back of his throat, the kind that only happened when an apex predator possessed human vocal cords. "That is probably true, but I can't shake the feeling that something deeper is going on."

Derrick wasn't one to argue with the chief's spidey sense. No one else had come close to holding so many packs together. The North America coalition was unprecedented in their history. So, he simply grunted, turning his attention to their medic Kiera as she emerged from the exam room.

A mere five-foot-one, Kiera was a submissive wolf of mixed Anglo and East Indian descent. She had grown up with him, Connell, and Mara. Not that they had spent much time together as children.

Kiera was one of the shyest submissives in the entire pack. As a child, she'd been scared of her own shadow, but Derrick had always had a soft spot for her—something he made sure she'd known. That was why he was the one she'd gone to whenever one of the other adolescent wolves teased her.

She had come a long way, but even he had been surprised when Kiera announced she was going to medical school right after college.

Many submissive went into care fields. Dominant wolves were ornery, difficult patients. A submissive's gentle nature was far more soothing in those environments where a hard case was injured or sick. But despite her brilliance, he'd secretly had his doubts Kiera would have the grit to make it through medical school.

Although it had taken her some time to grow into her role as healer, she had proven him wrong, of course. Kiera had a habit of surprising them.

Today lines of concern bracketed her mouth. "It was tricky because the female's so small, but we finally got her transfused. We've hooked up an IV. She's too weak to eat on her own at this point."

He'd suspected as much, but it was still a blow. Derrick swallowed. "And the boy?"

"In better shape, but he is also suffering from malnutrition. His gums are inflamed, and he had a minor infection in a front paw, likely from where one of his dinners fought back and took a swipe at him. But he won't need to be fed intravenously if he cooperates." She lifted her chin. "As long as we take care of his sister first, he is."

She broke off and shook her head, sympathy darkening her sweet features. "I have no idea how long they were out there, but it's a miracle they survived. The poor babies are covered in dirt and burrs. They even picked up a few ticks."

Derrick did growl aloud this time. The cubs only stirred on the hospital bed, the boy's ears perking up in that distinctly feline way. But neither reacted in fear, their little minds having accepted that they were finally safe.

A moment later the boy settled, curling against his sister in the loosely wrapped blanket Kiera had fashioned into a nest for them.

"But I think I got all of those," the medic continued in a lower voice. "They're both so small it wasn't that much fur to check."

She turned to him. "I mention this because I'd like you to stay on and do some skin-to-skin therapy. Or skin to fur in this case."

Derrick didn't need to ask what the therapy was. Last year when his friend Mack and his mate Liesa had their cub, the babe had come nearly two months early. The boy had struggled, and Derrick had been sure he'd spend months in an incubator. But every time he'd visited, he'd found the cub sleeping on Sam's bare chest or snuggled with his mother, her shirt open to allow the cub to lay against her with no barriers.

Weres were tactile creatures, and Derrick was a dominant alpha. His protective instincts were coded at the DNA level. "Whatever they need," he promised Kiera.

He and the chief exchanged looks. They didn't need further conversation. Both were going to do everything in their power to make their small patients safe and secure.

And there was no question that they would bring the asshole playing with them to justice. But first Derrick had to roll up his sleeves, toughen up, and cuddle some kittens…

CHAPTER SIX

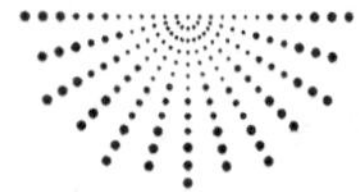

Four days later Derrick settled the girl cub in the crib Douglas had moved out of storage.

The boy meowed once, the high-pitched keen simultaneously indignant and adorable. Kylie had estimated his age between four and six years old—it was hard to tell until they shifted back to human.

However, no one was pushing for that. They weren't about to rush the healing process. Knowing their exact age would have to wait, but given the protest over sleeping in a crib, Derrick guessed the kid was at the higher end of that range.

He scratched between the little leopard's ears. "It's temporary," he promised. "I know you don't want to leave your baby sister alone."

Tiny teeth nipped at his fingers, punishing him for suggesting such a thing. He lowered his head to level with the little beast. "Now, I know a crib is beneath you, but we don't want her rolling out of bed and hurting herself. Baby sis is better, enough that she doesn't need to be at the clinic, but she's still weak. Also, we wouldn't want her waking up and thinking she's alone in a strange place."

The male cub butted his furry head against his fingers. Taking that for agreement, he wrapped the baby blanket around both cubs.

"You know, this is a special crib," he added. "The chief's kids used to sleep in here. A brother and a sister just like you two, but they're twins. Neither of them is home just now, but you'll meet them soon."

The boy sniffed at his surroundings. Even though the bedding had been freshly laundered, there was still enough residual traces for him to protest with another meow. "Yeah, I know it smells like wolf, but it's clean and warm."

It was best he grew accustomed to that smell now. Though Derrick had been busy with the cubs, the chief had kept him updated on the search for the parents. Things weren't looking good.

"I'm sleeping just down the hall, so I'll hear you if you need anything in the night." He picked up one of the baby monitor handsets next to the crib. "In fact, with this I'll be able to hear you from anywhere in the house. Just give me a shout."

Derrick scratched under the boy's chin, before using his free hand to stroke the sleeping girl. He had given her a bottle of fortified milk downstairs, one fitted with a nipple specially designed by vets to feed baby animals. The baby girl had purred for him, a sound that had seemed to surprise her brother. It also had the side effect of turning Derrick into a giant pile of goo.

And I don't even like cats. But these cubs were an exception.

Tucking the receiver unit for the monitor into a pocket he headed downstairs where the chief was waiting with Amy, Kiera, and another packmate, Nathan Hale.

They were sitting around the dining room, which doubled as an informal conference room. They had a formal one just off Douglas's office, next to the den downstairs, but they rarely used it unless the chief was meeting with an alpha from outside their territory.

Derrick nodded at Nathan, another former soldier who served in the upper levels of the pack hierarchy.

The chief motioned him to sit. "How are they?"

Setting the baby monitor receiver on the table, Derrick settled next to Kiera. "As well as can be expected. Still too skinny by half but loads better than when I found them."

He turned to the medic, who'd accompanied the children over from the hospital. "You did a good job with them."

The children trusted Kiera, recognizing her gentle nature instinctively. Neither had bonded with her to the extent they had with Derrick, but they were comfortable with her enough to be alone with her.

There were a few others on that shortlist now. Which was good for him, because he was itching to get out there and find the person who had abandoned them.

That person had a very difficult confrontation coming.

"I think you deserve more of the credit for their improved condition than I do," Kiera said, fidgeting in her chair.

She tended to do that more when Nathan was in the vicinity. He'd always thought it was because the other wolf was a less familiar dominant. Nathan had come to them from a satellite pack back east in his late teens.

That should have been enough time for her to grow comfortable with him. Especially since Nate had a calm and centered presence for a Were of his dominance—which was just a few shades less than his own. He really shouldn't have unsettled the submissive medic to this extent.

But Kiera was a special case. Outside of the hospital, she struggled around dominants. It made Derrick sad to think she always would.

"I've already run down their condition and prognosis to the others here," Kiera continued, sweeping her eyes over the others in turn, skittering over Nathan a touch too quickly. "If they keep on as they are, I predict they will make a complete recovery."

Despite the good prognosis, her voice hitched. "I hate to think what would have happened to them if you hadn't found them when you did—it was touch and go for a bit there with the little girl. Her brother did his best, and he's the reason she's alive, but a cub that small needs constant care and attention. Both cubs do really. That someone could just leave them out in the woods like that…."

Breaking off, she shook her head, blinking away the sudden sheen. Nathan leaned over and patted her shoulder. Color stained her cheeks, and she tensed, but after a beat she covered his hand with hers, grasping his fingers as if taking strength from him.

"Still no luck on tracking the parents?" she asked Amy. Kiera was still hoping the children's parents weren't responsible. She was doggedly hanging onto the hope that they had been kidnapped and then dumped when the kidnapper realized they were shifters.

Except there was no evidence that had happened. The techs had scoured the news reports and all active amber alerts, tapping into local police and federal databases. But there were no kidnapping or missing persons reports involving two children.

"There is no news on that front," Amy shared. "But they might not have been reported missing yet."

Douglas held up a hand when Kiera opened her mouth. "Yes, we know it's rare for two kids to go missing without a report in this day and age, but it may not happen for weeks—unless the body of a custodial parent turns up."

Downcast, Kiera nodded, leaning a little in Nathan's direction. "For their sake, I hope that's not what happened."

"We will learn more once the boy shifts back. Hopefully, he'll be able to shed some light." Douglas leaned toward her. "I'd like you to work on that with him, gain his trust, because I'm going to need Derrick and Nate on the investigation."

Kiera straightened in her seat. "Of course. I was planning that anyway."

The chief leaned back and turned to Derrick. "Good. Because we have news on the texts. My gut said this was more complicated, and as it turns out I was right. This isn't the first miraculous rescue we owe to an anonymous texter."

He gestured to Amy, who opened her laptop. An image of a small-town newspaper's website appeared on the screen.

The headline read, "Narrow Rescue for Family of Five" above a picture of a burned-out shell of a house.

"This is Rafe Hawkins's territory— he mentioned it to me a few months ago. The family in question was rescued by a member of his pack, a volunteer fire department in their town. I didn't connect it to our case because the first warnings weren't texted to the pack. It was an anonymous phone call to the local emergency service line."

Douglas tapped the table. "The call came in during the day. It was checked out by a police cruiser, but they didn't see anything wrong. Despite that, the officers knocked at the door, spoke to the owner, and determined it was a prank call. The fire didn't break out until the middle of the night."

Derrick scowled. "Arson?"

"You would think so." Douglas lifted a shoulder. "But the arson investigator's report identified the source as faulty wiring—apparently the contractor used substandard materials and then made a hash of the installation to boot. No accelerants were found."

He paused. "They would have died had Jacinta, a shifter firefighter, not driven past on the way home from a night out with her friends. And the only reason she did that was because of an email asking her to do a drive-by. She thought it was her supervisor messaging her based on the language."

He broke off and shook his head. "Jacinta admits she didn't give it a second thought until she passed by and found the place in flames. She got the humans out quickly and called her supervisor immediately after only to find out that the man didn't send the message. It came from an address very similar to his—it was off by just one letter."

"Someone was intentionally trying to make it look like a legit email from someone she knew?" Nathan asked.

"So it would seem," Douglas said. "But that in itself wouldn't have been difficult. That email address was listed on the fire services web page. No extensive insider knowledge of the players was involved—just a little technical wizardry to spoof the email."

"And they never traced it?"

"No. It was only used once. And Jacinta didn't scent any strangers at the scene. The house that burned was a good four miles away from their nearest neighbors. The mailbox was at the end of the lane. Jacinta only picked up the family members near the building.'

"The fire may have obscured a stranger's scent," Nathan pointed out.

"True. But it would have had to have been unusually weak for her to miss it. Rafe uses Jacinta as a tracker. She's one of his most experienced people. That and Rafe himself went to the house the next day to check out the surrounding woods. He didn't pick up any unknown scents. Nothing that shouldn't have been there."

Derrick grunted. That was enough proof for him—although there were plenty who would disagree, because Rafe Hawkins was a latent wolf. He couldn't shift, which meant he dealt with a lot of prejudice from their kind. But Derrick knew firsthand that the man possessed an alpha's strength and sharp senses.

Amy and the chief exchanged a look.

"There's more than just Rafe's weird case, isn't there?" Nathan asked the question on the tip of Derrick's tongue.

"That's right. To date, we've verified eight different calls, texts, or emails sent to pack members all across coalition territory warning them of some impending disaster." Amy tapped on the keyboard of her computer, bringing up a bulleted list.

Derrick scanned it. The tips were spread all over the country. They reported fires, cars going off the road in isolated areas, a lost hiker, even a mugging.

He homed in on the last warning. "This mugger. Does he have a record?"

"A long one," Amy confirmed. "And he has a history of aggravated assault as well. The perp was armed with a stolen gun that day, just pulling it out when the shifter intervened."

Interesting. "Then it's conceivable the message prevented a murder as well."

"Entirely possible. I asked around, and the guy was a suspect in at least one other homicide case, one that looked like a mugging gone wrong. But we won't know for sure, because it was a different gun and he's not talking. Police pegged him as a loner."

"And he didn't brag to anyone in his life about what he was getting up to? No friends who could have turned him in?"

"None that they could find."

Nathan narrowed his eyes. "So let me get this straight. We have at least eight verified cases of genuine forewarning that have ended with lives saved. No one knows who the person sending the messages is. There were no obvious suspects or people with enough insider knowledge to send the warning. Or at least none that we can explain."

"Sounds about right." Douglas scrubbed his face. "Which means the person who messaged us about the kids may not have had anything to do with their abandonment."

Derrick wrinkled his nose. "They could have still gone to get them days earlier. It wasn't as if they didn't know where they were."

Kiera took a deep breath. "What if he or she couldn't get to them for some reason?" she asked tentatively. "The cubs were in some pretty rough terrain."

"It wasn't that bad," he scowled.

"For a shifter," she pointed out in her gentle way. "But even though we're connecting these cases to our kind, it sounds as if we're dealing with some other kind of being entirely. I think we might be being warned by a witch."

Even though that same idea had been bouncing around in his head, Derrick still growled. "*Perfect.*"

He knew all witches weren't bad, but shifters had a long and unpleasant history with their kind. However, the chances of it being another kind of Supe was unlikely. Foretelling was a rare ability. He couldn't think of anyone with the ability who wasn't some long-distant legend. But he'd seen enough weird shit to believe it might exist.

"It could still be a fae," he pointed out. "Some of them have been known to have seer abilities. Although, anyone born with it would have been locked down by the Faerie court."

"That would explain why they can't intervene personally."

Nathan's face screwed up. "I thought upper-level fae couldn't touch certain metals like iron. Would one be able to use a phone or a computer?"

"Maybe. It's more plastic than metal these days," Douglas said. "Except for small components. But it's true the higher the caste of fae, the more sensitive they are to iron and its alloys. And a fae with this kind of ability would be high caste."

He leaned back in his seat. "We can't assume anything until we investigate further. I've sent an alert to the other alphas in the territory as well as the other shifter packs we're on speaking terms with about this matter. I didn't give specific details, but they know to inform our office if they've had any similar warnings in the past or if they get any in the future."

"I hate waiting," Nathan groused, his usual even-tempered nature cracking a bit.

Dominant shifters were men and women of action. They didn't like sitting on the sidelines.

Kiera gave him a small commiserating smile. "If it is a witch with the ability to see the future, isn't it lucky they chose to confide in our pack? Just imagine if they'd reached out to some other kind of Supernatural or a random human. At least we have the strength and speed to intervene."

"Maybe they did and were ignored," Amy sighed, her expression pensive. "This could have been going on for years...Imagine how powerless she must feel."

Derrick raised a brow. "She?"

"Or he. Or they." Amy shrugged. "It could be anyone. But I guess I was thinking it was a woman since the person hasn't ever intervened personally or stuck around to witness the aftermath."

There was an idea. "We don't know if that last part is true. Maybe they have been observing and went unnoticed."

Which hinted that Amy's idea their witch was female might be accurate. Unless they were pack, most shifters would have noted the presence of a strange male as a matter of course. But a female? A dominant soldier like him and Nathan might, but as sexist as it was other pack members were less attuned to threats from females. One might have gone unnoticed.

He turned to Kiera after confirming that the fire and the abandoned cubs were the only cases involving cubs or children. "You haven't noticed any outsiders in the vicinity of the clinic? No one trying to catch a glimpse of the cubs or asking leading questions?"

She shook her head. "No, nothing like that. We had a few people coming in for regular services and checkups, of course. But the cubs were kept out of sight."

"No walk-ins?"

"A few for small accidents like cuts that required stitches. All very ordinary."

"All pack?"

"Well, no, of course not," she admitted. "We serve the broader community, and not everyone is in the know."

"What about the new girl, the one who goes around in a blue hoodie?" he asked, a sudden suspicion in his head. "Was she around?"

Kiera's head tilted back. "Meghan? Yes, she was. She got a flu shot the day you brought the cubs in."

Her chin wrinkled; her head cocked to the side as she studied him. "Don't you remember? You passed right by her when you ran in with the cubs."

Fuck. Derrick's indignation drowned out his satisfaction at finally learning the girl's name. "No," he growled. "I was too focused on the cubs. Did this Meghan see them in cat form?"

"Um, I think so." Kiera hesitated. "But my assistant covered. She told her that one of the nurses was also a vet tech. Meghan just nodded and said she hoped they would be okay."

Douglas flicked his eyes to him, wondering where he was going. "Do you think this woman is the witch?"

"Probably not," Derrick said. The woman had been playing with her phone just as he received a text, but that didn't mean anything. She could have been doing anything on it. "But I recently learned that she flew under the radar and never got checked out. I didn't even know her name until just now. Kiera is the only one who knew what it was."

The medic winced. "Well, she said it was Meghan."

Douglas frowned. "Did she not present identification? An insurance card?"

"Well...no," Kiera said, clasping her hands in front of her on the table. "Meghan lost her wallet. When asked, she confessed that she didn't have health insurance. That last isn't uncommon, so I gave her the shot. I remember suggesting more tests—she's very thin and pale for someone of her coloring. I thought she might have a vitamin deficiency. But then Derrick came in, and I forgot all about it. I don't think she stuck around much after that, but I can't say for certain. I was busy with the cubs."

Derrick didn't like the description of the female's condition, but Douglas didn't show any reaction.

"Well, not having an ID or obvious resources isn't a crime," the chief said decisively. "As I understand it, we don't have a definitive address for the girl. She could be squatting in a lake cabin for all we know."

He turned to Nathan. "I want you to track her down and question her."

Derrick sat up straighter. "But—"

"I know you are chafing at the reins to do something, but the best thing you can do for the cubs is to stay available. At least for a few more days. Nathan will do the initial recon and report back to you with his first impressions of the girl. In all likelihood, she has nothing to do with the cub case."

Disappointed, Derrick sat back in his seat. "Yes, sir."

CHAPTER SEVEN

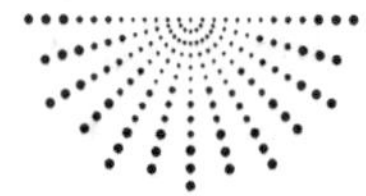

Derrick prowled around the cabin exterior, frowning at the wrongness of the scent near the small two-room cabin Nathan had identified as belonging to the mysterious Meghan.

The woman had pulled another disappearing act, slipping out of town without any of them being the wiser.

"Can you smell it?" Nathan asked. The other soldier had run out with him when Derrick had declared that he was coming out to check the cabin for himself. Although the cubs were doing better, they hadn't shifted back to human.

In addition to Kiera, the chief had invited Diya and Frankie Reddy-Young, a same-sex shifter couple who had been on several adoption waiting lists for a few years. They had come close to adopting a little girl from India once, but the adoption had fallen through. He had never heard why.

Douglas had suggested the Reddy-Youngs might be a good fit to foster the cubs, but he first wanted to know if they could handle the situation if it didn't turn out to be permanent.

There was still no trail to trace the parents, although Amy and the others were still working on that. But despite the lack of leads, they might still find an innocent parent or guardian at the end of this. So even though Douglas was convinced of Diya and Frankie's suitability as parents, the fact that the cubs might not end up here permanently might be too hard on everyone involved.

Fostering wasn't that common in the shifter community. Most shifter kids who lost their parents were adopted straightaway, typically by relatives or friends of the family. Pack alphas were diligent when it came to caring for their most vulnerable members.

For now, Douglas and the Reddy-Youngs were treading carefully, but Derrick had seen Diya and Frankie with the kids. The little girl cub had consented to drink a bottle as she was being held in Diya's arms, the boy sitting next to Frankie while the latter read an adventure story. They weren't cuddling, but he was paying attention as she read. Derrick took that as a good sign.

The Reddy-Youngs didn't care that the cubs were another species. Derrick took that to heart. If the worst happened, the cubs would find a home with the couple. Meanwhile, he had a puzzle to solve.

"There is something off about the woman's scent," he decided. That was why Nathan had come back with him to the cabin. The woman in question wasn't around, her absence unexplained, but Nathan had been harping about the odd olfactory cues he'd picked up around the cabin, so he'd decided to come back for a second sniff.

What the difference was, he couldn't quite say.

"Is she evil?" Nate asked.

It wasn't as silly a question as it sounded.

"Black witches smell like death. Many black spells have a certain profile that leave traces of ozone. But this is not like that." He knew that was what Nathan suspected, why he'd come hoping for clarification Derrick could not give him.

"I can't tell what's different from out here," he finally admitted. It was not unpleasant, but there was a hint of otherness, a tiny suggestion that got both his and Nathan's hackles up.

The other Were stuck his hands in his pockets and grunted. "So long as she's not here to refresh the scent, I doubt we'll get anything more definite. It's fainter now than it was before."

"Yeah." The wind off the lake would have swept most traces away.

Even on the protected side of the structure, traces left from physical contact degraded in the sun. Unless the girl returned, the only alternative was to break into the house where the physical evidence was protected from the elements.

He turned around to suggest just that when Nathan sighed. "It could just be the area. We're not far from the Haunted Hollow. You know things get wonky near it."

Derrick snorted aloud, turning his head to look back at the other man. "Been spending time with the old folks in the pack?"

"My niece, actually. She's nine, and her friends dared her to stay out there after dark."

"Ah yes." Derrick grinned, the sudden levity bringing a grin to his face. "But she's a bit early. We normally don't start obsessing about that spot in the woods till middle school. It's our spook central. Did your niece take the dare?"

"Of course. She's a chip off the old block...although she didn't mention to her friends that she had company."

"Let me guess. Her big strong uncle hid just out of sight in wolf form."

Nathan smirked. "Only while she took her little videos to post to her social media as evidence."

"Video proof," Derrick guffawed. "*Damn.* In my day you had to stay out there all night to prove yourself. Your friends had to sneak out of their own houses in the middle of the night if they wanted to know if you stayed the whole time or not."

"So did you spend the night, or did you cheat?"

"Damn right I spent the night. I was a legend."

Who cared that Connell had also been out there with him? People expected spectacularly brave deeds from the chief's son.

"Well, I have to admit I'm kind of glad Sabrina didn't have to go that far," Nate said. "Because if I have to be honest, the place did give me the creeps. It's almost as if—"

"You heard a voice," he finished.

"Yeah." Nathan wrinkled his nose, grinning sheepishly.

It hit Derrick then—Kiera's distraction around Nate had nothing to do with discomfort.

Well, what do you know? And it wouldn't be a bad match for her… except Nate didn't look at Kiera like an interested male. Pity that. Because upon reflection it would have been a solid match for his favorite medic. Nate was a decorated veteran and a good man to have in a tight spot. But despite his proven bravery, he had that even temper and calm aura, like a placid lake.

Nate kicked a nearby rock. "All right, I thought I saw something too. Like a less dark spot moving in the shadows. But it was gone before I could be sure. It freaked Sabrina out."

"Yeah," Derrick nodded in commiseration. Gesturing with a jerk of his head, he started another circuit around the cabin, this time peeking through the windows. "I've seen weird shadows there too—stuff that can't have been cast by anything in that clearing. But it's just a trick of the light."

"And the voices?" Nate asked, following his lead

"Just the wind, picking up snatches of other people or animals."

That was what Douglas had said when the pack's young kept sneaking out of their houses at night. But the Haunted Hollow was part of their local lore. Interest in it went up and down in waves.

The elders of the pack maintained the haunting was real but that the younger generation was wrong about the location. His grandfather had told him it had been at the western ridge back in his day. Later reports had it moving down, migrating until it was finally in the valley, almost as if it were making its way across their territory.

Nathan stopped in front of the cabin's right-hand rear window, the one facing the lake. "Hey, who did you say owns this place?"

"Vicky Gillan. They're an elder wolf. She moved out of the territory to the California coast six years back because she wanted to be closer to her grandkids."

Once Nate had tracked down which cabin the girl had been staying at, it had been easy to determine who owned it. Vicky hadn't been to town for a couple of years, but she kept the cabin up for when her grandkids would spend summers here once they were a little older.

"And she gave it to this Meghan rent-free?" Nate asked.

Derrick lifted a shoulder. That raised a red flag for him too. "The girl was talking to her about wanting to visit this area. Then she performed what Vicky called a great service—she found a family heirloom thought lost for years."

He moved to stand next to Nate. "Vicky was so grateful she decided to offer the cabin free of charge. All Meghan had to do was perform a little light maintenance on the place."

"Ah, that's what I thought." Nathan pointed through the window. "If that's the case, then we might have grounds for coming in."

Derrick followed the line of sight from Nathan's finger. The cabin consisted of a single bedroom and a kitchen slash living room. The couch was visible, a battered brown corduroy number with a patchwork quilt thrown over the back.

At first, he didn't see what Nathan was talking about. He was about to point out the dirt on the kitchen counter off to the left—it looked more like potting soil, but then he spotted the sandwich on the small coffee table in front of the couch.

"Is it moldy?" The half-eaten sandwich was stained with a bit of tell-tale green.

Nathan nodded. "I'm pretty sure that plate hasn't been touched since I was here last. Neither has the mug next to it."

Pursing his lips, Derrick considered that. Vicky had gushed about the girl. She'd commented on Meghan's quiet and respectful manner more than she talked about the heirloom Meghan had found.

"I think we should call Vicky," he said, pulling out his cell phone and placing the call.

When he shared what he was seeing through the window, the older woman was alarmed.

"That's not like Meghan at all," Vicky said, concern in her tone. "She's a very neat person. Something must be wrong."

"That's what I thought too."

Though he didn't know Vicky all that well, he remembered her face, and she knew him. He didn't need to explain what he was doing out here. The pack monitored the welfare of all the people in their territory.

"That is why I was calling," he said. "You're the owner of record on this cabin. I'd like your permission to go in and make sure nothing is wrong."

Vicky hummed, hesitating.

"I don't think she's here," he said, not needing to explain to another werewolf about the strength of the scent around the building.

"Hmm, well, I know you're a good boy," she said, making Nathan smirk. "Meghan's a very timid sort, but if she's not there I guess it's okay. If something happened to her, you'll track her down, right?"

"Oh, I will," he promised, exchanging a significant look with the Were next to him.

"Just make sure you don't scare her." Vicky made a high-pitched sound. "Meghan is a dear girl. A very gentle human."

"There's no scent of blood or anything like that out here, but I don't want you to worry. I'm going to find out where she went," he promised.

"Good. Let me know what you find," Vicky said, breaking off to scold one of her preschool-age grandkids. "And say hi to your mom for me."

Murmuring his agreement he hung up, gesturing for Nathan to follow him.

"Door or window?" the other man asked.

"Door." The window in the front of the house wasn't locked, but he didn't want to slip inside the house like a criminal. A woman living alone wouldn't react well to that. And he had the landlord's permission to enter.

Moving to the front, he knocked on the door loudly. He waited for a beat and then opened his wallet, sliding out the credit card-sized folio that held his lock-picking tools.

Nathan's eyes widened. "Do you carry those all the time? Are you a cat burglar in your spare time?"

"Ha-ha," he groused. "But a lot of our elderly come back to visit the area. Most of them are still sharp, but occasionally one will lock themselves out. Learning to pick locks was a lot cheaper than letting them bust the doors open all the time."

Bending over, he fiddled with his tools, slipping a thin bar and lifting the lock mechanism's pins with his gonzo hook until he heard a click. The door swung open.

"Hello?" he called out, knocking again as he stepped inside. There was no reply, so he moved deeper into the room.

Despite having gotten a look at the inside from the window, Derrick was not prepared for the sight that met his eyes.

CHAPTER EIGHT

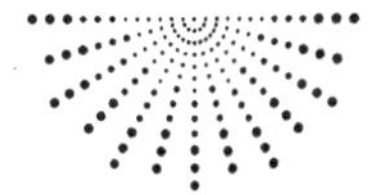

"What the hell?" Nathan asked aloud, coming in behind him.

Confused himself, Derrick walked around the rectangular room wide-eyed. What had looked like empty decorative ceramic pots from the outside were anything but. They covered every surface, and each one was filled with dirt.

But there were no real plants—not unless you counted the moss and weed sprouts that lined some of them.

"It's not potting soil," he said, after taking a pinch to examine it closer.

Derrick sniffed it. "I think she dug this up from the ground outside."

"What was she trying to grow?"

Drifting to the kitchenette, he shook his head. There was more dirt in bowls and basins on the counter. There was even one in the sink.

A drop of water welled from the faucet, dropping to the dirt. It was followed by another, a slow but regular drip. He assumed the sink was leaking, but when he tightened the taps the drops stopped falling.

"Weird." The other Were sniffed, pivoting to take in the entire space. It wasn't large, but the vessels of soil seemed to be everywhere.

"Is the bedroom empty?"

"Yeah," Nathan confirmed after taking a peek through the open doorway. Neither had picked up the sounds of breathing, but he wanted to make sure.

Derrick stepped into the small bedroom, checking the floor on the other side of the bed and underneath it.

"Nobody?" Nathan asked. A Were would have smelled decomposition, but he wasn't leaving anything to chance.

"All clear." He got to his feet.

The cabin was too rustic for a built-in closet, but it had a small wardrobe in one corner. Opening and closing the doors, he found shelves containing a small amount of clothing. A few personal items were set out on the counter of the adjoining bathroom.

"Meghan could be away for work," Nathan mused.

"Vicky didn't mention her having a job."

"At least there are no signs of a struggle."

"It certainly appears as if she simply walked away. As for the clothes, I don't know." Derrick scratched his head. "She's been wearing almost the same thing every time I've seen her. It could be that she just doesn't have a lot of clothing."

"If she's not well off like the chief thinks, that might be the case." Nathan tilted his head. "Her scent is barely stronger in here than it was outside."

Derrick had noticed that too. But at least he could distinguish Meghan's essence from the rest now. It was faint sandalwood mixed with something flowery. Very pleasant, although it was peculiar.

As a dominant werewolf, he could dissect a scent down to its particulates. And this flower wasn't something he was familiar with. As for the enveloping layer that accompanied it, he realized that mysterious other note was the tang of soil—a scent that was a touch acrid with metallic tones. Nevertheless, it smelled alive.

"I guess she doesn't spend much time inside." There were a pair of Adirondack chairs facing the lake outside with a small table in between. "Meghan may pass most of her time out of doors."

It was as good an explanation as any. "C'mon. Let's toss the sandwich in the bin and take out the trash."

"Won't she notice we came inside?"

"Maybe. Maybe not." It depended on how observant she was. Given that she'd dropped everything and left without throwing away her sandwich, they could be dealing with someone who had memory problems. That sort of thing wasn't always restricted to the old and infirm.

Hmm…Maybe he'd better take a run around the lake now that he had the scent. Vicky hadn't mentioned any health issues, but if Meghan was prone to memory lapses she might have gone out and gotten lost.

"I'm going to leave a note," he decided, fishing around the drawers for pen and paper. "We'll say Vicky asked us to check on her, and we saw the moldy sandwich and entered to make sure."

He found what he needed on the counter next to the fridge. There was no phone, so she must have used it to write grocery lists.

Derrick was adding his name and phone number to the bottom of the note when some movement caught his eye. He froze, blinking in disbelief as a small, hooded figure fell over onto the couch.

CHAPTER NINE

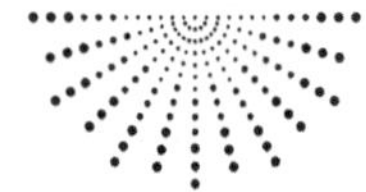

Derrick swore, yanking on Nathan's arm before running over to the immobile form on the couch. The other Were had bent to grab the trash from under the sink, so he missed the part where Meghan had appeared between one blink and the next.

And it was his mystery girl. She was huddled in a ball, her arms wrapped around her knees.

Her hair was covered by her trademark blue hood, but her face was unobscured. A delicate nose and chin were paired with a small rosebud mouth that had surprisingly lush lips.

Meghan's skin was a little darker than he expected based on the few other Meghans he'd known. It was closer to toasted caramel, and her hair was very curly and dark except for the ends. The bit that protruded from her hood was tipped in gold.

Tellingly, she hadn't reacted to his or Nate's presence. Her eyes stayed shut tight even as Derrick went from hovering to crouching in front of her.

He reached out to touch her shoulder, squeezing lightly. "Meghan? Are you okay?"

No answer.

"Her breathing is labored," Nathan pointed out needlessly as if Derrick hadn't already noticed how hard Meghan's lungs seemed to be working. Her slight breathing had an alarming raspy, rattling sound to it.

Using two fingers, he felt for her pulse and swore bloody murder. "She's freezing."

Sitting on the couch next to her, Derrick gathered the strange and slight woman in his arms. It was like hugging an ice cube.

Curious, Nate put his hand on her forehead. "*Shit.* It's like she climbed out of a meat locker. How the hell is that possible? The sun is low, but it's still at least eighty degrees outside."

Rubbing his hands up her back and arms, Derrick agreed. The hairs on the back of his neck were standing on end. "There's no way she came in from a hike while we weren't looking."

But more alarming than the way she had just appeared was how she wasn't even shivering, which sent off blaring alarm bells in his brain.

He could hear Nathan getting on the phone, asking Kiera to run out here with her medical gear.

Derrick leaned back, putting enough space between him and Meghan for him to pull off his shirt. Then he grabbed the hem of her sweatshirt and began to tug it over her head.

"What are you doing?" Nathan asked, his head drawing back as Derrick worked off the sweatshirt. Meghan was wearing a sports bra that provided as much coverage as many exercise outfits women in the pack favored.

"We have to treat this like hypothermia," he said, tossing the sweatshirt aside and pulling the girl against his bare chest. His nerve endings went crazy as her icy skin pressed against his, but he held on. "Skin to skin is the fastest way to warm her."

Shifters ran hotter than humans. That had bothered some of his overnight guests, who complained he was too hot to cuddle at night, but Derrick was never more grateful for that trait than he was right now.

Reaching behind him, he pulled the quilt off the back of the couch, wrapping it around the girl's back and around their sides to create a cocoon of warmth.

Adjusting her weight, he hitched her higher against him, so her faint breath fanned down his pectorals.

"C'mon, Meghan, open your eyes," he urged as he continued to stroke her back and arms.

Her progress was excruciatingly slow, but eventually the girl's breath strengthened, becoming even and deeper. The rattle disappeared, and the skin of her cheeks grew pink as her body began to warm. Then she shuddered, her thick brown lashes fluttering.

Rousing as if from a deep sleep, Meghan pressed against his chest, rubbing her cheek to his pecs. She sighed softly, almost happily.

Her head tilted up at him as she opened her eyes. The color was almost as startling as her drowsy smile.

Clear amber irises blinked up at him, a color so light and bright it was as if they were lit from within. A dark ring surrounded them, the contrast making the light color startling by contrast.

Meghan raised her arms, stretching as if waking from a nap. She wrapped a lazy arm around him, seemingly unconcerned at finding herself half-dressed in a stranger's lap.

She hitched up a little higher, pressing her lips to his briefly before nuzzling his neck.

"Derrick honey, did you get the eggs?" she murmured in a husky voice.

He froze. "*What?*"

He hadn't yelled, but the girl startled as if he had, pulling back away from him.

For a moment they stared at each other, the incipient panic in her eyes growing before she put her hand flat on his chest.

The touch burned. Then it was gone as she abruptly pulled away. Meghan landed on her backside on the floor, her breath coming in rapid pants as she panicked violently.

CHAPTER TEN

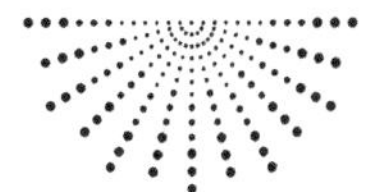

Meghan stared up at the wolf, trying to steady her breath. *Derrick*, her mind supplied. His name was Derrick. That was what the lady at the sandwich shop had called him.

She had wondered for so long what it was.

Wait, this couldn't be happening. She was imagining him again. That was all. Disappointment settled in her gut like a brick, but she didn't fight it. Living in fantasies was dangerous.

Fighting for breath, she pushed back a wave of nausea and dizziness, the former from her trip and the latter because Derrick wasn't wearing a shirt in her vision. All that golden skin over taut, defined muscles short-circuited her brain.

She closed her eyes and opened them, but the apparition was still there. This was about the time she realized he was speaking to her.

This is real. Her breath sped up at the realization.

Derrick had left the couch. He was crouching next to her. Movement behind her made her jerk. A second large man was standing behind Derrick, his features slack with confusion.

"Here," he handed a blue sweatshirt to Derrick, who pressed it into her hands.

Meghan belatedly recognized it as her own. She wasn't wearing a top, just her bra.

Cheeks flaming, she snatched the thick pullover, pressing it against her exposed skin as she scooted backward.

"Hey, it's okay," Derrick said, showing her his palms. "We're friends of Vicky's, remember? She asked us to come and check on you."

Meghan frowned. "What? Why?"

Derrick gave her a gentle smile. "Because of the sandwich."

He glanced behind him at the other man. "I guess you didn't hear me. I was saying that we're good friends with Vicky and she sometimes has us check on the property—you know, in case something needs to be fixed. We saw the rotting sandwich on the table through the window and called her. She explained that she lent you this place and was worried about your welfare. Vicky gave us permission to come inside to make sure you hadn't fallen ill or suffered an accident. You can call her if you like to confirm this."

"Oh." She looked around, avoiding his eyes. The sandwich she'd been eating wasn't on the table anymore. How long had she been gone?

Derrick made a noise as if trying to attract her attention. The wolf was startlingly handsome, and she was having a hard time looking directly at him. Blushing, she pulled her sweatshirt over her head. When she was done, he held out his hand.

She shook it tentatively, allowing only the briefest of touches.

"I'm Derrick Sheridan." He jerked his thumb to the other man.

"That's Nathan. Like I said, we're friends with Vicky. Do you know where you were?" he asked, his head tilting to one side.

Meghan didn't answer.

"You were pretty cold," he continued. "That's why I'm like this."

He gestured to his bare chest, his expression growing sheepish. "I was trying to warm you up. I have a little survival training, so I attempted to share my body heat."

The color in his cheeks deepened under her wide-eye scrutiny. Derrick coughed and grabbed his shirt, tugging it on. "So do you know where you were?"

"Uh." Meghan racked her brain, but no convenient lie came to mind. So she told the truth. "Sorry, I don't remember."

Both men stared at her. "You don't?"

Shaking her head, Meghan got to her feet. Derrick followed suit, taking a step back and putting his hands behind his back. But the non-threatening posture didn't give her any more confidence. Even though her mind told her these two were protectors and weren't a danger, she was having a hard time convincing her body of that.

Lifting a shoulder, she avoided the question. "Thank you for checking on me. As you can see, I'm fine now."

She edged to the door, but the wolf—*wolves*, her brain corrected—stayed stubbornly where they were.

"Are you sure you're feeling all right?" Derrick lifted one dark eyebrow. "That was…kind of weird."

Meghan laughed shortly. The sound made Derrick twitch, but he said nothing.

"What about food?" the other man asked.

Confused, she turned her gaze in his direction. It was harder than it should have been. Now that he was here in front of her, she wanted to keep looking at Derrick. The urge to crawl back into his lap was almost overwhelming.

"What about it?" she asked, forehead puckering.

The other wolf was as aesthetically pleasing to the eye as Derrick. He was tall with a leaner wiry frame corded with muscle. Classically handsome with sandy brown hair, he wore an open expression she remembered as being typical for him. She hadn't been watching this group long. But Meghan studied all the local young men because she had been searching for the one standing next to him.

"We had a look around when we, uh, couldn't find you. There doesn't appear to be a lot to eat in the cupboards. If you like we can do a grocery run for you, maybe pick up more sandwich fixings if that's the sort of thing you like."

Meghan hid her surprise at the generous offer. Nathan was always thoughtful, she reminded herself.

"Oh, it's okay." She tugged at the hem of her sweatshirt before shifting to stand with her back to one of the small decorative tables Vicky favored. Hiding her hands behind her back, she stuck her fingers in the planter she'd left there, running the soil through her fingers.

"I'm going to get groceries tomorrow. Wednesday is my regular shopping day."

Derrick's face sobered. "Today is Saturday."

A pang of dismay made her face fall. She tried to hide her consternation, but she could tell from the wolves' reaction that she didn't do it well or fast enough.

"I mean Sunday," she corrected softly. "Sunday is my shopping day."

Taking a deep breath, she went to the door and opened it. "Thanks again for checking on me. I'll call Vicky and let her know everything is fine."

It looked as if Derrick was going to be stubborn. He planted his legs and crossed his arms, but Nathan poked him hard in the back. They exchanged another significant and very lupine look. Though he scowled, Derrick uncrossed his arms and headed for the door.

He paused outside the cabin. "We can't leave yet. If it's all right with you, we're going to wait out here for Kiera, the doctor from the clinic—I think you might know her. While you were unresponsive, Nathan here called her. She's coming over here to check on you."

Meghan's lips parted, gripping the doorknob. "I don't need a doctor."

But Derrick shook his head. "It won't take long. I hear her car now."

He gave a bright smile, one too tight to be genuine. She was testing his temper. Even the good wolves didn't like being gainsaid.

But Derrick was making a hell of an effort to appear as if he wasn't angry. He gave her a friendly wave and went out to meet the car driving up the lane.

THE MOMENT KIERA stopped her car, Nate was there. He opened her door and gave her a quick debrief in a low voice that didn't carry to the cabin.

"Well, this should be interesting," she muttered, heading to the door. She made a shooing motion with her hand, warning Derrick to give her and Meghan some distance.

"*Go,*" she urged when he didn't move.

He ignored her of course. The stubborn wolf just leaned against a wide tree trunk on the other side of the clearing where the cabin was located. She could smell his agitation. Derrick was really worked up.

She knew his protective instincts had been riled by his discovery of the cubs, so it wasn't all that surprising that he'd go all dominant alpha male right now. But she didn't want his hyper-masculine presence to agitate the sensitive girl she'd met at the hospital.

Biting back a sigh, she knocked on the cabin door. She'd known Vicky had found a caretaker for this place but hadn't realized it was Meghan. She had assumed it was another wolf. And Meghan had read as human to her senses, but she was second-guessing that now after what Nathan had told her on the phone.

Kiera sternly told herself not to turn around and look for Nate when Meghan finally opened the door.

Meghan gave her a nervous smile. "I'm sorry Derrick called you. Really, I'm fine," she said, her eyes flicking past Keira to the idiot wolf faking nonchalance outside. "You didn't have to come out here."

Kiera's own protective instincts kicked in. She returned the smaller woman's smile, her eyes calculating the changes in her appearance since she'd seen her last. Her face was paler, the gold in her skin tone muted. Though she remained as lovely as when they'd first met, Meghan was noticeably thinner than when she'd seen her last.

"I know you are probably tired of nosy neighbors messing in your business," she told her with a grin. "But this is a small town, and you're talking to a doctor who's related to a good quarter of the residents. They're going to hound me if I don't check you out. Plus, you look a little peaked."

She held up her medical bag. "Why don't I give you a quick exam right now?" She jerked her head at the men behind her. "My overly concerned friends can wait out here."

Meghan hesitated, but then she stepped back and waved Kiera inside. She closed the door behind her and moved to sit on the couch.

Kiera remained standing. She set her bag on the small coffee table and took out a stethoscope.

"Should I take off my sweater?" Meghan asked.

She nodded and Meghan pulled off the navy hoodie. "Twice in one day," she commented with a wry twist of her lips.

Kiera pressed the chest piece over her heart. "Twice?"

A copper tinge burnished the girl's cheeks. "Derrick took off my sweater and hugged me," she explained. "He said I was too cold. I guess it scared him."

Her intuition was doing cartwheels, but Kiera kept her expression placid. "Yes, Nathan mentioned how icy your skin felt. Does that happen a lot?"

Meghan hesitated. "Now and again."

"That's a little odd in this weather. Is that why you're always wearing a sweatshirt?"

Nodding, Meghan clasped her hands together, leaning forward when Kiera pressed the stethoscope to her back. She listened to her breathing, not picking up the rattle Nathan had described.

"It is."

Humming noncommittally, Kiera continued her exam. She waited for her patient to speak. Most volunteered information instinctively to fill the silence, but Meghan wasn't typical.

It was obvious something odd was happening here. The girl's evasiveness certainly supported that theory.

But she doesn't smell like a witch. Not that Kiera was bigoted against witches that way. It went against her nature to let another being suffer, no matter who or *what* she was. This was why pack alphas were generally advised to let their healers treat everyone, even pack enemies—as long as they didn't pose a threat.

"Well, you're breathing sounds much better than what the boys described."

Meghan snickered. "You call *them* boys?"

Kiera was only thinking of Derrick when she said that. Nathan had always been a man in her eyes, but she nodded anyway.

"They may be full-grown now, but they will always be boys when they don't get their way. Am I right?" she asked, trying her best to establish some sort of rapport.

Meghan lifted a shoulder. "I don't know many men."

Join the club, she thought, almost laughing aloud. But the urge to play big sister was too strong. There were few women in the pack less experienced than her, but Meghan's was so sweet and innocent it almost made her teeth ache.

"They're all similar in some respects," she said with a knowing smile that didn't reflect her reality.

Kiera couldn't speak from experience. She could count the number of men she'd dated on one hand, but she'd heard enough similar comments from female friends and relatives to feel comfortable repeating them.

"Deep down each has a little boy inside," she added.

"I'm not sure that's true of Derrick."

Kiera's ears perked up. She wasn't imagining that note of interest in Meghan's voice. "Oh, don't get me wrong. Derrick is one of the good ones. He just wants to make sure that you're okay."

Meghan nodded. "He's very kind."

Kiera straightened her cursory physical exam over. "You do appear to be fine now. Your heart sounds normal, as do your lungs. Your reflexes are a little sluggish for my taste but within the normal range for hu—for a woman your age."

Kiera mentally bit her tongue. She had almost said "humans" instead. Recovering, she reached out to pat the girl's shoulder but stopped when Meghan shied away.

"Sorry," she said, drawing back.

Kiera saw the small shimmer in her light-brown eyes, but Meghan looked down at her hands to hide the incipient tears. "It's all right. I'm just not a big toucher."

"That's okay," Kiera said, considering her young charge with pursed lips. "But I would like to talk to you about something else. You said you have had other episodes where you get cold like that. Is it always that extreme?"

"I haven't taken my temperature, so I'm not sure what you mean by extreme. It *feels* very cold."

"And you have problems breathing after?"

She nodded.

"Do you have memory lapses associated with these incidents?"

Meghan blinked, hesitating. "Sometimes," she whispered.

Kiera frowned. "I'd like to do more tests. Do you think you can come back to the clinic with me?"

She could tell the answer was no before Meghan shook her head. "I would like to stay here and sleep a bit."

Sitting on the coffee table in front of her patient, Kiera set her stethoscope aside. "A fugue state where you can't remember what you did can be a sign of a more serious condition. The fact that this appears to be happening on a regular basis is troubling."

Meghan's fingers laced together tightly. "I wouldn't call it a fugue state. I just get muddled."

Her sensitive nose picked up the other woman's sudden spike in anxiety. Kiera decided not to press her on the exact nature of her symptoms, but she couldn't help asking. "Do you think it's a good idea to stay out here so far from your neighbors? The nearest cabin is a good five-minute walk away. That may not seem like a big distance, but when you're in medical distress it can feel more like five hundred miles."

This earned a shrug. "I'm grateful for your concern, but I'm afraid I'm not in a position to move."

"Do you have a job?" She hadn't heard of anyone hiring Meghan in town, but people worked remotely quite a bit these days.

This time Meghan hung her head. "I, um...I have trouble holding down jobs. But I'm not starving or anything. I have some money from rewards."

"Rewards?"

Meghan lifted a hand to gesture to the cabin around her. "Like the cabin. Vicky lent it to me after I found her great-grandmother's ruby bracelet. She wasn't offering a reward at the time because she never thought she'd see it again—it had been lost for years—but when I found it, she was so grateful she told me I could stay here."

She gave Kiera a small look that seemed to ask for her understanding. "Vicky doesn't like renting it out," Meghan continued. "She says the residual smell of strangers in her space bothers her. But she doesn't mind mine. I'm a friend."

Kiera leaned back, her mind going a mile a minute. "A friend who returned a priceless heirloom to her."

Meghan's grin transformed her interesting elfin face to something arrestingly beautiful. "Oh, I'm sure a jeweler could put a price tag on it. I doubt it was worth all that much."

"I imagine it held a lot of sentimental value for Vicky. So, you've found other things that you've received rewards for?"

"Yes."

Kiera didn't know what to say. She finally settled on. "You must be lucky."

"I guess so." Meghan's expression was wry and not entirely happy.

"Health issues aside, I mean," Kiera corrected with a wince. She made an impulsive decision. "You know, I live in the middle of town. My place is down the street from the clinic. I have a spare room you could stay in."

Meghan's mouth opened, but she didn't speak right away. Finally, she cleared her throat. "That's very generous, but I can't have roommates. Thank you anyway."

There was a note of finality in her tone. Kiera knew it meant the case was closed.

"I respect that, but you seem so nice. I would hate for anything to happen to you. How about we schedule some tests to see if we can get to the bottom of your chill attacks? Maybe we can take some scans and draw some blood? We can tell a lot about the body from a few simple tests. It won't cost anything if money is tight. The clinic does a fair amount of *pro bono* work."

She could feel the girl's resistance, but Meghan lifted a shoulder. She looked up, her gaze on the door, and Kiera knew she was picturing the idiot wolf on the other side of the clearing. "Maybe I can swing by later? I have some shopping to do."

That was the most she could ask. "Great." Rising, Kiera headed for the door. "I hope you can come to the clinic soon. Tomorrow would be best."

Meghan nodded. Her hand went out, and she dropped some dark stuff into a bowl sitting on the coffee table.

Was that *dirt*?

Okay, that is weird. But she didn't comment. Instead, she simply said goodbye and left, taking a lot of troubling new thoughts with her.

CHAPTER ELEVEN

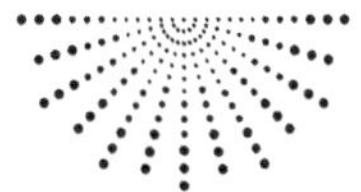

Derrick couldn't sit at the table while Kiera presented the details of her meeting with Meghan to him, Nate, and the chief. He was too wound up, his skin itching to go back out to the cabin on the lake.

Kiera didn't disclose any private medical details, but she didn't correct him or Nate when they insisted something was going on with the girl. "I just wanted to wrap her in bubble wrap and do everything I could to protect her."

Douglas, seated at the table next to Nate, twitched a brow. "Well, if Kiera reacted that way, I guess the pair of you were feeling the same impulses."

Kiera was a healer, but he and Nate were upper-level dominants. Their protective instincts were finely honed. Derrick could no more turn off his need to take care of weaker members of the pack than he could cut off his own arm. The drive was built into his psyche. He'd been born that way.

So yeah, to say he was feeling protective of Meghan was the fucking understatement of the century. It didn't matter that she was an outsider. She had come to their territory after performing a service for one of their pack elders.

But clearly there was some seriously shady shit going on.

"I had the same urge," Nate offered. "Especially after the way she just popped into existence like that."

They had described the details of their visit, why they had entered, and the way Meghan had simply appeared. They also had mentioned the odd way she had stored dirt in whatever receptacle she could find.

The best they could figure it was some sort of nervous tick. Derrick was seriously hoping she didn't eat it. A quick internet search had confirmed that was a real disorder often caused by the body's attempt to get the nutrients it needed when it was malnourished.

And Meghan had looked so thin…

"Could she simply have evaded your senses?" Douglas asked thoughtfully. "Perhaps with a spell?"

Nathan shook his head. "There was no way she could have come in and sat on the couch without us noticing. And Derrick was looking right at her. One second the living room is empty and then bam, she's falling over on the couch, almost frozen through in this muggy heat."

He passed a hand over his face. "Stranger or not, I was relieved when she recovered, but I doubt I'm as concerned for her as some others. Of course, *I* didn't get a kiss, so that's understandable."

Nate, the bastard, grinned and waggled his brows in his direction.

Douglas raised an eyebrow. "She kissed you?"

"It was more than a kiss," he said, his voice perilously close to a growl—an unwise tone to take with his alpha.

But he was too worked up to be wise at this moment. Something about Meghan had flipped all his switches.

He turned to Douglas, fighting to get his bearings. "She knew me."

"Maybe she does," the chief said reasonably. "You're fairly visible around town.'

Derrick thrust out an arm, passing it roughly through his hair. "This was more than that."

Cupping his hands, he gestured as if Meghan were there in front of him. "I had her in my arms. The cold had departed, and she was rousing, waking up as if from a deep sleep. I expected her to look up at me and start screaming. That would have been rational. But there was no panic. Not a hint of it, because she *knew* me."

The chief pursed his lips. But Derrick didn't need to explain to this group how unusual it was for a woman to wake up in a stranger's arms and not freak out.

"Meghan recognized me. And not from a handful of glimpses around town. There was no surprise on her face. She looked at me as if she'd spent years waking up with me."

That was it. The recognition hadn't just been personal. It had been…intimate.

He broke off and slashed the air with his hand. "For fuck's sake, she even called me by my name."

A corner of Douglas's mouth pulled back, but he didn't chastise Derrick for his intensity. The chief was used to dealing with wolves in various stages of freaking out. Being the chief's nephew might also get him a slightly longer leash than another wolf, but Derrick didn't abuse that privilege.

"And yet all of you agree she's not a witch," Douglas said, looking at them in turn.

"If she is then she's one unlike any other I've met," he announced when the others merely shrugged.

Douglas wasn't impressed with his opinion. "But it's possible?"

"Yeah," he admitted with some reluctance. "What she told Kiera about finding stuff certainly points at some magical ability. But she might not know what she is."

The chief growled. "That doesn't mean she's not dangerous. We all know how much damage witches ignorant of their own nature can do."

A great fucking point. Derrick had almost forgotten how his cousin Mara had almost died because a male witch who didn't know he was a witch became obsessed with her.

"We could also be dealing with a human under magical duress," Nate said, voicing the same idea Derrick had been turning over since Kiera had pried him away from the cabin. "It could be a curse."

He put his hands on his hips. "I think we need a magical consult from a witch. A powerful one."

A normal alpha would have bristled at the idea of bringing a witch into pack business. But even though he would not admit it, Douglas was dating one.

Hope Li was Logan Li's mother. Logan was Connell's mate and the current Air Elemental. A powerful Supernatural who could call up tornadoes and hurricanes with a flick of her fingers, Logan was charged with keeping order in the Supernatural world. Only four women were chosen to be Elementals at any one time. They came from formative magical families, which made Logan's mother Hope a very powerful witch indeed.

Derrick liked Hope, especially since the woman had been instrumental in saving Mara's life when that male witch finally tried to kill her. But she confused him.

Hope was smart and stylish with a perpetually cheerful, calm expression. A professor of military history who studied the bloodiest battles in history, she said things like, "'Now Derrick, at least the local flora and fauna will be renewed. Fire is an important part of the ecosystem' when one corner of the state burned down.'"

No one had died during that fire, of course, or the comment would have been wildly inappropriate. But it was only one example of the woman's otherness. Hope saw the world from a different lens. And Douglas was very taken with her.

"It is just too much of a coincidence that we have some mystery person texting us warnings that led to the discovery of two abandoned cubs," he said. "Now there's this girl who goes through life finding things so often she can live off the rewards. Do you think Hope can come out here?"

Douglas nodded, not bothering to hide how pleased he was. "It sounds as if this Meghan could go either way. She could be a witch playing some game or a victim. I will give Hope a call and ask her to come to give her assessment."

The chief's quiet exuberance faded a touch. "You all realize this means Mai will come with her."

That went without saying. Hope and her sister, the chain-smoking and surly Mai, went everywhere together. Mara adored the bitchy witch. Derrick wasn't as big a fan, but he appreciated the other woman's forthrightness.

"I'm good with that. Just make sure to give them the third-floor guest room." That one had a balcony. Mai could smoke without having to stomp down the stairs or worse—scare the shit out of him again by casting a levitation spell on a broom and flying it out the window.

Mai liked to poke fun at certain stereotypes.

"Noted," Douglas grunted, getting to his feet. He gave Derrick a resigned look. "I take it I don't have to ask which one of you is going to be monitoring Meghan, do I?"

Nate glanced at him and put his hands up like he was surrendering. "Not my mystery."

Derrick's mouth flattened. Nate was enjoying this too much. But all he said was, "Good."

CHAPTER TWELVE

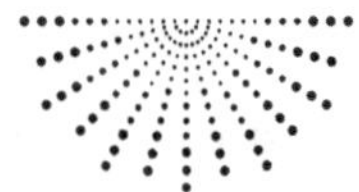

Meghan should have been surprised to see Derrick so soon, but she wasn't. The wolf showed his face at mid-morning, although she was certain he'd been watching the cabin since well before breakfast.

That was why she didn't blink when he appeared in front of Vicky's defunct vegetable patch where she'd been digging around barehanded.

He held a paper sack full of groceries.

"Hi," he said, his chiseled features schooled into a placid and non-threatening expression. He was toning down those ultra-masculine dominant vibes for her sake. It was very sweet.

Meghan stared at him with a considering expression. *This must be the right time.* It had to be. But her tension didn't leave her. Because there was no way of knowing. And she didn't think she could stand it if she were wrong.

His too-perceptive gaze was watching her intently, forcing her to bow her head to hide the turmoil of her thoughts. The fact she couldn't focus even now made her angry. But there were too many disjointed memories. They danced across her mind like a kaleido-scope or a puzzle she could never assemble.

She was lost in thought a little too long for the werewolf's comfort. When she finally looked up, he was looking at her with such concern, and she sternly reminded herself to stay in the here and now. It was the only way to cope.

Derrick cleared his throat and knelt in front of her. His eyes were lighter than his normal ginger brown as if they were warmed by his concern for her.

It was practically criminal to let her mind wander away when in the presence of such a handsome male specimen, but up close she felt helpless. All she could do was stare.

"Do you remember me?" he asked, his head cocked to the side, that same soul-warming solicitude in his slow, careful movements.

The laugh escaped before she could stop it. Oh dear, if only he knew.

But the sound only seemed to deepen his worry for her. *Well, you do look like a madwoman, scrabbling in the dirt with the attention span of a gnat.*

"Derrick," she said. "Yes, I remember."

She had kissed him just yesterday. Or at least she thought she had. But he didn't mention it, so maybe she was wrong about when that was.

He nodded slowly. "You knew my name yesterday before I introduced myself. Did you hear it in town? At the diner maybe?"

"Uh." she blinked. "I must have, I suppose. Or someplace else. I can't recall where I heard it."

"Yeah. Living in a small town can be like that. Everyone just knows everyone. You absorb information about them without even trying."

He hefted the grocery sack a little higher. "I wasn't sure if you were aware that the grocery store closed early on Sundays. I didn't want you to miss your window to get supplies, so I picked up a few essentials."

He showed her his teeth, the gesture too gentle to be a smile. "I hope you don't mind."

Derrick held the bag out to her.

Meghan stood, slapping her hands together to shake the dirt off. But she was careful to leave some of it on her palms.

She knew the wolf wasn't going to give up until she took the bag. But the fierce bit of her inner self, the one she recognized as pride couldn't simply take it.

"I can't accept these unless you allow me to pay for them."

Some might have been surprised to learn that Meghan didn't take everything that was offered. After all, she lived off rewards, staying in homes not her own. But she wasn't a beggar. Or a freeloader.

A man related to one of her patrons had called her that once. The word had stung fiercely. It also made her annoyed. She *always* performed a service in exchange for her rewards. Always.

But she had performed no such service for Derrick. Instead, he'd done one for her, warming her from the bitter cold.

"You accepting these is payment enough for me," Derrick told her with a grin. "Consider it a belated welcome-to-town gift."

He shuffled to one side, still doing his best to appear harmless—a tall order for someone so large and muscular.

"Why don't I put these inside? Then I can come help you plant whatever you're planting. Is it some sort of fall crop? Carrots? Beets? I think those would tolerate a little frost, and they mature quickly."

His eyes ran over the turned-over earth in the little garden patch. She had used Vicky's small spade to dig so she could reach the richer living soil below the surface, so it *did* appear as if she was gardening. However, there were nothing to plant. His expression said he hadn't missed that detail.

He'd also seen the inside of the cabin, with her little safeguards scattered around in whatever container she could find. But that damnable pride didn't relish Derrick seeing this proof of her strangeness again.

"I'll take it, thank you," she said, holding out her hands for the groceries. "But I don't need help planting. As it turns out, I lost my packet of seeds."

"That's too bad," he said, handing her the sack. "We can run out and get some if you like. I parked a little down the road."

He was lying of course. He'd run out here. His kind didn't sweat much, so it wasn't noticeable. And if she said yes to him, he'd simply run out to where his car was and drive back. It would take him mere minutes. His kind was so fast.

Derrick read her distraction as hesitation. "Of course, if you don't want to be alone in a car with a strange man, that's understandable. I always tell my female relatives that—never go off with strangers. Or new acquaintances."

"Wise words, but in this case rather silly," she said. "We have perfect privacy here. If you wanted to hurt me, a secondary location would be redundant."

Derrick's head jerked back a fraction, and she almost bit her tongue. Implying that he would hurt her was a great insult to a wolf of his ilk. She almost apologized but remembered he'd started that line of conversation.

And you're not supposed to know his true nature. Not yet.

He held up his hands, giving her a winsome grin. It transformed his features, reminding her of lazy mornings full of sunshine, languorous heat, and the smell of clean skin. But they weren't memories she should have. Meghan knew that much.

These had bled through.

"That's why I'm going to stay out here," he said. "While you put away those groceries."

Shifting the bag in her hold, she bit her lip, considering him for a long moment. As much as she needed to keep her secrets, she didn't want him to get bored and leave.

"It's all right. You can come inside while I put them away." Meghan gestured at the cabin door. "I have coffee."

Derrick loved coffee. And he took it black with just a bit of sugar, which was good because she didn't have any cream. Meghan would also find her cache of money because she *was* paying for the groceries.

Seemingly pleased with her invitation Derrick held out his hands as if to take the sack, but she shook her head. "I've got it."

Meghan stepped inside of the cabin with his heat at her back.

Gesturing to the couch in silent invitation, she headed for the kitchenette with the bag in her hands.

She didn't make it.

CHAPTER THIRTEEN

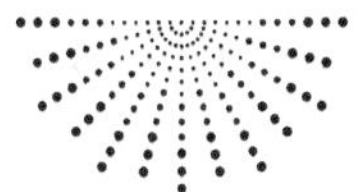

Derrick sprang from the couch with a startled shout. Meghan was gone. She had disappeared before his very eyes.

One moment she had been carrying the groceries to the kitchen portion of the room and then she had jerked forward, almost as if she'd been tripping. And then she was gone as if she'd fallen into a hole that had opened in front of her.

The way she had disappeared was unnatural too. She hadn't just blipped out of existence the way Nathan had claimed she'd appeared last night. No, her body had literally fallen through a tear in the universe he couldn't see—her front disappearing before her torso and back. Her curls, flung behind her by her sudden imbalance, had been the last to go.

Rushing to the spot where she'd vanished, he thrust his hands out, hoping to reach into whatever hole she'd fallen into so he could pull her back.

"Fuck," he growled when his hands stayed resolutely visible. Whatever opening Meghan had fallen into was closed now.

Derrick strangled the howl that rose to his throat. The girl's sudden and bizarre disappearance had shocked him to his very core.

I was here to check up on her, he told himself. His task had been to assess the threat if any, that Meghan posed. But after yesterday he knew that was bullshit. He was here for two reasons. To satisfy his curiosity and to protect her.

The visceral memory of her freezing cold body coming to life in his arms made the beast that lived inside him throw himself at the walls of his head. It was almost rabid in its rage.

His wolf wanted out so it could find Meghan.

Derrick took a slow breath. This was the closest he had come to losing control of his beast since he was a teenager. The first flush of hormone overload was the most dangerous time for werewolves. Or at least it had been for him.

Except this moment threatened to eclipse any of his teenage rages.

But Derrick couldn't afford to let the beast slip the reins. His wolf was a touch more animal than some of his peers when stressed. He *had* to find Meghan. And he would need human reason to do it. Forcibly he pushed back the beast, expecting a fight.

But the wolf calmed sooner than expected. His other half recognized the need for quick action.

Derrick started running through the small cabin, calling Meghan's name. Coming up empty, he ran outside, circling the cabin over and over.

Nothing. Meghan was gone.

He shoved a hand in his jeans, intending to pull out his phone so he could call for reinforcements. But it wasn't there. Cursing a blue streak, he retraced his steps, finally finding the phone on the couch. It had fallen out of his pocket when he jumped up.

Then a disheveled Meghan stumbled out of nothing clutching the now-grubby grocery bag in her hands.

CHAPTER FOURTEEN

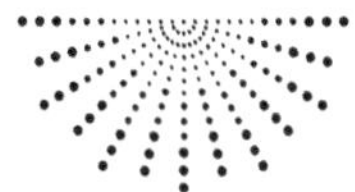

Derrick's hands closed over Meghan's thin shoulders before he was consciously aware of moving.

Fuck. She was cold again. Not as much as yesterday, but enough. To say something was fucking wrong with the universe was a big fucking understatement.

Her glazed features were like a knife to the heart. "What happened to you? Where did you go?" he asked, trying not to shake her.

The slight movement of her body made the stench of the bag in her hands waft in his face, but he was too far gone to gag.

Blinking, Meghan looked up at him. "Hi...um, Derrick. What's wrong?"

"*What's wrong?*" he asked in disbelief, his hands squeezing her reflexively.

She flinched.

Swallowing, Derrick forced himself to loosen his grip on her delicate limbs. She was so light her bones might have been hollow, like a bird. "You disappear in front of me and you're asking me what's wrong?"

Her lips trembled, but Meghan shook herself and forced them into a smile. She began to speak, but her voice broke. Clearing her throat, she swallowed audibly and tried again.

"Don't be silly," she said hoarsely. "I didn't go anywhere."

Derrick hissed. He swallowed, forcing his voice smooth. "Meghan, sweetheart…the groceries are rotten."

Startled, Meghan shifted the bag. She picked one of the items at the top—a pear. The rotted fruit disintegrated in her hands, the fermented liquid mess landing on the floor with a splatter.

Meghan burst into tears.

Tearing herself out of his arms, she left him holding the bag as she staggered to the sink. Meghan rinsed her hands, the rotted fruit residue mixing with the soil in the pan under the tap.

Derrick put the sack down on the floor, moving behind her. He made sure his footsteps made noise so he wouldn't startle her, but she jumped when he put his hands on her shoulders.

Then she did the weirdest damn thing—second to disappearing. Meghan turned off the tap and pivoted so she was over the flat baking dish filled with dirt on the counter.

Then she started to wash her hands with it. Tears streamed down her face. A few landed in the dirt. Spots of green appeared there. But it wasn't mold.

Tiny plants were sprouting, their growth happening in fast forward.

CHAPTER FIFTEEN

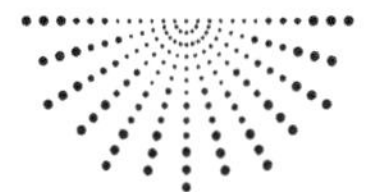

Meghan shuddered as the heat of Derrick's hands seeped through her thin shirt. She hadn't been wearing a sweater, because she hadn't wanted to soil it while digging around in the garden, so she'd been caught unprepared when a bubble appeared without warning.

She hated when that happened, hated the cold.

And Derrick's warmth was so inviting. He was like a furnace at her back. There was nothing she wanted to do more than to lean back and soak up that heat. But she couldn't risk him that way…

"You shouldn't touch me," Meghan said in a small voice, her head down. "It's not easy for anyone else to fall into one of my bubbles. They try to keep other people out, but it can happen. And if it does, you'll die. Nothing that lives can survive them. Only me."

Meghan braced herself for the loss of his touch, but she had underestimated the wolf. Derrick was a warrior, incredibly brave and beautiful. Also, a foolhardy idiot who reacted to mortal danger by embracing it tighter.

Hands settled more heavily on her shoulders. He turned her to face him. "Can you explain?" he asked, wiping the traces of her tears.

His gentleness made her want to cry more. But instead of tears, she let her pain out in words.

"I've met you before."

His brows rose. "You have?"

Meghan looked into his eyes and nodded, prepared for him to push her away or to say she was lying. But he needed to hear the words. It was time.

It is time, isn't it?

"I don't know," she said, answering her own question. Which was naturally misinterpreted.

Derrick's head pulled back. "So, you don't know me?"

"I sometimes get confused." Meghan touched her forehead. "It doesn't help that I usually only have myself to talk to. I don't like being around people too much, for obvious reasons. People who've caught glimpses of me disappearing don't always react well."

"Yeah, I bet," he muttered. His thumbs stroked her shoulders. "Whatever is happening to you is very unsettling. I don't blame you for getting mixed up."

He clasped her dirt-streaked hand and guided her to the couch. Puzzled at his willingness to keep touching her, Meghan sat next to him.

It was very awkward. The wolf was very large as a man. Derrick took up most of the room, but the weirdest part was holding his hand as if they were...normal. A man and a woman holding hands, like the movies she sometimes saw on the library computers.

"I *have* met you before," she clarified. "But it was only before for *me*. From your perspective, it hasn't happened—you were a bit older than you are now."

Meghan peeked at him from under her lashes, trying to gauge his reaction.

Derrick's lips were parted. He looked like a very handsome fish with his mouth gaping like that. But it was obvious he was having a hard time accepting her words as truth.

He thinks you're crazy. The few people she had confided in always did.

"It's okay if you don't believe me." No one ever had. But she had hoped he would be different…because he had told her he was.

His fingers squeezed hers. "Hey, I didn't say that. It's just a lot to process. Time travel."

He rubbed his face with a hand. But not the one that held hers. Derrick didn't stop touching her, even for a moment.

"But I don't see how you could be lying, because you popped back with evidence."

Meghan frowned. "I did?"

"Those groceries show signs of at least a few weeks' worth of decay."

"Oh…er. Yes."

Derrick sighed, but the deepness of it made it sound like a growl. "I suppose you could have popped into a place that was so unhealthful that it was filled with spores and mold, but you were freezing when you got back, which would have preserved the food."

He grimaced. "I'm afraid to ask how long you've been actually gone?"

"A few days." She took a deep breath. "I dropped the bag in the first bubble and was forced to go forward into another to avoid some obstacles."

He inched closer to her until his thigh was touching hers. "What sort of obstacles?"

She chuckled mirthlessly. "I'm not sure what it was this time. There was noise, like shouts and the sounds of dogs. It might have been a hunt. I end up in some dangerous places sometimes and can't trust that the people I'll run into will be friendly or willing to listen to whatever story I can concoct on the fly. I ran until I found another bubble."

"I think I get it. These bubbles can overlap and lead to skips and hops in time. Nothing is linear."

"Yes!" Meghan said, excited that he understood. Then she sighed. "I think I was in that second one for about a day before I could retrace my steps."

She bit her lip. "I'm not always able to do that."

"They're not static?" Derrick asked. "Your bubbles aren't just doors we can't see?"

"No," she said shaking her head. "They move, floating all around like soap bubbles, except no one else can see them. *I* can't always see them. Not until it's too late."

His deep voice swore unintelligibly.

"Some bubbles are chasms or pits," she continued. "I can sometimes avoid those, but if I'm not careful I fall in. Sometimes I can climb back out, although it can take some time. And some bubbles are windows—you can't go through those."

His eyes lit up. "But you can see through to the other side?"

She nodded. "Yes, sometimes. It has come in handy a few times in the past."

Derrick grinned. "I bet it has…especially if the windows show you where someone lost a precious family heirloom."

"Yes." But her pleased satisfaction that he understood faded quickly. "Less common are the bubbles that stretch out to where you can see what's at the other end—like a short hallway or corridor. I have gotten better at recognizing *when* and *where* is on the other side, but it all depends on if I've been there before.

"Unfortunately, that's not the case most of the time. And sometimes the bubbles surprise me. They slide in on their side, so narrow I don't see them until they are on top of me. I slip through. Then they burst open unexpectedly, leaving me with no idea when or where I am."

Her eyes grew distant as her mind reflected on the wonders and horrors she had seen. There had been plenty of both. Derrick watched her, seeming to understand.

"There's no telling where I'll end up until I'm there. Occasionally, I can figure it out by the position of the stars. I've studied the constellations for that very reason—although at times even that hasn't been enough. Sometimes the skies have been so foreign that to this day I don't know where those places were. One time I was convinced I was actually on another planet."

She sighed. "But even those sorts of bubbles aren't the worst...the worst are the black holes."

Alerted by the hushed dread in her voice, Derrick wrapped an arm around her waist. He tilted her face up with a finger under her chin. Guilt flared. Meghan was too weak to stop him, soaking up the small contact greedily.

"What are they?" His voice was husky.

"The worst kind of bubble," she whispered. "Super-heavy, like the black holes astronomers describe. When one opens, there's no escaping them—even if they're on the other side of the room. They always suck me in."

She wondered for a moment if she should tell him the rest, that she believed something evil had figured out how to manipulate those black holes to capture her. But she decided not to. Derrick had enough to process.

And this last tidbit took him a long while to digest. She was starting to think he was going to spend the rest of the afternoon holding her hand in silence when he turned to her with whiplash wolf speed.

His gaze roamed over her face, a hint of possessiveness in his gaze. "And just how well do we know each other?"

She hesitated but decided to answer honestly. "Our previous meeting was brief. I landed in a backyard, and you were there."

Her lip trembled as she relived the relief that swept through her at what he'd told her that fateful day. It seemed that relief had been premature.

"You knew me on sight," she continued in a low voice. Meghan removed her hand from his grasp. "You told me I had to keep going, to find you earlier and..."

Derrick tensed. "And what?"

"You said everything would be all right. You *promised*." This time her smile took real effort. "I guess I hoped that when I did find you it meant that this was a fixed point—a place and time where the bubbles didn't exist."

She had read about fixed points but could no longer remember where. Perhaps it was a note she had written to herself.

Meghan looked down at her hands. "But the bubbles are everywhere, in all times."

"Why did you kiss me?"

Startled, she jerked her head up. She had almost forgotten about that.

"I think it was my first kiss," she said, looking ashamed. "The fact that I don't remember why I did it is almost unforgivable. I had been away and suddenly, I was warm and in your lap. I couldn't remember how I had gotten there or why I was caressing you."

It was completely out of character for her.

He frowned but nodded. "I believe you."

For a second, she marveled at how accepting he seemed until she remembered Derrick was a werewolf. His kind had senses so perceptive they could smell truth from lies. She'd have to be a sociopath—a very committed one who believed her own lies—to fool his nose.

How she knew this about werewolves was a mystery for another time.

Derrick glanced at the table. "Do you mind answering another question? What is with the dirt?"

Oh. Of course, he would wonder about that.

"Remember that I told you I can sometimes tell where a bubble leads?"

Meghan held up a soiled hand. "Well, this helps. The ground beneath our feet varies. Some is just dirt or sand. But some is true soil with a unique complement of bacteria and fungi. Each is tiny, but it's a life, one that was born in a specific time and place."

"You can track their signature," he said, his quick mind following her logic seamlessly. "Like a biological geo-locator, you can track in time as well as space. But I thought you said nothing alive survived your bubble."

This last was a question.

"That's because it's a void with no air or heat—no atmosphere to speak of. However, many of the microbes that live in the soil are anaerobic. They don't need oxygen or at least very much of it."

It had taken her a very long time to figure that out. She reached out and took a pinch of soil from the pot in front of her. "Also, I think I carry a small amount of air with me, bound to my skin and lungs. Otherwise, I don't know how I can live when others don't."

"Magic is a tricky bitch," he said with a commiserating chuckle that didn't sound very amused. "But your reasoning makes sense. You can carry traces of life but not something bigger, like a plant. Anything bigger would die."

"Yes." She decided to trust him with another truth. "But if I were touching a plant, it probably wouldn't happen in the first place. Most bubbles slide around big living things like trees or people. Mostly. But it's surprisingly difficult to go through life literally hugging a tree. And if a black hole bubble pops up, even that doesn't help."

Derrick rubbed his face, leaving a big streak of dirt on his cheek. He'd forgotten he'd held her soiled hand.

Biting back a smile, she pointed at his cheek. "You got some schmutz."

He gave himself a little shake, his head pulling back a little. Then he laughed, the sound hearty and genuine. "A time-traveling witch just used the word schmutz."

"Vicky used it to describe the bracelet. It had slipped off her wrist in her backyard after the clasp broke. It was pretty dirty when I found it."

Meghan paid close attention when a person spoke to her. She did her best to emulate their speech patterns and vocabulary without being too obvious.

Fitting in was the key to her survival.

"How long has this been happening? Do you know where you're from? Where or when your family might exist?"

Meghan pushed back the swell of loneliness his words inspired. "Those memories are too distant now. I can only recall pieces."

And some of those I don't want to remember. Because then she'd have to see the woman lying so still and cold in the tall grass—the one with skin darker than hers, but the same hair…dark curls edged in gold.

Derrick had a hard time accepting that. "So there's nothing? No clue of where you came from or how you got this way?"

Helplessly, she shook her head. "It started when I was a child. All I remember is a distant vista of a city with many spires. But I've never found a picture of it in any library."

His lip curled. "Maybe because it doesn't exist anymore?"

That was a possibility she had considered many times. "My birthplace may be a pile of ruins, its history long forgotten."

That part didn't bother her. Not anymore. It was the idea of what she might have had there, had and lost, that was a far more painful subject to consider.

She rose to her feet. Derrick grabbed her hand and scowled. "Where are you going?"

Flinching at his stern expression, she stammered. "I-I was going to get you a towel."

"Oh. Sorry." He huffed and gave himself a little shake. "But I'm okay, thanks."

"No?" She frowned, tilting her head. "I guess werewolves don't mind being dirty."

The reaction to her words was unexpected. Derrick looked as if he'd just won a bet.

"I knew it," he gloated. He snatched her hand back, using his free one to point at her. "I knew you knew."

"When I met you—"

He held up a hand. "Stop. I don't want to know about our first meeting. Nothing about me or what happens to me. I don't want to risk my future with too much knowledge. There are rules to time travel."

"*There are?*" she asked, her mouth dropping open. Where had he learned them? Did this mean there were others like her?

"Well, according to the movies," he apologized, realizing she had read too much in a flippant comment. "But clearly, none of those apply to you."

"Oh," she answered, crestfallen.

Derrick took one look at her downcast expression and scrambled to his feet. "C'mon," he said, tugging her to the door.

Confused, Meghan stumbled after him. "*What?* Where are we going?"

He picked up the rotten groceries with his free hand and kept towing her to the door. "Someplace where I can keep an eye on you."

CHAPTER SIXTEEN

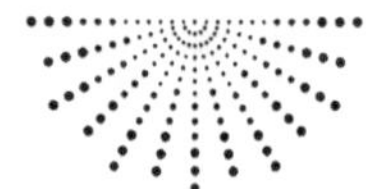

Derrick managed to toss the bag in the garbage, lock up Vicky's cabin, and drive to the chief's house with one hand. It was harder than he imagined it would be, but he possessed the sharp senses and preternatural reflexes of a shifter. He was able to muddle through without feeling he was endangering his more fragile companion.

Meghan protested, of course, insisting that he could let her go. But the woman had disappeared before his eyes. He wasn't going to let that happen again.

His quiet companion was naturally apprehensive about going to the chief's house but quit arguing halfway there, mainly because she was starting to flag, slumping in the seat.

He thought it was because telling her story had taken so much out of her, but her drawn features and general exhaustion finally penetrated his thick skull—she was exhausted.

Meghan had been fine when she was out in her garden, but in the few minutes she was missing she experienced more than a *day* someplace else. Had there been food? From her pallor and the dark circles under her eyes, he guessed she hadn't slept.

When she started to nod off on the drive, he pulled her against him and told her to go to sleep. She did so without a murmur, her head resting on his shoulder.

Her trust in him filled him with equal parts pride and anxiety. Derrick didn't just want to protect this girl. His nature demanded it. But what she was dealing with was a mind-bending conundrum he could barely understand.

Derrick was a wolf in his prime, a trained and highly decorated soldier. He'd participated in covert operations all over the world, both in the Rangers and on behalf of the pack. In some well-informed circles, he was considered a hero—a man you could depend on to save the day and bring everyone home safe. But this situation with Meghan was beyond him. He couldn't follow her into her bubbles. And if he couldn't do that he couldn't *help*.

That had never happened to him before. *Is this what feeling powerless is like?* Because it fucking *sucked*.

Meghan didn't rouse when he pulled his truck in front of the chief's house. He unclipped her seatbelt and gathered her in his arms, expecting her to wake. When she didn't, he shrugged, arranging her slack limbs so that her head continued resting on his shoulder.

He closed his truck and went up the stairs cradling her in his arms.

Alerted by the sound of his engine, Amy met him just past the mudroom with a few sheets of paper in her hand. Her eyes were on whatever was printed on them until they snapped up, detecting the newcomer.

"Hey, Derr…" Trailing off, Amy's head drew back. She held up a finger, no doubt preparing to launch into a lecture, but he forestalled her by moving Meghan's hair to expose her face.

The exhaustion and thinness of her cheeks were enough for Amy to close her mouth. She pivoted and retreated.

He started for the stairs but checked himself when he realized none of the bedrooms had what he needed—some kind of insurance against Meghan's ability. And as much as he would like to keep holding her, it wasn't practical.

Racking his brain, he considered and discarded several possibilities, deciding on the library just off the sunken living room. It had a couch and more importantly, several large potted plants.

Alerted by Amy, the chief appeared at the threshold of the library a minute later.

"Can you bring me that?" he asked Douglas, gesturing to the potted Yucca palm tree by the window.

"The plant?" Douglas asked, blinking once. His tone matched Derrick's subvocal whisper.

Nodding in confirmation, Derrick kept holding Meghan's hand as he circled the couch to reach the window, removing the tie holding the curtain open.

Gesturing, he showed Douglas where to put the heavy planter. The chief and Amy exchanged a look but neither said a word as Douglas set the palm next to Meghan's shoulder.

Crouching in front of her, he moved Meghan's hair again, stroking the skin next to her ear to wake her.

Her eyes cracked open.

"Don't worry, you can go back to sleep, but I'm just going to leave this here," he said, nudging the palm a touch so he could tie her to it without having to bend her arm awkwardly.

He looped the soft cord around her wrist, then around the trunk of the Yucca so that her palm rested around the thick base.

Still blinking sleepily, one of Meghan's fine dark brows rose sardonically.

"I know, I know." He sighed. "Humor me."

Derrick passed his index and middle finger lightly over her eyes, encouraging them to close again. She obeyed without argument—a novelty from the women in his life.

Rising, he backed off, meeting the eyes of his uncle and leader.

Douglas had seen a lot of shit in his day, but Derrick could tell this was a new one, even for him.

In silent agreement, the three of them retreated to the dining room table.

"I take it we aren't dealing with a threat to the pack," Douglas began, sitting back with his arms crossed. He pinned Derrick with a look. "Is she cursed? Or is she a witch?"

"Uh. Both. I think. Well, maybe just cursed." Derrick huffed and rubbed his chin. "Nope. I forgot about the plants sprouting at her touch. It's both."

He held up a hand when Amy opened her mouth.

"Hold the smart-ass remarks for the end, because this one is a doozy," he said, trying to decide where the hell to begin.

"Can you try and explain something this year?" Amy groused, unable to help herself when getting the story took too long for her taste.

"Okay, fine," he snapped. "So, our friend Meghan—that's her only name by the way. She doesn't remember her family at all—Meghan is a time-traveling witch," he announced. "Or at least that's the closest description either of us can come up with. Bonus, she can't control it."

Amy started laughing.

"I'm afraid I'm not joking."

She stopped. Her nostrils flared.

Douglas shut his eyes, opening them, and blinking several times. "Are you sure?"

"Pretty fucking sure," he confirmed, explaining how Meghan had vanished and reappeared with a bag of rotten groceries. He also described her reaction, what he'd seen and smelled as she told him her story and the genuineness of her reactions.

"She met you in the future?" Amy asked, her features screwed up as if tasting something bitter.

"Yeah. And apparently I sent her to meet me when I was younger. I'm supposed to help her," he finished, staring off in the direction of the library, wishing he could see through the walls. "But I have no clue how. Anything that's not her that gets trapped in those bubbles dies. From the description, it's like fucking outer space in there—no air, no light. Just a vacuum that she alone can magically survive."

"And how does being tied up to my potted palm help?" Douglas asked.

"It might not," he admitted. "But most of the bubbles, for lack of a better word to describe them, sort of slide around living things or other people...except for the ones that don't. But most of them do."

The chief passed a hand over his face. "Does she present a danger?"

"Well, if you want to be technical about it..."

Douglas caught his eye, his expression flat.

"Okay, yes, she does," he sighed. "A big fucking hell yes. But it's not intentional."

The chief sat back, tapping on the table once. "We have to move the cubs and quarantine the house."

"That won't be necessary." Derrick sat up straighter. "The cubs can stay on here. I'll take Meghan to my house. I know it's not ideal, but Priya and Frankie were going to start by spending the night to get the cubs accustomed to their presence. We should stick to that, for their sake. Once the children are comfortable with them, they can relocate to their place."

That had been the plan all along, and from the texts he had been getting from Priya, getting to know the children was going well.

"Fine," Douglas agreed after a moment of reflection. "But we have to figure out a way for you to visit the children without Meghan's problem endangering them. They've been traumatized enough, and I don't want you to drop out of their lives so soon after their rescue."

"Never," he promised. "I'll figure something out."

Amy dropped her sour pucker and leaned forward. "So, the little witch *is* our mystery texter, right? We've confirmed that?"

"Uh...well, no."

Amy's face was a mask of disbelief. "*No?* Didn't you ask her?"

"No. It kind of slipped my mind."

Amy couldn't believe it. "Seriously? How could you forget something like that?"

Derrick scowled. "Excuse me for not getting that far down my list of twenty questions—what with the fabric of reality tearing open in front of my eyes. But I'll get right on that once she wakes up."

The thorny submissive threw up her hands. "Oh, come on. That would have been my first question."

"Had you been there, I think you would have had other priorities too," he snapped back. "We're talking about a woman in trouble here."

"Oh, stop acting like you're not loving that part," Amy sniped good-naturedly—well, as good as her nature got. "Your kind eats this stuff up with a spoon."

"My kind?" he echoed.

"You dominants are all the same. Put a damsel in distress in front of you and look at what you do." She waved a languid hand and sneered. "Any opportunity to don your cape and save the day. It's especially gross when it's a young female you want to bone."

Derrick growled. "I don't want to bone her. I am *helping* her."

Amy laughed. "Please. The way you carried her in here was way more possessive than protective. You may as well beat your chest like Tarzan. I can still smell the pheromones you were pumping off."

What bullshit. "She was *asleep*," he protested. "She hadn't—"

"Children," Douglas interrupted.

"Oh, come on," Amy said. "If I can't tease him—"

"That's not what I meant." Douglas stood up. "I think I hear the children in the library."

Hustling, they followed him out, Derrick's warning about the plant not being enough spurring them on. And because the universe was getting its rocks off by being perverse, the cubs were exactly where they feared. Or at least the little female was.

Meghan had just woken up, so he caught the moment when the confusion of sleep cleared and she realized a little cat was trying to climb up on the couch. The cub's little nails snagged the sleeve of her long-sleeved t-shirt, pulling at her arm.

Her breath caught. She sat up as the cub succeeded in jumping up on the couch.

"Oh, hello," she crooned. Her hand reached out to pet the cub, who meowed at her plaintively. But she stopped herself, a look of intense longing on her face.

"Who are you, beautiful?" she asked in a thready voice.

"You don't recognize her?"

Startled, Meghan looked up, noticing the three of them for the first time. Quickly her eyes zeroed in on Douglas. She froze, the limbic lizard brain reacting to the threat he posed.

This was a common reaction to the chief among Supernaturals.

How humans missed the power and potency of the man was a mystery that had always puzzled him. But their kind only saw the surface, which in Douglas's case was that of a handsome dark-haired older man with a distinguished touch of grey at his temples. He looked like a cross between a lumberjack and a professor, not friendly but open and intelligent.

Human women threw themselves at him, completely oblivious to the dangerous predator prowling beneath the surface.

But not Meghan. She instantly recognized the threat Douglas posed. And that made sense. How many times had her life depended on her ability to size up people at a glance? She had probably lost count.

Derrick stepped forward so she would know he was there. "Meghan, this is our pack leader, Douglas Maitland It's okay. He doesn't bite."

He grinned when she continued staring at the chief, so much that she hadn't noticed the cub pressing its paws on her thighs as it nosed at her in curiosity.

Meghan scowled at him adorably, the teasing breaking her stupor. "Hello," she said, nodding politely.

"And this one is Amy." Derrick gestured to his least favorite submissive. "She does bite."

Amy smacked him, the sound loud enough to catch the cub's attention.

"Hi," she said, addressing the witch. "Derrick's been filling us in on your special circumstances. I'm the pack IT specialist, one of the ones you sent a text to, telling us where to find the cubs," she added with a nod at the little cat.

"I did what?" Meghan asked, a pucker appearing between her brows.

She glanced down at the cub, who was standing on its hind legs as it determinedly made biscuits with its front paws against her jeans.

"Where were they?" she asked, her bewilderment clear in her clouded expression.

"You didn't text their location?" Douglas asked.

Meghan bit her lip and winced. "I might have and forgot. I do that. Or I haven't done it yet. That happens too."

Sadness permeated the air as she drew back from the cub. "That's not safe, little baby."

Meghan glanced up at him, her expression forlorn. "You should take her," she warned, worry creasing her brow.

"No problem." Derrick scooped up the little cub and sat on the couch next to her.

He could tell Meghan hadn't expected that. She edged away, sliding to the other edge of the couch.

"Don't worry, sweetheart," he said, bringing the cub a little closer. "Our smallest guest likes you. I think we can risk a small cuddle. If I'm holding her, it should be safe, right?"

Amy snickered at the endearment, nudging the chief in the side with her elbow. "Told you so," she said smugly in a low voice.

Derrick ignored her, focusing on Meghan as he hefted the cub closer to her.

"Go on," he encouraged. "She can't get caught in your bubble if I'm holding her."

"I guess that's true," Meghan murmured. She reached out but stopped before making contact.

The little cub pushed against his palm, straining towards her hand. The little cat closed the distance, meowing in satisfaction as Meghan finally gave in.

"She's so soft." Meghan leaned closer, scratching the girl behind her ears.

He could feel her fascination and longing to hold the adorable cub so clearly it made his heart ache. How long had it been since she'd allowed herself the luxury of a human connection? To enjoy a simple touch?

"No, I don't think you would have forgotten helping this little one. It's just not the kind of thing a body forgets," he decided, settling the cub in his lap. "But I think there's a way to check. Can I please borrow your phone?"

He had felt the imprint of the device in her pocket when he'd carried her inside.

Her big eyes fixed on the cub. Meghan handed the phone over without protest.

Derrick blinked at the old Nokia, a type of cellphone that had been ubiquitous over a decade ago. Known for its durability, the little brick could take heaps of abuse and still work. It had been his first phone back in the day, a hand-me-down from his father.

Not a surprising choice, all things considered. But he did admire her ability to text so quickly on such an old device. Those keys were damn tiny.

He passed the phone to Amy, who began pushing buttons, navigating into the messaging menu.

Derrick held his breath, a fake smile plastered on his face. Was he wrong about Meghan being the one? No, he couldn't be. Could he?

As if on cue, the phone in his pocket vibrated, and Amy nodded. Meghan was their mystery texter.

Something tight unfurled in his gut. *Good, this is good.* He only had one mind-bending mystery to deal with.

"But the messages guiding us to the location are not here," Amy announced, handing the phone back to Meghan. "Unless you deleted them. Did you?"

Meghan, who had been too engrossed with the cub to pay much attention, snapped her head back up. She shook her head. "No. I never delete anything in there. Given the way I jump around, sometimes checking the phone's messages and outgoing calls is the only way to see where I've been and where I still have to go. It's sort of a second brain."

She lifted a shoulder. "Being perpetually confused is one of the pitfalls of a non-linear life."

"I can imagine," Douglas rumbled, not unsympathetically. "I've known a few psychometrists, even a foreseer or two in my time. But their abilities were nowhere near as disorienting or dangerous as yours."

Meghan nodded without meeting his gaze, which she was having serious trouble holding. "I used to write everything down in a note-book, but I don't anymore after I lost it sometime in eighteenth-century England. Unfortunately, the local vicar's wife found it. That mishap almost got me burned as a witch."

Christ. Derrick pressed closer until their thighs were touching.

"How is the phone safer?" Amy asked the question he was wondering himself.

"Even if a person from the past got it off me, they wouldn't know how to use it." She glanced up at all of them in turn. "That's only happened once. I told the woman who found it that it was a toy for children."

"Did she buy that?" Derrick asked.

"I don't know," she said, almost apologetically. "I grabbed it and ran for another bubble."

"*Mmh.* Smart. You don't want to lose it," he said, slipping the Nokia into the front pocket of her sweatshirt. "You need this phone to save lives...including the one in front of you and that family in Alaska."

CHAPTER SEVENTEEN

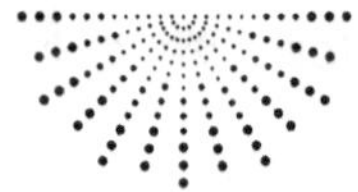

Meghan jerked, her lips parting as she took in the cub in front of her with new eyes. Loose threads suddenly came together.

"I do remember Alaska. A fire, right?"

"Yes," Douglas confirmed.

"I thought you knew about the cubs," Amy frowned. "Because you were at the hospital the day Derrick found them."

Flushing, she turned to Derrick and then back to the small, aggressive female. She couldn't very well say she had been stalking Derrick, could she?

They're wolves. That might be permissible here.

"I went there because I had seen myself there," she said, muddying the truth a touch. "But you say I have something to do with bringing these cubs here?"

The little leopard cat meowed and batted the air.

"Derrick will fill you in on those details later," Douglas said decisively. "In the meantime, I will contact a few specialists to confer on your case. We'll be sharing the details of your affliction, but rest assured the witches we intend to speak to are trustworthy."

"You know good witches?"

"Yeah, the chief's dating one on the down-low, so you can rest assured they know how to keep secrets," Amy chimed in, miming zipping her mouth shut and throwing away the key.

Douglas glared at the young woman before taking the cub from Derrick's hands. "Anyway, our consultants may wish to speak to you soon, so expect that call, Derrick. I'll take this one up to bed."

"I will, thanks," Derrick said, giving the cub one last cuddle before making their goodbyes.

DERRICK USHERED Meghan back to his car, driving a short distance before parking in front of a modern-looking two-story farmhouse.

She liked the structure immediately, its grey stone facade, dark blue slate roof, and huge picture windows.

But Derrick didn't give her a chance to admire the stylish house. He guided her inside, straight to the kitchen. After urging her to sit at the counter, he pushed a tray of kitchen herbs toward her.

"Hug that while I fix you a plate," he ordered, snatching up a spatula and pointing it at her threateningly.

"Very well." Meghan laughed but obediently circled her arm around the planter. She was exhausted but also too hungry to sleep without something in her stomach.

He bustled around the kitchen, pulling out a pan and eggs, cheese, chanterelle mushrooms, and ham.

"I hope you don't mind an omelet," he said, turning on the stove. "It's sort of my go-to quick meal."

"I don't mind at all," she said, hoping he couldn't hear how her stomach was growling.

She knew he had when he cut off a hunk of cheese and put it on a plate as he continued to prepare the omelet.

"I don't have too many plants, but we'll figure that out tomorrow," Derrick said watching her out of the corner of his eyes as he flipped the omelet without looking. "As for tonight, I think it's best we share a bed."

"W-what?" Meghan mumbled around the piece of cheese in her mouth.

He didn't answer until the omelet was done and deposited on her plate.

"I think we should share a bed tonight. Strictly platonic, of course," he said as he opened the fridge, pouring her a glass of orange juice. "I don't have a convenient potted palm to tie you to, so I will have to do."

He set the glass next to her plate, studying her as if trying to gauge her reaction. "Not that getting a big plant is a viable long-term option. Like you said before, you can't go through life hugging a tree, or lugging around a huge potted plant."

He cocked his head to the side and gave her a dangerously beguiling grin. "Not with those skinny arms. Eat up."

"You can't share your bed with me," she said taking a small bite of omelet. "I keep telling you that it might not be safe."

"Don't worry about that," he said, straightening and puffing his chest out. The move highlighted his broad shoulders and muscled upper torso, as he no doubt intended. "I'm not about to let myself get sucked into one of your bubbles. And I'll be damned if I let you get lost in one on my watch."

He broke off, his expression intentionally blank. "On the other hand, the shower *is* going to be a challenge," he said in a too-neutral tone. "Because dragging a palm in there would only wash the soil out of the pot...clogs the pipes."

Blushing, Meghan put her fork down. She had polished off more than half the omelet already—the chanterelles took the simple dish to another level. But she couldn't eat and talk about such things at the same time.

"Er, um, I don't usually use the shower or the tub," she explained. The awkwardness of the situation made her want to crawl under the counter and hide from him. "I can't risk being caught unprepared...you know...without my clothes. I take a bar of soap to the lake. Or river. The ocean a few times..."

"Oh." Derrick mulled that, a touch of red staining his cheekbones. Then light dawned in his eyes. "*Oh*, because there are living things in the water. Like algae and diatoms. Have you ever been taken from a lake or river?"

"No. Not yet thankfully." Technically, she had fallen into a bubble right *after* bathing once as a teenager. It had led to downtown San Francisco in the swinging sixties where a naked teen was welcome. Too welcome, really. But Meghan had no intention of telling him *that* story.

"Then you never get to take a hot shower or warm bath?" Derrick asked.

"No," she sighed.

"That sucks."

He had no idea. "It's not that bad in summer."

"But winter…" he trailed off. "It must be torture."

"It's not pleasant," she admitted. Clearing her throat, she picked up her fork again, because she had a pretty good idea what he was about to offer…and she wasn't sure she could say no.

"Well, maybe there's something we can do about that too," he replied, his eyes fixed steadily on her. "Tomorrow."

Face flaming, Meghan dropped her eyes to her food. She shoved in forkfuls of omelet until she had choked down the delicious meal with help of big sips of juice.

When she was done, he cleared her plate, rinsing it and putting it in the dishwasher before taking her hand. He led her to his bedroom.

Meghan took one look at the huge four-poster bed and felt faint. The room spun, and she swayed.

Derrick picked her up and set her down on the edge of the bed. He unlaced her leather shoes.

"I smell like the lake," she warned, a touch breathless, as she stepped out of the weathered sneakers. Then he edged a potted orchid on the bedside table closer to the bed. He gave her a pointed look until she picked it up.

"I'm a wolf. I'm not going to complain about you smelling of the lake."

Rounding the bed, he stripped his shirt off. He took a pair of pajama bottoms out of a drawer. "Am I right in guessing you're going to want to sleep in your clothes?"

"Yes." She answered far too quickly.

But Derrick didn't seem offended. He unsuccessfully hid a grin and went into the bathroom. He was back in less than a minute, bare-chested in light linen pajama pants.

"Sorry I didn't think to stop and pack you a bag, but I do have a spare toothbrush fresh out of the package on the sink. If you take the orchid with you, you can go and use the facilities."

"Okay." Still blushing, she took the plant to the restroom.

The master bathroom was spectacular. It was almost as spacious as the cottage living room with double sinks and a big bathtub with many jets and a separate shower stall. It even had a separate shower stall in the corner. It too had a double shower head, which made her wonder just how often Derrick showered with a guest.

Images of nubile and busty women werewolves danced through her head. *I bet none of those guests were invited out of pity because they might get sucked into another time or place.*

Depressed she washed her face using both hands, taking the risk of letting go of the plant. Because, really, would falling through the floor be all that bad a thing at this moment?

Wiping her face, she counted to a beat of ten before returning to the bedroom, orchid in hand.

Derrick had dimmed the lights, but the sight of his tanned and extremely well-defined chest damn near made her trip anyway.

He was sitting up in the bed, propped up on two big pillows. He had his phone in his hand and was typing rapidly.

He glanced up briefly before resuming typing. "Just making a few notes for tomorrow. I hope you don't mind going on my rounds with me."

Recovering, she hustled to the bed. She dived under the covers next to him, which was quite stupid really, given how she was fully dressed.

"That's no problem," she said, unsure of what he meant. "I don't exactly keep a schedule."

Nodding, Derrick set his phone aside, slipping it into a charging dock—an item she had only ever seen on Vicky's television—before turning off the light.

The room was not fully dark. Derrick had left the window's shutters partially open, and there was enough moonlight spilling over the foot of the bed for her to make out most of the furniture.

He turned, angling that picture-perfect chest at her. "Tomorrow, we get some answers," he promised, reaching out and tugging her into his arms, making her the little spoon.

Meghan froze. "You're just going to hold me all night?"

She sensed more than saw his confusion. "Is that weird?" he asked.

"It's *not* weird for you?"

"Not really. Weres are pretty tactile. We touch and hug each other all the time. It's important for our cub's development. Teens too."

His breath fanned the top of her head. "Sorry, is this very uncomfortable for you?"

"Um. No." Describing the sensation she was feeling cuddled into his body as uncomfortable wasn't precisely correct. But she couldn't find the right words if her life depended on it.

"That's good then." Derrick's voice was already starting to slur as if he was one of those annoying people who went to sleep instantly.

Her theory was proven correct when Derrick's arm went slack around her, his breath evening out.

By rights she should have stayed awake all night, tensing at his every slight movement. But this was Derrick, the man she had been searching for longer than she could remember.

Instead, Meghan twisted until the front of her body was pressed against his glorious chest muscles. And she fell asleep with a smile on her face.

CHAPTER EIGHTEEN

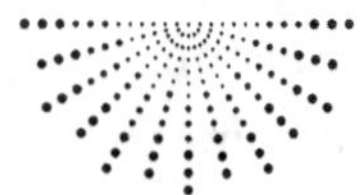

Meghan was aware of Derrick's hard and warm body next to her before she opened her eyes. When she did, he gave her a melting smile that would have made her weak in the knees had she been standing.

But she didn't get to enjoy the sensation because the doorbell rang. He swept her up, carrying her out into the living room before depositing her on the couch, the potted orchid in her lap.

Blinking sleepily, she watched, bemused as he accepted a box from a teenage girl wearing a name tag Meghan couldn't make out at a distance.

"Is that her?" the teen whispered, avid curiosity on her face.

Derrick gave her an indulgent look. "You'll meet her later," he said, his tone warm but firm. "Thanks, Jenny."

He shut the door on the girl. Her last glimpse was of the girl craning her neck to gawk at her.

"I take it you know her." Meghan hugged the pot closer, like a teddy bear.

Derrick gave her one of those endearing lop-sided grins. "I know everybody. Jenny is Moira's daughter. Moira runs our local flower shop."

She glanced down at the orchid she was holding. "You ordered more flowers?"

"Of a sort, yes," he said, starting to open the box.

He didn't strike her as the type. His house was very masculine. "I had no idea you were so fond of such pretty, delicate things, but I guess I should have given that I'm holding the evidence."

"Actually, my mom bought that orchid, but I did plant those kitchen herbs on my own." He opened the box, setting aside the lid. "But I was brainstorming while you were in the bathroom last night, so I sent Moira a message before we went to bed."

"You ordered this last night? For me?" Warmth that had nothing to do with his masculine beauty pooled inside her.

"Yeah." Derrick's rumpled hair was sticking up on one side, but his tousled appearance only made him more appealing. "Lucky for us Moira opens the store early to accept deliveries, so she whipped up something for me first thing this morning."

He held up a long woven rope made from some silvery grey-green plant.

"What is that for?" she asked, not without trepidation.

This was Derrick, she reminded her suddenly pounding heart. Just because he was proudly holdup up a rope, there was no reason to be alarmed.

"Moira and I bounced some ideas off each other last night on a wearable plant." He held the braided length out to her. "At first, I suggested a fresh flower lei of some kind—the kind you get in Hawaii —but that left the problem that it wasn't alive after the flowers were plucked. Then Moira suggested an air plant."

He held up one end of the woven length, pinching it between his fingers. "I'm not entirely sure what that is really, but Moira assured me that it was alive and doesn't require a pot or soil. It absorbs its water and nutrients directly from the air."

Pulling it out the full length, he held it up over his head. It stretched to the floor with enough left over to coil at his feet. "This is related to a Tillandsia plant, but I've been assured it's much softer. Judging from the length, this is several dozen plants woven together."

"Wow." Touched and surprised, she reached out to touch the rope. Derrick obligingly picked up the coil and dropped it in her lap.

"I know it's not a perfect solution, but every little bit helps, right?" He slid the box lid back on.

"I should ask Moira if you can shower with it. I suspect the answer is no, because she told me to mist it lightly. But if you do want to give that a whirl with a bit of this maybe we can sacrifice a portion of it. You could wear a couple of feet like a belt under the shower stream and still have enough left over to wrap around yourself like a sash as we go about our day."

Her throat thickened. "Thank you," she whispered. Blinking, she set the orchid aside and picked up the rope. "And I'm going to take the hint and go shower."

"I didn't mean it like that—I like your smell."

"Sure you do." Laughing she got to her feet.

"I do," he protested

"Uh-huh." Meghan paused, biting back the smile. "Um, now that I have this handy dandy tether, should I use the shower in a guest room?" A house this size had to have more than one bedroom. More likely three or four.

"No," Derrick scowled. "The air plant is just insurance. You and I are still going to be joined at the hip until your magic consult happens."

Meghan took a deep breath, shuddering involuntarily. "And what if these experts can't find a solution?"

"Hey." Derrick put his hands on her shoulders, his big hands engulfing her much smaller frame. "Don't think like that. They are going to find a solution. These people we are talking to are some of the most talented witches in the world."

"I don't doubt that," she said, trying to take heart in the confidence in his voice. *You came all this way because you believed in him, remember?* But what if the best of the best failed to find a solution to her problem?

You are unique. And Meghan had learned the hard way that this was a bad thing.

A touch on her chin. Derrick stared down at her with wolf-light eyes.

"I'm not supposed to share this, but it's not just the talent of the witches that makes me think they will be able to help you. It's also because they have access to some seriously badass magics—including an ancient repository of knowledge chock full of books on the subject. It's a collection spanning centuries. Longer even. I'm pretty sure they have stuff as old as the written word in there—spells preserved on animal skins or carved on rock tablets. Your city of spires is in one of those records. It has to be."

He gave her shoulders a final squeeze and straightened up. "They're going to figure this out."

Swallowing her misgivings, she nodded. "That does sound promising."

"Believe it." He stuck his thumb in the direction of the stairs. "Now, if you feel like changing into something else, there is a chest full of spare clothes in the room next to mine. You'll find things in your size —some should be new."

"New?" Exactly how many overnight guests did Derrick have for him to stock supplies for them?

"It's a pack thing," he explained before she could feel the stirrings of jealousy. "We strip down to run as wolves else the clothes get caught on our other form— they disintegrate. That's rare, but at the top tier that happens more often than not so we can shift unencumbered."

"You all keep spare clothing in your houses for packmates?"

"Yes. Or in special waterproof caches in the woods. But doing it this way—in our houses means the clothes are laundered regularly. Even though you are on the small side, I'm sure you'll find clothing that fits."

His eyes ran up and down over her body. "Although, you may need to roll the pants up at the ankles."

He waved toward the kitchen. "I'll get the coffee on in the meantime. You do like coffee, right?"

"I've never had it," she admitted with a sheepish grin. "But I like hot chocolate."

Derrick smirked and backed up to the cabinets, removing a yellow and red cardboard cylinder. "I've got this great Mexican stuff—Chocolate Ibarra— that you're going to love."

"Sounds good," she said. "I'll try to be quick."

Murmuring another quiet "thank you" she headed back upstairs, gathering the long plant rope so she wouldn't drag it behind her.

CHAPTER NINETEEN

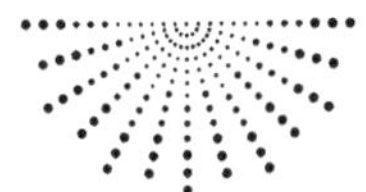

Joining Derrick on his rounds was surreal. At first glance, it appeared as if he wasn't doing all that much. He drove them around in his big truck, almost aimlessly. Because his face and manner were so relaxed, it took her a moment to recognize he was scanning the area for trouble.

"Are you police?" she asked as he maneuvered the vehicle down a winding lane bordered by scrubby pines on both sides. "Is this a patrol of some kind?"

He threw her a quick grin. "I'm not on the force, although the sheriff and his deputies are some of ours."

"Werewolf cops?" she asked.

"We make decent police officers. Good soldiers, too. It's in the blood. But that's why you started sending some of your warnings our way, isn't it?" He glanced over at her, reaching out to adjust her air plants.

Meghan had initially coiled them around her upper torso like a beauty queen's sash, as suggested. But she would have crushed it between her back and the seat wearing it that way, so she wore it looped around her neck. It sat against her chest in coils, like one of those over-the-top multi-strand pearl necklaces she'd seen in a magazine once.

"I *did* do that," she said in realization, her brows drawing together.

A vague recollection of getting advice about how to best use the information she picked up came to her, but only snatches of it. "Someone told me once that warning the police or fire department in advance of a catastrophe wasn't going to cut it, not unless they were shifters. Because shifters, as a rule, were both curious and capable. So if they were the ones who got the warning, they'd be more likely to intervene."

"Do you remember who it was who said that?"

Meghan wracked her brain. "No. My memory gets a bit fuzzier the more bubbles I pass through. The words I remember fine, but not who said them." Her eyes widened. "*Hey*—maybe it was you."

Derrick made a rumbling noise in this throat. "I don't know whether to laugh or not. Your existence breaks all the rules. It could very well have been me sometime in the future talking to a younger you."

A memory of his lips on hers flooded her with heat. Blushing, she turned away, pretending to watch the scenery out the window. "I think sometimes I know things I'm not supposed to—that they come from some other time I haven't lived yet but will. Like ripples reaching back. That muddles things too."

"I can imagine," he murmured, glancing at her with curious wolf eyes.

"You don't think I'm crazy?" She often did.

"Not at all. *You* having memories of your future makes more sense than a witch being able to foretell the future without time travel."

Her chin wrinkled. "Even if I haven't lived it yet?"

"Yes—because of the quantum."

Meghan blinked. "What?"

"Do you understand the theory of quantum entanglement?"

"No."

"Neither do I, but I watch a lot of sci-fi movies."

Derrick grinned when she laughed. "To me, it makes sense that you would glean information about the future, because you of all people might be capable of being in two places at once. One mind at two different points in your lifetime connected across the bridge of time formed by one of your corridor bubbles."

"But my mind would be different, wouldn't it? If I were at a different stage of my life."

He shrugged. "I didn't say it was a perfect theory. But magic makes a lot of the impossible possible."

Meghan ran her teeth over her lip as she considered him. "

You are very...understanding. The few people I've confided in haven't always reacted positively or been so open." Then she snorted lightly. "But that makes sense too. After all, you turn into a wolf."

He made a humming noise, his eyes fixed on the road. "Well, you'd be surprised. Just because a man or a woman is a shifter, that doesn't automatically translate to their being receptive to new ideas. Some of the most narrow-minded jerks I've ever known have been shifters. Comes with the territory, I guess. One trait we all share is stubbornness."

"Then why are you different?"

"Dunno. Different life experience? My position in the pack means I've traveled, seen more shit—a fair amount of it weird." He snickered. "Some of the weirdest stuff has been here at home, although things were pretty quiet until you got here."

Her stomach sank. "I'm sorry," she whispered.

Derrick jerked his head at her. "Oh, *hey*, no. I didn't mean it like that. I'm glad you are here. And not just because I was getting antsy for a little action."

His fingers drummed a staccato beat on the steering wheel. "A dominant wolf like me is hard-wired to protect. I see you and want to help. Honestly, you couldn't stop me if you wanted me to."

He cast her a serious, sidelong glance. Meghan flushed, her core temperature rising beyond comfortable. It made her glad he had the air conditioning on in the cab.

"Knowing you were out there, just stumbling through time, needing help—it bugs the hell out of me."

He meant it too. Derrick had that drive to defend and safeguard. Yes, it was a somewhat more common trait in shifters, but in him the dial had been turned to maximum.

"Do you have any idea how old you were when this started?"

She frowned, trying to compare the mental picture of herself at the start to the children she'd seen over the years. "Eight or nine? Maybe a little younger."

His sigh was heavy. "And you've just been…existing like this ever since? Passing through a bubble, dancing through space and time?"

"Dancing is a rather cheerful way of looking at it," she said, a corner of her mouth pulling back. "I always thought of it as falling."

The words were light, but they didn't reflect the reality of her bleak existence. One she wasn't sure she should share.

Now that he'd taken charge of her in his way, Derrick seemed to take her past experiences personally. It *would* hurt him to know how close she had come to starving or freezing to death.

Things had been grim for a long time until she learned to trust her instincts about people and places. There were good people in the world—as a child she had met a few who had genuinely wanted to help her.

They thought her abandoned or homeless, and she let them believe that. But her lack of control meant none of those people had stayed in her life for very long.

She hadn't been able to hold onto them.

More than anything Meghan was afraid Derrick was going to be another of those helpful people she would be forced to let go of. Sighing, she looked down at her hands, wishing they were stronger.

"I know you want this crazy traveling to stop, and I want that too," Derrick said as if sensing her emotional downturn. "But you have done a lot of good already." His big heavy hand moved off the steering wheel to gesture. "And you can potentially do a hell of a lot more—like with the cubs. Sometime in the future, you're going to send me a message that I'll get three days ago. And when I do, I'm going to go and save those abandoned babies, because of you."

Hearing the words so closely parallel her thoughts filled her with emotion too overwhelming to name.

Time slowed—a new and novel sensation. The moment grew heavy, weighted with power and purpose.

Derrick was right. Even though he would never say it, she had a responsibility to help whenever and wherever she could. But what if she couldn't help without traveling? Was she going to have to leave him?

Heat covered her hand. Startled, she glanced down to see his big fingers covering her much smaller ones.

"I know how tired you must be of living this way. I can smell your exhaustion. And I am *not* saying you have to keep traveling. If anything, I'm saying it has to stop."

He squeezed her fingers. "But I just wanted to remind you that this curse of yours has also been a blessing, for those cubs you found, for that family in Alaska. And I have faith that you're going to get control of it and once you do? The sky is the fucking limit for you."

His optimism lifted some of the gloom pressing her down into the seat. But not all of it.

"After meeting that little cat cub in person, I feel anxious and guilty. I want to help them *now*. But I have no way of knowing what bubble leads to the right time or when I'll encounter it."

He pulled in front of a small cluster of white low wooden buildings at the end of a long narrow lane. "It *is* going to happen. We know this."

She nodded weakly. "Yes, I know. I just wish that I could force the right bubble to appear in front of me. I fantasize daily of being able to reach out and grab the right one whenever I want."

Derrick turned in his seat. "But don't you will it sometimes? Or at least influence it? Because I gathered from what you said that you found Vicky's bracelet *after* she told you she lost it. Was that wrong?"

"No, you're right. It did happen in that order," she confirmed. "But I've never thought of that as willing it to happen because…"

She trailed off.

"Because what?" he asked.

Meghan lifted a shoulder. "Faster connections like that only happen when I'm starting to get tired or hungry."

She looked down at her hands, afraid of his censure. But she wouldn't keep any secrets from him. "In the beginning, I had to steal or scavenge in fields and orchards for food. But as I got older more and more opportunities like the Vicky situation started to crop up. In return for my help, I was rewarded with money or favors that led to food and shelter."

Meghan frowned, fingering the length of tillandsia, which had sprouted several tiny flowers despite the fact weaving it into a rope must have stressed it. "I guess that could be considered influencing it in some way, but it's not conscious or anything like that. I wish it was. God knows I've tried forcing it. But that doesn't work."

Derrick sat up, straightening his wide shoulders. He raised his brows but didn't comment about the flowers. "Still, it *does* sound as if you can affect it on some level, almost as if there's a fail-safe to keep you alive."

He tapped her hand and opened the driver's side door before stepping out. "I think that's a very hopeful sign your ability can be controlled. We just need to figure out how."

Unconvinced, Meghan unfastened her seat belt. "Are we stopping?"

She had assumed he had pulled off the road so he could avoid driving while distracted.

"Yes, I have something to show you."

He came around to her side. He opened the door, and she slipped out of the tall cab, standing on the running board, while she accepted his outstretched hand so she could jump down. It was quite a tall truck.

Derrick checked his watch, the corners of his mouth lifting. "Any minute now."

Meghan took his outstretched hand and followed him around the back of a wooden building. It was one of three set at precise right angles to each other with a narrow space left to walk between them. The fourth side was left open to the woods, leaving a wide clearing in the center that had a playground with small plastic slides, swings, and miniature climbing equipment.

She was about to ask what they were doing when the back door to the central building opened, and a torrent of little bodies spilled out.

Meghan's breath caught as a mix of cubs and children ran to the equipment with happy cheers and childish chatter. Most were on two legs, but quite a few were on four.

"This is Creekside School," Derrick explained as he waved to an adult who had to be a teacher. "It's pre-K up to fifth grade and is exclusive to pack members. Once they get a little older and we don't have to worry about spontaneously shifting, they attend Atticus Jones —a combined middle and high school.

"That one has a mixed population, including humans. Most of them are pack, but not all, so our kids don't go there until they have a handle on both their shifting and can keep quiet about it."

He waved again as a few of the children spotted him and let out little howls and whoops of joy. "C'mon. I'll introduce you."

Meghan looked at his outstretched hand in dismay. "Oh, Derrick. I'm sorry."

"You don't think it's safe enough?" he asked, gesturing to the loops of braided air plants around his neck.

"It might be. But it might not." Meghan watched the children and cubs with undisguised longing. Could she really risk any of those little lives?

Derrick's large hands covered her shoulders. "Hey, it's okay. I didn't mean to stress you out. If you're not comfortable, we can leave soon. But I have to take care of something first."

Taking her hand, he led her to the very edge of the clearing and nudged her until she was leaning against the trunk of a tall pine. "Yeah, I know," he said when she caught his eye. "But please do it anyway."

He walked back to the playground, intercepting a curious cub who was coming to investigate the stranger in their midst. But a weirdo decked out in a plant liana did not compare to Derrick coming to visit.

Depositing the cub he was holding with his friends, Derrick strode into the fray like Gulliver in Lilliput.

He was welcomed like a superhero, with cheers and childish cries of excitement. Human and wolf cub alike surrounded him, climbing his long limbs like a tree.

Playing along, Derrick went down on all fours, allowing himself to be buried in little bodies before breaking free with a mock-roar of victory. Then he proceeded to pet and cuddle his many admirers, occasionally tossing one in the air so high she almost screamed in fright.

But they weren't scared at all—forcibly reminding her that these were shifter children. They weren't as fragile as their human counter-parts. That and there were likely many future adrenaline junkies in the crowd.

The group might have kept carrying on in this way had the teachers not helped Derrick out. They herded the wolf children away, leaving him free to maneuver to the couple who had exited the schoolroom deep in conversation.

It took a moment for Meghan to realize the women in question weren't talking to each other. They were speaking to the cubs each held—leopard cubs, the only cats in the yard.

Her lips parted as she realized it was the first day of school for the rescued children, an occasion Derrick wouldn't let go by without making an appearance to show them his love and support.

The women must be the Reddy-Young family, the couple fostering the children. One of them, a tall elegant Indian woman knelt and put her cub down, the larger one Derrick had told her earlier was a boy.

Curious wolves and children surrounded the male cub, making his hackles visibly raise. But Derrick knelt, putting his hand on the boy's back. His lips moved as he gave him a good scratch.

She was too far away to hear what he said, but the cub relaxed under Derrick's caress.

Eventually, he waved some kids closer, making introductions and cracking jokes that made the human-shaped kids laugh. Then the smaller cub struggled in the other women's arms, silently asking to be let down as well.

Soon both leopard clubs were jumping and playing, mixing with their wolf counterparts like the children they were.

Tears made her eyes swim. Meghan dabbed at them with the edge of her sleeve, stepping forward a bit in the process. The noise abruptly changed, going from the sound of children at play to cars zipping along the road.

Blinking, she turned around. Meghan was standing in downtown Lake Veris now, right in the middle of the road.

And she was directly in the path of a black SUV.

CHAPTER TWENTY

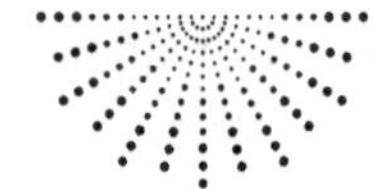

Yelping, Megan threw herself to the side of the road as the black car thundered past, the man behind the wheel honking his displeasure with her as he drove on.

That was Edgar, she thought, recognizing the driver. She had appeared in the road right in the wounded wolf's path. Bless his reflexes.

Breathing in rapid pants, she moved farther from the road, her head twisting this way and that trying to figure out where she was.

Then she saw him. *Derrick.*

Thank god. She was still in the Lake Veris of his time. Shuddering in relief, Meghan lifted her hand, about to call out to him when he turned. His eyes passed right over her as he went inside Jeannie's Deli.

All the air left her lungs. Meghan flinched, the emotional punch hitting hard because it was so unexpected.

He doesn't recognize me.

"It's okay," she told herself, repeating the words a few times before she could think clearly. *You just traveled back in time, back to a point where you haven't met yet.*

Judging from the length of Derrick's hair and the shade of his tan, she hadn't strayed too far back.

Putting her hands in her pockets, she began to walk, slowly at first and then faster.

Meghan needed a newspaper, or access to a computer—anything she could trust to tell her the correct date.

The little brick Nokia was a comfortable weight in her pocket. *Remember what Derrick said.* Maybe she had willed this to happen. The why or how remained to be determined, but there was hope. She hadn't gone far.

Gathering herself, Meghan skirted the busy shops on Elm, the picturesque main drag in the center of town. Trying not to tremble from the aftershocks of cold, she ducked into the library.

She went straight to the computer, typing in her credentials, holding her breath as the slow device finally logged into the main screen, displaying the date.

It was three days before the cubs were rescued.

Breathing fast, she began to text. Derrick's phone number was burned into her brain, but she also tried the other pack numbers he had written down for her yesterday.

It's a damn good thing you can remember numbers.

Once she was done sending her warnings, she took off the rope of air plants, setting them on top of a trash can in a residential neighborhood. A riot of tiny fuzzy pink and purple flowers dotted the entire length now.

Her new wolf friend would be disappointed, but she couldn't keep wearing it without calling attention to herself. It wasn't as if it worked.

Also thanks to Derrick, she had a little cash in her pockets, so she stopped for a sandwich at the cafe. She tried not to be disappointed when he wasn't there.

The impulse to run to him and explain everything to him now was strong. But experience had taught her not to mess with her own timeline. She had to meet people in the order it happened or bad things followed.

Sandwich warm in her pocket, Megan began to trudge to Vicky's cabin.

CHAPTER TWENTY-ONE

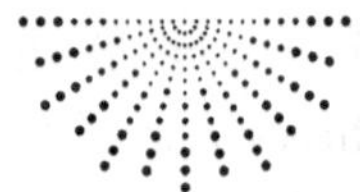

"Thank you for coming out today," Diya said, her watchful eyes fixed on her foster cubs.

"I wouldn't miss it," Derrick replied. "How's it been going?"

"Better than I would have guessed," she said. "A few bumps but nowhere near as many as you'd expect under the circumstances. The little girl is settling in better, which we expected given her youth. She has only cried a few times at night."

"For her mother?"

"No." Diya gave him a sober look. "For her brother."

Derrick grunted. Well, that certainly said a lot about their family situation before the rescue. "Has the boy shifted back to human yet?"

Given the trauma they had experienced, it wasn't unusual for shifters that young to prefer their animal form. But it wasn't healthy long-term. Shifters were dual-natured. They needed to maintain a balance between their human and animal forms or risk developmental issues further down the line.

"He has actually," Diya said, making him relax. "For meals and sometimes in his sleep. He even speaks—monosyllabic responses, but it's farther than I thought we would be at this point."

"Good. It's a decent start. I take it he hasn't shared any details yet?"

"No, and we didn't want to push the issue. I'll wait till the better half says it's time."

Diya's wife Frankie was a therapist. Her patient load was mostly adults and a few teens, but Derrick knew her training had included quite a few child psychology classes.

"They couldn't be in better hands," he said, giving her a quick hug.

He looked over his shoulder to see if Meghan was watching—not because he wanted to make sure the embrace had read as platonic. He tensed, doing a double-take as he spotted Nathan escorting Meghan around the corner.

They were coming from the opposite direction he had left her.

Diya noticed his consternation.

"Should I…?" she asked, gesturing at the pair.

"No, it's fine. I've got this." Derrick jogged over to Nate and Meghan, trying not to look as if he'd just been smacked across the face.

"Guess who I found walking here?" Nathan said, trying and failing to sound jovial and nonchalant.

Meghan looked up at him, biting her lip. She was wearing the same pants and shirt, but it smelled stronger of detergent and fabric softener than it had a few minutes ago. It was as if she'd washed it this morning and pulled it on as soon as it was dry.

The air plants were gone.

"You've been traveling," Derrick said through a surprisingly stiff jaw. It had nothing to do with the fact Nathan was holding Meghan's hand.

Nate coughed. "Um, here." He transferred the hold. Derrick's muscles eased as Meghan's fingers twined with his.

She squeezed him reassuringly. "I have good news. The cubs are safe."

"So you didn't go far?" he asked, trying to sound normal.

"Not far," she said quietly.

He gestured to her liana-less neck. "I take it they didn't help."

"No, I'm sorry," she sighed before taking a deep breath and giving him a bracing smile. "But it was a good idea."

"That's fine," he said thickly, hoping this last trip hadn't led to missing meals or passing through freezing cold wormholes. Speaking of...

He took both her chilled hands, chafing them to warm her. "It was worth a shot."

"I'm not cold," she protested.

"Oh." He stopped rubbing her hands. "Sorry, Weres run hotter, so it's hard to tell."

Someone cleared their throat, and he looked up to see Nate watching the two of them. "I guess we're good here, right? I can leave her in your hands?"

He didn't miss the innuendo in the other man's tone, but it was tempered by concern. He kept glancing at Meghan as if he were worried she would disappear on the spot.

Join the club, buddy.

He clapped Nate on the arm, unsubtly pushing him toward the parking lot. He'd been so caught up in the cubs and their welfare that he hadn't noticed his packmate's big red Ford pulling in. "Yeah, I got this. You can go ahead and take off."

"Thank you for the ride, Nathan," Meghan said with studious politeness. "I would have had a hard time finding this place without you—I didn't pay that much attention on the ride over."

Nathan smiled. "No worries. As for this place, it's out the way for a reason," he said jerking his thumb at the mixed crowd of children. "But it was my pleasure. If you ever need a taxi, feel free to flag me down. Even if you need it three weeks ago. Just make up an excuse, like you missed your bus."

Derrick pressed his lips together and nodded in agreement. He didn't know why it bugged him to picture Meghan and Nate alone in a vehicle.

"Most members of the pack would do the same, so you should feel free to flag someone down—if you see a familiar face you're comfortable with, that is. Stay away from the vacation people," he added hastily.

He wanted to add a dozen other caveats but decided to zip it when he caught Nate's gossip-hungry glance. He waited for the other man to leave before pulling Meghan under his arm.

"Are you really okay?" he asked.

"Yes," she said. "I admit I got a little jolt when I realized I'd slipped back. But at least I was able to send a bunch of messages about the cubs—all the ones you received anyway. I'm sure of it."

"That's good," he said, trying to smile. He was damned grateful the cubs were safe, but he couldn't help feeling unsettled at the realization she had slipped away and he hadn't even noticed.

And this was with Nathan escorting her back before I missed her. He imagined if he'd looked up and she hadn't been there. He was too disciplined to freak out in front of the children, but that didn't change the fact he would have been losing his shit on the inside.

His phone buzzed. The text was a mixed blessing.

"Hope and Mai got in touch with the chief," he said after scanning the brief message. "They've hit a wall, so they're moving on to the T'Kaierian archive—that big magic book repository I told you about. They were supposed to call us after lunch at the chief's place but postponed a few hours so they can make their way there. But it's all good. We can head back to my place and relax for a while till they can make the call."

"You don't have anything else to do?" she asked, glancing back at the crowd of children. They were still playing, not having noticed their little drama.

"Not really," he lied. But halfway home he pulled over unexpectedly.

Edgar's black SUV was in his driveway, the partially filled garbage can lying over on its side next to it.

Sighing, he drove on, making a mental note to text Nate when he got home. He didn't want to let go of Meghan long enough to pick up the mess.

Once there she gently let go of his hand. "I need to use the restroom," she said.

Closing his eyes, he nodded. "Of course."

As much as he wanted to grab onto her and never let go, this situation was untenable.

He decided to make lunch, putting on the television so he could think about anything else. A bit sick of sandwiches, he steamed some soup dumplings and made a salad with thin rice noodles and slices of fried spring rolls.

Meghan was back before he was done preparing their meal. She crossed the open space to the kitchen corner and peeked into the salad bowl. Her stomach growled, making her grin sheepishly.

"What is this? It smells so good."

Glad to be of service in some way, he scooped some into a smaller ceramic bowl. "It's a Vietnamese dish I had in France during one of my tours. They call it *salad des nems* over there, which is spring roll salad. It's pretty popular in the states too, but the way I had it in France had this incredible sauce none of the local places use, so I experimented until I could recreate it. Are you allergic to peanuts?"

"No, peanut butter is one of my staples."

"That's good, because the crunch of peanuts is what makes this dish," he said, sprinkling several spoonfuls over the top of the bowl.

He handed it over with a pair of chopsticks...which she did not know how to use.

After the third failed attempt to pick up a piece of spring roll, he grabbed a fork from a drawer.

"*Nooo,*" she laughed as the noodles slipped from her chopsticks. "I want to get this."

Her mirth was infectious. Chuckling, he set the fork down. "Okay, here. Let me show you."

Derrick moved her fingers, adjusting her grip before taking his chopsticks and demonstrating.

Her chopsticks made their shaky way up to her face. This time she didn't drop the bit of spring roll and noodles before she was able to scoop the lot into her mouth.

She kept giggling as she chewed. Charmed to his toes, he joined in, his deep chuckle blending in with her light dulcet tones.

"I did it," she cried, holding up her chopsticks in victory after swallowing.

"Good job." He smiled. "I guess you haven't had all that much Asian food yet."

"Oh, I have tried some. I like sushi and lots of Chinese dishes. But I always get takeout. The servers take one look at me and throw in a fork instead of chopsticks. I'll have to practice more."

"Well, until you get the hang of it, this is a perfectly acceptable way to eat." Derrick brought the bowl closer to his lips and used his chopsticks to shovel a big portion into his mouth.

He chewed appreciatively. "Mmm. My version of the sauce isn't as good as my favorite resto—what they call restaurants in France—but it's close. I would keep tweaking it, but I think the gap lies in the difference of the American versus French ingredients, not their actual composition at this point."

"I love it. I hope it's not hard to make."

"Nah. It's more like assembling. If I have the stuff on hand, it's a simple dish to prepare. But you don't have to worry. Even after we fix your problem, you can come by for lunch. Anytime."

The words came out with a nonchalance he didn't feel. They *were* going to find a way for her to gain control of her abilities. And once she had it, she might even keep traveling. After this incident with the cubs, she'd feel obligated to continue in case she was able to save lives.

But Derrick didn't want Meghan going anywhere. He bit back a sigh, telling himself he was just being a good dominant. But the little voice in his head insisted on being a smug little bitch. And it was whispering that all his excellent reasons for keeping Meghan close were starting to feel like convenient excuses.

You can always rent her a room. His house had two spare bedrooms and an office that could be converted into a fourth bedroom in a pinch. He had the space. Plus, it would be nice to have someone else around.

Derrick sometimes missed the camaraderie of close quarters that he'd experienced as a Ranger. But he wouldn't miss the loud resonant snores of his teammates.

Yes, a woman would be a far better roommate. And his protective instincts about her traveling might calm down if she agreed to stay here permanently.

She was almost done with her meal when he invited her to pick a movie from his collection while they waited for Hope to get back to them.

"What sort of things do you like?" he asked, half afraid she was going to say foreign films. Derrick loved good food and always found lots to love no matter what corner of the globe he found himself in, but he hated squinting at subtitles.

"I'm not sure. I can't say I have very strong preferences. I just watch the not-so-new releases at the library," she said kneeling in front of his television, still holding her bowl.

His console had built-in shelves crammed full of DVDs and Blu-Rays he rarely touched.

"We can find newer stuff online," he shared as she ran her finger along the spines of his collection. "I have subscriptions to all the different streaming services."

"I don't think that will be necessary. I haven't watched very many movies, so there's plenty here that is new to me." She pried out a female-led action-comedy from between two gore-fests.

"That is one of my favorites," he shared. "And bonus—it passes the Bechdel test."

"What is the—"

The rest of her words were snatched from the air as a roar filled the room. A gaping dark hole opened in the far corner.

Meghan dropped the disc and the bowl. She threw herself forward, trying to grab his coffee table, but her hands slipped off the slick lacquered surface.

Crying, she began to slide across the room, turning and tumbling toward the gaping doorway.

Derrick was already moving, but it felt as if he was slogging through molasses.

He leaped over the coffee table, snatching at Meghan's hand.

His fingers grazed hers. The instant he did, he heard it. The *snarl*.

But it was too late. Meghan was too far for him to take hold of. With nothing to grip, she flew back through the opening.

It closed around her instantly, leaving him alone with the echoes of her scream.

CHAPTER TWENTY-TWO

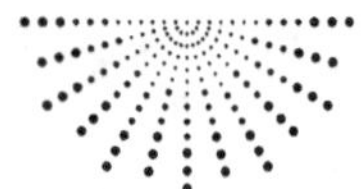

"As you can see, the opening affected the space around it—it didn't just suck the girl in. It would have taken whatever was between it and her as well."

Douglas held up his cell phone higher, panning it around the room slowly so Hope and Mai could see the mess the black hole had left.

Derrick had called the chief a few minutes after Meghan had disappeared so violently—after he'd run all over the property, searching every bit of the house and exterior. He'd even scoured his neighbor's yard, looking for any sign of Meghan or a bubble.

But there was no sign of her. And she would have come back if she'd been able to. *Fuck.*

That was when he sounded the alarm. The chief, alerted by the stress in his voice, had hustled over with the cavalry. In this case that included Nate, Kiera, Amy, and her army of techs.

Kiera and Amy started opening the cases Nate carried in for them. They were full of diagnostic equipment. Kiera took readings and Amy recorded the data while Nate watched over them both, just in case...

But the most gut-wrenching and disturbing episode of his life had left very little evidence for them to document.

His coffee table had flipped over, the coasters and other objects that used to rest on it scattered everywhere, some in pieces. His flatscreen was on the floor, the glossy surface cracked. But everything that had been in the opening's line of sight was gone. A vase and table, the one he used to drop his car keys onto.

Derrick scowled and patted his pockets. His keys were on him, not lost in oblivion…like Meghan.

Everything else was still in its place. Even the flowers in the delicate glass vase on the dining room table behind were fine, a few stray petals lying undisturbed on the wooden surface.

"The hole was focused on her. Like someone sighted Meghan with a laser sight and sicced it on her," Derrick growled, his mind struggling to accept it.

A force powerful enough to punch a hole in the world and suck one small girl out? It was the stuff horror movies were made of. It had certainly felt like being in one.

"By rights, it should have destroyed the room," he continued. "But it didn't."

"Do you believe there was human-level intelligence behind it?" Hope asked. Douglas swung the phone around so he could see her.

"It would explain the snarl I heard—I think it was human. Male. Pissed off when I touched her. It didn't have the bass or resonance to be a shifter's growl, but that's a guess. The wind was too loud to be sure."

"You didn't see anything beyond the threshold?" Hope asked, her face too close to the screen.

The woman was a highly skilled witch and a heck of a history professor. But she was a Luddite when it came to modern technology.

"Let me hold that," Mai snapped, offscreen. Derrick caught a glimpse of open sky and more of Hope's head, enough to see her chick bob flying around out of control.

"No, I didn't see anything. It was just as she described it—a black hole with turbine force sucking power." He squinted at the witches on the screen. "Are you in a convertible?"

"No, dear. That wouldn't be a very good way to get to T'Kaieri. We're flying there now."

"Boy has a point," Mai rumbled, still offscreen. "We could have done what they did in that children's movie and enchanted a car. A Chevrolet would be a damn sight more comfortable than this."

Derrick raised an eyebrow. "You're not on the broom, are you?"

"Of course not, dear," Hope chided. "That would be far too uncomfortable. We're on the trunk."

The camera panned down, showing him a bit of Hope's waist and thigh. It was resting on the oversized leather apothecary bag they took everywhere with them.

But it looked even bigger now, as if the witches had magically stretched it. As big as a steamer trunk, the bag held everything you could imagine. Too many things for the volume, even in this stretched-out form.

Derrick had always imagined the interior was enchanted to be bigger on the inside like Hermione's bag in Harry Potter or the Tardis. But he'd been afraid to ask.

And right now you also don't care. "I thought Meghan was being a bit cagey about the holes—not dishonest," he clarified. "I believe she told me everything she knew about the bubbles and how they worked. But I had a feeling she was leaving something major out."

Hope frowned thoughtfully "Like what? Something that would have reflected badly on her?"

"No, nothing like that. More like…" Derrick paused, looking at his chief, mulling it over.

"More like she was afraid big bad Derrick wouldn't be able to handle it," Amy sniped from across the room.

Derrick shot her a look of utter disgust. The one the chief gave her must have mirrored it, because Amy dropped her eyes.

"Sorry," she murmured, true regret in her tone. "I didn't mean it like it sounded. I just think that Meghan might have hesitated to mention she was being menaced because she knew you couldn't do anything about it."

"A viable hypothesis." Hope's voice was tinnier, as if she were farther now. "There may be an intelligence behind these black holes that she is aware of on some level. Regardless, we must trust in the girl's resourcefulness. She's been living in this reality for a very long time."

"Yeah," Mai chimed in. "Meghan's made it this far without help. But don't worry, my young friend. We're calling in the big guns. I was able to reach Logan before you called, and she and Connell are on their way back to you."

"That is good news," Douglas said. His expression didn't change, but his scent did. Satisfaction with a hint of relief. The latter might have been for Meghan's sake, but it was also the fact Connell was on his way back. Douglas went very long periods without seeing him.

"Yes," Derrick echoed, trying to inject some enthusiasm into his tone. "That's great news."

"Douglas, I'll text you when we land." Hope was shouting now to be heard over the wind that had picked up in the background.

"Please do," the chief replied, inclining his head before hanging up. His formality was a dead giveaway that something was up between them, but Derrick found it hard to care at the moment.

The only person he wanted to gossip with wasn't here.

Douglas threw an arm around him, drawing him in close so they touched foreheads. Startled, Derrick tried to pull back. Technically the chief did this all the time, with the submissives or children.

"I don't believe you met Meghan just to lose her now. Have faith. Picture her returning, safe. It will happen."

The shifter version of "if you can dream it, you can be it."

He opened his lips to correct the chief's assumption that Meghan was his. But he clamped his mouth shut. Now was not the time. He'd focus on getting her back first.

And if there was human intelligence behind her problem, he'd also use the time to figure out how to rip the bastard's head off.

Yeah, that was a goal he'd happily visualize into reality.

CHAPTER TWENTY-THREE

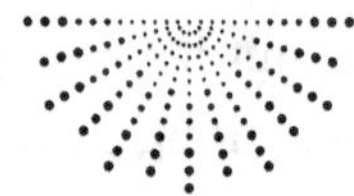

Meghan tripped over a root. It sent her flying, but she adjusted, hitting the ground in a roll. She still hurt everywhere, but at least she didn't get the air knocked from her lungs.

Yes, there would be bruises. But she couldn't afford to dwell on that. She had to keep going.

He would be coming. He always did.

Wincing, she picked herself up and began to run, trying to get her bearings without losing her footing or crashing into the tree trunks crowding her.

The moonlit woods resembled those around Lake Veris, but there were no landmarks, nothing to orient herself. It could have been pine forest anywhere in the world. And it was freezing. Too cold for Colorado.

You could be wrong, she told herself, hoping despite the grim appearance of the landscape. She could have traveled back to Lake Veris in the dead of winter.

Meghan slowed down to a jog. She knew from past experience that she couldn't keep running flat out. Not in this kind of cold. It was better to conserve her strength and stretch out the time she could stay mobile. Because when her energy ran out, she'd be at the mercy of the cold.

Topping a rise, she spotted the lake a few hundred yards away.

It is Lake Veris. She hadn't gone far. But the scene was subtly wrong.

Snow dusted the shore. Moonlight reflected off the pristine white, the only source of illumination. The shore was black otherwise—there were no vacation cabins, no warm golden lights dotting the darkness. It was either years before they were built or so far in the future they had been removed for some unknown reason.

That didn't matter. It was familiar enough, something to hold on to. Derrick might not be here. The people she had met, her new friends might be gone, but this was their land. It belonged to his pack. And they had called this home for a long time.

Except that didn't make sense. Why would *he* bring her here, a place where she might potentially be able to seek out help?

Because there is no help.

Just like there was no safe place. This might be Lake Veris, but he might have brought her here to show her exactly how alone she was.

If the pack did live here, they could be in the middle of a war during this period. Derrick had told her about their violent history and how hard they had worked to overcome it.

For all you know the next wolf you meet might go for your throat. Was this an elaborate trap? *Except you already know he doesn't want you dead.* She'd have died as a child had that been the case.

Unsettled by her thoughts, Meghan stopped walking, training her ears for the smallest sound. But she could discern nothing beyond the rustle of the wind through the pine. The only sign of life was her own breathing.

Then the wind off the lake changed course. A strong gust ran over her with icy needles, penetrating the thick sweatshirt as if it wasn't there.

Chaffing her hands didn't help warm them. Pulling her hood over her hair, she shoved her hands in the front pocket of her sweatshirt.

Then she began to walk again, looking for a bubble to take her away before he found her.

Meghan had been wandering for a good hour when a soft growl froze her in her tracks.

She turned around and came face to face with the biggest black wolf she had ever seen—one who was looking at her with bared fangs.

CHAPTER TWENTY-FOUR

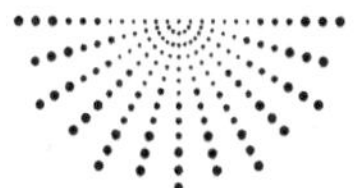

The wolf was huge, even bigger than Derrick in his animal form. It was standing on top of a fallen log. That should have put them at eye level, but the beast was so big she was looking up at him.

Another growl, this one deep enough to make her eardrums vibrate. It advanced toward her, licking its chops.

"P-please," she said, taking a big step back. Meghan pulled her hood down hastily so he could see her face. "I'm sorry. I know I'm not supposed to be here."

The wolf ceased growling, slowing. But it didn't stop advancing. Edging back, she shuddered and tried again.

"I didn't mean to violate your territory. I wasn't meant to come here at all. I was brought here against my will… Err, are you a Maitland?" she asked tremulously.

The wolf's muzzle drew back.

"I know some shifters. Wolves," she volunteered in a breathy voice, trying to decide how much to share.

How would a strange shifter react if she told him she was a time traveler?

Not well. "They're not here, my shifter friends. I—I lost them. But I want to get back to them."

The wolf cocked its head, studying her. Then it walked forward, slower than before. It moved its head in a half-circle, pointing down with its muzzle in an almost imperious command.

"Oh." Quelling a tremble, Meghan leaned down. *Please don't bite me. Please don't bite me.*

The beast leaned in until its massive jaw was an inch from her head. Hot breath made her hair flutter as it sniffed her.

Meghan swallowed, bracing herself for it to unhinge those massive and swallow her whole.

The wolf made a sound suspiciously close to a harrumph. Backing away, it sat on its haunches with an air of mingled puzzlement and frustration.

"Do you smell him on me? My shifter friend?"

The wolf continued to stare at her as if it expected her to sprout horns or wings.

"I guess you do. He's not a Maitland though," she added lamely.

The wolf made a sound in its throat. It rose abruptly and left, disappearing into the woods.

"Okay, then." Sighing, Meghan got to her feet, her stiff cold muscles stretching reluctantly.

A shirtless man emerged from the woods. His hair was grey, his face carved and craggy, but there were clear traces of Douglas Maitland in his features. He was wearing a pair of rough canvas pants—the precursor to jeans—and his feet were bare.

If he felt the cold, he showed no signs of it.

"No. The shifter you smell of is not a Maitland. He is a Sheridan."

"*Oh,*" she said, not bothering to hide her surprise. "I had no idea you could tell that."

"Not all family lines can be distinguished. But some can. Strong family lines." The stranger narrowed his eyes at her. "The Sheridans fall into the latter category. The fact you carry the scent of one in your skin is the only reason I'm not ripping you apart, *witch.*"

His dark eyes lightened to wolf bright yellow. "I still might. Because the Sheridan you smell of is unfamiliar to me—a near impossibility."

Meghan gulped. "I'm not a witch," she protested.

A disdainful snort. "Sit, witch" he ordered, pointing to the fallen log.

Sighing, she obeyed. He left and came back five minutes later with a beaten metal case and a sac.

The case ended up being a tinder box. He used it to start a little fire. Inside the sack was a hunk of cheese and a piece of bread. A few minutes later and she was holding a steaming cup of watered-down wine infused with cloves and other spices she couldn't name.

Closing her eyes, she drank, warming herself by the fire. A few other wolves came, drifting out of the trees. They stayed in animal form, giving her the evil eye but keeping their distance.

The grey-haired man didn't shift back, staying human so he could speak to his people. He conducted his little conferences in low tones, saying nothing loud enough for her to catch.

Meghan finished her drink and huddled under the blanket. She was starting to get sleepy, but she didn't ask the wolves if there was a shelter nearby. If they wanted to provide one, they would. Asking wouldn't help.

Besides, it might still be cold, but thanks to the fire and the spiced wine she wasn't suffering.

You should be out looking for a bubble. But she didn't move. It wasn't as if the wolves would let her leave. She still wasn't sure who she was dealing with, but it was clear they found her suspicious. The grey-haired man wasn't about to let her go on her merry way.

She was fairly certain he was a Maitland alpha, one a few generations removed from Douglas. Was it his grandfather? What had been the man's name?

Damn. She should have asked Derrick more questions about the pack's history.

Her question was soon answered when he pressed another hot drink into her hand a few minutes later. "My name is Atticus," he volunteered with a growl.

"Oh, like the—" Meghan bit her tongue. But his words confirmed her guess. This was Douglas's grandfather, the Maitland alpha who had founded the Columbia Basin Pack.

Atticus smirked. "The what?"

He stared at her long enough for her squirm. Her skin was crawling so badly it felt as if it were about to walk off her. *Alpha shifters*, she swore mentally. "Like the school," she whispered.

There was a long silence. "If I ask what school, canna I expect an honest answer?"

Meghan looked down at her lap.

"Forget I asked." Atticus began to walk away. He began to give instructions, louder this time, instructing the other wolves to prepare a shelter for her.

Whatever they had planned took some time. Tired and worn out, she huddled close to the fire, laying as close as she could, risking going up flames from stray sparks.

Ignoring the wolf powwow being conducted in the shadows, her mind went straight to Derrick. Her body ached, longing for his protective arms.

You'll get back to him, she told herself. In the meantime, she would allow herself a few foolish fantasies. Things he never needed to know about.

While she was lost in thought, her lashes began to flutter and close. Behind her lids, the light of the fire began to sputter and go out. Too quickly. Far too quickly.

Meghan's eyes flew open, breath visible as the temperature plunged. The flames died, crusted over in ice—a physical impossibility that signaled *his* arrival.

Scrambling to her feet, she whirled, looking for the wolves. "He's here!" she shouted, waving her arms wildly. "Run, *run!*"

CHAPTER TWENTY-FIVE

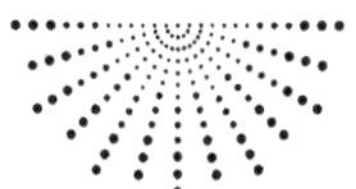

The damn stubborn shifters ignored her, of course. Atticus thrust his arms out, his claws unsheathing as he scanned for the threat.

But this evil was not hiding. That wasn't what he did. He was there in the shadows—which went from normal dark to the inky black of the void.

Growling deep in his throat, Atticus threw back his head and howled, the sound all the more disturbing for the fact it came out of a human throat.

All around them other howls answered, the chilling war cry bouncing off the rocks and trees to reverberate back, the echo vibrating in her ears. It was sound designed by evolution to strike fear into the hearts of anyone who heard it.

But as terrifying as the sound was, it paled in comparison with the creeping shadows.

Inky black tar crawled out of the murk, coalescing into a tall ascetically thin form in a caped cowl. The shadow man turned toward her.

Meghan hadn't been this close to him in years. She used to believe he was a giant. Seeing him now with adult eyes, she could see he was a man of average height. But that realization didn't make him any less monstrous.

A bone-white face was illuminated in the moonlight. Sunken eye sockets and thick bulbous lips parted with a hiss. Meghan drew back, revolted as the slack skin rippled, the surface of his skin bubbling like a pot of milk about to boil over.

Bile rising, she shouted again, telling the wolves to leave. "You can't fight him. If he touches you, he'll kill you!"

That was how the woman she thought was her mother had died—she had been trying to help Meghan.

She had failed.

But the stupid wolves didn't listen. There were a half dozen now. They surrounded their alpha, spreading out into a half-circle, advancing in front of him.

"Ruun girrlll," Atticus snarled, his eyes glowing a brilliant feral yellow as the wolf began to take over. He tore at his pants as he shifted, the black wolf ripping out of him with a luminescent blue glow.

Turning on her heel, she prepared to do just that. She got to the cover of a thick pine tree trunk, panting and looking behind her.

The shadow man was facing the wolves, his attention on the threat. He raised his hands, and she heard him hiss.

Forgetting her for the moment, he started closing in on the wolves, his rolling and shifting gait unnatural, like a bobbin rolling up and down as it crept forward—more automaton if one was made of oil and toxic waste.

Whimpering, she dug her fingers into the bark of the tree, her breath coming in ragged pants. *I can't go.*

What if one of those wolves out there with Atticus was the Sheridan he'd mentioned? If the shadow man killed one of Derrick's ancestors—if *any* of them died—she would lose him.

The world would lose him.

Her vision darkened, but she fought back the panic, intentionally scraping her palms on the bark. Too hard. Until she drew blood.

The shadow man whirled, his nostrils flaring as if he could smell it.

The massive wolf turned to her too, a bark of warning that did an excellent job of conveying how he was unhappy with her.

But she didn't care. If the shadow man took even one of these shifters, the world she desperately wanted to get back to might not exist. Not if she let the wolves fight him.

This was her battle. And yes, she was still terrified, but she was something else too. Meghan was *angry*.

"*GO*," she told the wolves. She almost missed the echoing resonance of her voice. It thrummed through her, her blood coursing through her like it was a stream of bright hot magma.

The wind had picked up, whipping her hair. Fingertips tingling, she pointed to the wolves. "*MOVE.*"

The snaps and cracks of breaking wood were so loud she was convinced her bones were snapping. That was how it felt. The pain made her want to crumple to the ground, but the rage coursing through her kept her on her feet.

She raised her arms. Broken fragments of the shattered pine trunk sharpened to spears and razor-like shrapnel.

Pressure filled her head, filling her ears until she was deaf. Her field of view was rapidly narrowing when she let her arms fall. Struggling, she pushed through the air like it was thick mud. The cloud of stakes and spikes flew toward the roiling darkness of the shadow man.

An unearthly scream filled the air, the sound of a wounded animal from hell. It was so loud it penetrated the pressure blocking her ears. But the shadow man was no normal beast. She wasn't even sure he was mortal. Meghan had stood her ground.

She'd managed to hurt him, and now he was angry. But her strength was gone.

Meghan fell forward, Derrick's name on her lips. But she didn't hit the ground. Instead, it swallowed her up, the darkness fast on her heels.

CHAPTER TWENTY-SIX

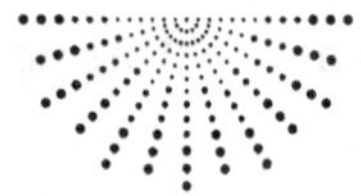

Meghan's vision was blinkering in and out when a pair of leather-clad legs filled her vision. Rolling on her back, she saw a short Asian girl standing in front of her.

Someone snarled at her back. Meghan's mouth gaped, and the woman called behind her.

"Derrick! Get your furry butt out here."

Then strong arms were lifting her. As she was carried away, she saw the girl raise her arms just like she had in the woods. The stranger was standing in front of a black hole, gale force winds sucking at her. But the tiny woman stood her ground, not giving an inch despite the fact the world should have folded up around her.

Her fading vision showed her a nightmare. The shadow man thrust his head and arms out of the hole. His roar filled the world, and Meghan tried to scream, to warn the woman to get away from him.

Her voice came out in a raspy whisper. "Don't touch him. Touch kills."

It turned out the warning wasn't necessary.

The woman glowed with deadly starlight. It gathered inside her, pulsing like a wave until it was concentrated enough to fling at the invader, electric-white energy making contact with white-hot fire and the smell of ozone.

Screeching, the shadow man fell back, and the hole collapsed on itself with a sound like the crack of a whip.

The sudden silence made her brain snap, a muscle stretched too far. Meghan passed out.

Warmth and movement. Strong arms in the dark.

Meghan roused in the shower, Derrick murmuring urgently in her ears. Relieved and overwhelmed, she started to cry.

Derrick existed. She hadn't changed his past, erasing him from existence.

The Asian woman was there too. She was standing just outside the shower, a huge dark-haired man at her back.

"Do you consent to have your clothing removed?" she asked, enunciating each word as if Meghan were hard of hearing.

Which she probably was. Warm iron-scented liquid was dribbling from her nose and maybe her ears, only to wash down her chest as a clear shade of pink

The big man—who resembled Derrick quite a bit—said something Meghan couldn't hear.

"We must make sure. I mean, look at her. She's this close to passing out," the small woman said, holding her fingers a centimeter apart.

A deep-throated rumble made her chest vibrate. Derrick had growled at the woman. She should have scolded him for it. But Meghan was so happy to be in his arms that she took comfort in the sound, rolling around in it like a puppy in a pile of leaves.

"What did I tell you about getting between a dominant wolf and his mate?" the man warned his small companion with a chuckle. "And don't poke him again if you want that hand back."

The woman clucked her tongue. She looked over Meghan's head. "Don't take too long—we have to talk."

Then she and the man were gone.

Derrick finished removing her clothes with urgent hands, cutting them off with his claws. She was naked and in his arms.

"Is this okay?"

"Yes, yes." Meghan pulled his head down, pressing her lips against his face, kissing everywhere she could reach.

Derrick pressed her against the slick shower tiles, holding her with one arm as he used the other to tear his pants off.

His mouth covered hers, his kiss hotter than the water pouring over them, hotter than the plasma bolts the strange Asian girl had thrown. "Good. Don't leave me again."

CHAPTER TWENTY-SEVEN

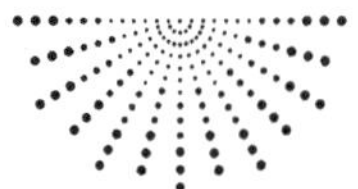

Derrick rubbed her back with a huge towel, making a soft terrycloth cocoon where she was nestled against his front as he sat on the edge of the big whirlpool tub.

"It will be hard to dress if I'm in your lap, like this," she said. But she didn't budge, her muscles lacking the desire to move.

Her first lovemaking experience had been everything she had ever dreamed of—had she dreamed of such things. She hadn't. But she would now. Every night if she had her way.

"Challenge accepted," Derrick murmured.

"*No*," she pressed her face against his chest. "I don't want to get dressed."

He passed the hand over her hair, drying it gently. "Neither do I. There's nothing I want more than to go straight to bed and stay there with you for the next month. But we can't do that."

Derrick pulled away so he could see her face. His hand moved her hair off her face, his fingers working through the curls. "Your magical consult is here."

"The Asian woman."

He nodded. "That's Logan, my cousin-in-law. She's mated to Connell, the big bastard who was with her."

Her brow puckered. "And Connell is your cousin?"

"Yes, and his mate is an Elemental."

She must have looked blank, because he quickly explained that an Elemental was a very powerful type of witch.

Meghan didn't follow everything he said about the balance and the Mother, but she didn't need to. The only thing she cared about was that Logan had taken on the shadow man and done the impossible. She had driven him away.

If anyone knew how to stop the monster, or when and where the city with spires was located, it would be Logan.

They found a stack of clean clothes outside the door, including a shirt and pair of pants that were much closer to her size than what she typically wore.

"I don't think these are Logan's clothes," Derrick observed as he held the shirt, a soft green tunic, against her chest to gauge the size. He snapped the tags of the bra and panties which had been included. "She's a shrimp."

"Logan seemed plenty big to me," Meghan said, taking the shirt and pulling it down over her midriff.

"I know. She takes up three times the space someone her size should. I think the power she wields distorts your brain's perception of how big she is."

Once they were presentable they went into the hall, Derrick's hand holding hers tight.

But the house was empty. When she asked why, Derrick blushed. "I think they cleared out to give us a little space." He tapped his ear. "Sensitive hearing."

Meghan's face flamed. "Oh," she said, trying not to die of mortification.

Derrick took her chin with his fingers, gently tilting her head back to look at him. "We have nothing to be embarrassed about. Wolves are carnal creatures. Having sex in a full house is hardly the most embarrassing thing one of us has done. The stories I could tell you..."

He trailed off and cleared his throat. "But not about me. I'm practically a monk."

"Sure you are," she laughed. Meghan had never seen Derrick with any women, but she had noted the way they looked at him. A man of his obvious strength and virile good looks never had to spend a night alone unless he wanted to.

She had read a romance that described the hero as a panty-melter. That was what Derrick was. A panty-melter. One who blushed as she admired him.

Derrick cleared his throat. "We'll discuss this later."

He sat down on the couch, tugging her into his lap. Wrapping one arm around her, he took out his phone and texted with one hand, presumably to tell the others the coast was clear.

Tired beyond endurance, Meghan drifted off, safely tucked under Derrick's chin. When she woke up she was being poked and prodded by a superhero.

Logan Li was a gamine powerhouse. Long-limbed despite her diminutive size, she moved with a grace that reminded Meghan of a prima ballerina she had seen dance on the library's computer.

"Hey," Logan grinned at her, taking her vitals as Meghan blinked sleepily.

The Elemental's eyes almost glowed, her expression hyper-focused, as if she were looking at the most fascinating puzzle. "Super cool to meet Derrick's witch."

Meghan sucked in a breath. So she was magic.

"So that's official?" Derrick asked. "She's a witch? Not a cursed human?"

"Oh, hell no. This kiddo packs a punch, don't you, Meghan?"

A gentle breeze passed over her hair. Logan sniffed, lips parted almost as if she was tasting the air.

"Are you smelling me?"

Logan's expression curdled. "Sorry. My abilities have taken a distinctly lupine aspect since I mated with this one." She jerked her thumb in Connell's direction. "But I am certain. You're a witch. A rather unique one."

Meghan started to protest, the denial automatic. But her memory brought back the image of flying pine shards, and she looked down at her hands, remembering how they had hurt.

She told Logan what happened. "They still ache," she said, holding up her fingers. "Deep inside."

"Yeah, channeling that much raw power will rattle the bones." Logan took her hand, testing her fingers to make sure there were no hairline fractures or breaks. "That's why witches of your ability use spells. A properly cast spell filters the power, harnessing it to complete the chosen task, and uses nothing more. Less wear and tear on the body that way. Not that there are a lot of witches with your kind of raw power walking around. Most are weaker."

"But don't the weak ones need spells too?" Derrick asked.

"Even more so, but for the opposites reason. With weaker witches, the spell gathers what power they have, focusing it like a laser. Sometimes they make an offering or sacrifice a life to give the spell the fuel it needs."

Logan straightened, rocking back on her heels. "But I'm guessing you've never had to do that last part. You've got the juice to power spells without an additional source of energy."

Meghan's face tightened. "I've never cast a spell. I don't know how."

Logan made another wolf-like noise in her throat, much more delicate than Derrick's growls and rumbles. "Not surprising if you've been bouncing around since you were a kid. You've had no training."

She looked back up at Derrick, who nodded in confirmation. "When her power activates—if bouncing through time can be called a power—it's involuntary or unconscious. Except when that creepy oily fucker punches a hole in our reality and drags her away."

Startled, Meghan tipped her head to look back up at him. "You saw the shadow man?"

"We all saw him," Connell broke in.

The tall dark-haired Were rubbed his face. "Creepiest thing I've ever seen, and I've been going around with my mate on her missions for years now. We've fought trolls, cult handmaidens—even a fae zombie berserker. This was more disturbing."

Derrick's hands squeezed her tight, hard enough that she nudged him in protest. "Sorry." He stroked her back in a soothing circle.

"That's okay," she yawned, trying not to slip off into sleep again. Her hazy vision settled on Connell. He was very handsome. Almost as handsome as Derrick. There was a lot of Douglas in his face but also…

Meghan gasped when she realized Connell's face was a younger version of the grey-haired man in the woods. "Douglas. I have to speak to Douglas."

"I'm here."

Meghan twisted in Derrick's hold, belatedly realizing there were a lot more people in the room than she had realized.

The chief was sitting at the dining room table, having a conversation with Nathan and Amy. Half a dozen others milled around them.

Discomfited, she huddled into a smaller ball in Derrick's lap, looking over his shoulder at the chief with burning eyes.

"Nobody died, right? When Atticus met the witch in the woods and the shadow man came, did anybody die?"

She broke off as he frowned in confusion. "Do you know about that?" He had to know the history.

"Wait…" Douglas's face clouded over before clearing. "You're speaking of the night Atticus Maitland met a quadroon witch in the woods by the lake?"

"Err, I think so." She blinked. "What is a quadroon?"

Douglas winced and lifted a shoulder. "It's the word Atticus used to mean a mixed-race person. But the details of her—your—physical appearance were a relatively minor note in the annals. He spent far more time describing the witch's odd speech and the bizarre clothing she wore: a thick protective jumper and pants that were with stitching fit for a queen. This was when clothes were still made by hand, not machines, so the fact your pants were so well crafted was a jarring detail to him. Such precision was usually reserved for the elite."

"When was this?" Connell asked, frowning at his father. They looked so much like each other and so much like Atticus when they scowled, it was not hard to draw a connecting line of relatedness from one to the other.

"It was shortly after Atticus settled in this area, officially founding the pack after the clan wars decimated our numbers," Douglas replied. "It was made up of an amalgamation of survivors from multiple clans."

He passed a hand over his face. "What was left of them anyway. But that group was special. It was unprecedented—the cooperation of so many former enemies. It set the stage for the alliance that would become the North American coalition."

Douglass snorted suddenly. "Atticus interpreted the events of that night as a portent of the future."

"Why? What happened to the wolves that night?" Derrick asked. "Did that creature get any of them?"

Meghan closed her eyes, preparing for the worst.

"There were no casualties."

Shuddering, she fell forward. Derrick's big hand covered her chest, pushing her back against him instead. "Meghan was worried she had changed the past. If one of those wolves had died…"

"We might not be here now," Douglas finished. "I understand. What I meant is that Atticus had been having trouble with another pack of wolf shifters from the south. He wrote that he was considering moving his pack up north until he encountered the witch. He guessed she was from the future, in part because of her odd speech and clothing, but mostly she smelled like an unfamiliar Sheridan. To him, that meant our pack successfully held this territory—by any means necessary."

A corner of Douglas's mouth crooked up. "So Atticus did the unthinkable. He began to try diplomacy." The chief scratched his chin. "That might not have worked with a wolf of lesser standing, but Atticus had proved himself in many a bloody battle. When other pack leaders realized there was an option to fighting him—one that left them to run their packs with some autonomy, they took his deal. His son, my father, completed the task of unification."

Derrick rumbled something under his breath. His chin rested on her hair. "*See.* You help even without trying."

"As far as I can tell our history is intact. But I defer to the expert." Douglas gave his daughter-in-law a significant glance.

Logan's eyes widened. "Oh, I'm not sensing anything big enough to be a timeline shift. However, I'm getting all sorts of weirdness from this one."

Her delicate hands passed over Meghan, swooping in circles. "And it is super *duper* weird—in fact, it's hard to look at her directly because she's vibrating on a frequency your eyes can't detect."

Meghan's face fell. "I am? Like the shadow man?" She touched her face. "His face bubbles, like a pot of custard boiling over."

"I was too busy blasting him to notice that." Logan wrinkled her nose. "But congratulations—you've put me off custard forever. Never making it again."

Connell snickered. "Like you needed an excuse to hate on it."

Logan pointed an accusing finger at her mate. "Tapioca and custard are gross and you know it. It's rice pudding or bust."

She turned back to Meghan. "Besides, this sounds a little different. Your vibe is more like a rapid oscillation, almost as if you were sitting on a speaker blasting deep bass."

"But you've never seen anything like it? Or like the shadow man?"

Logan drew herself up to her full height. That shouldn't have been impressive, because she was barely over five feet, but she *felt* taller to Meghan. "Not personally, but my mom and aunt are at the T'Kaierian archive. If there's even a hint of a similar thing happening in recorded history, that's where the record will be."

Meghan nodded, swallowing hard. "So we wait?"

Logan shook her head. "Actually, no. We have quite a lot to do, starting with figuring out exactly when and where you came from."

Derrick absently rubbed her arms, always trying to warm her. "You need to know where in the past the city of spires is?"

"It would help. While some aspects are universal, each civilization has its own flavor of magic. Meghan's is sufficiently distinct that knowing where she's from would be a boon. There are also a few things I want to try—think of them as diagnostic tests."

"What do you need to get started?" Derrick asked.

"I have most of the ingredients," Logan said. "I asked some of the kids to go out and gather the rest while you were, *ahem*, showering."

Blushing, Meghan looked down. But Derrick just squeezed her to him, unfazed in that male way that neither hid nor boasted of their intimacy. It was theirs and it was private.

"One thing—we should move this show to the chief's house," Logan advised.

"Why?"

"The spell Mai and my mother cast last year, protecting it from supernatural attack, is no longer active, but it can be revived with a few incantations and fresh ingredients. With a little work, we can tweak it and try and get some temporal barriers in there. It'll take less time than setting up a new spell here, as it's rather intricate."

Meghan glanced back at Derrick, silently asking for clarification. "This was done back when I thought we might be invaded. I'll tell you the whole story at the chief's house."

Derrick turned to Logan. "Is that spell powerful enough to keep the shadow man at bay?"

She lifted a shoulder. "I honestly don't know. But it's worth a shot."

Meghan could tell Derrick didn't like that answer, but she took comfort in Logan's honesty and obvious skill. Maybe her helter-skelter life was finally going to come to an end.

I might get to stay with Derrick.

He reached around her to squeeze her fingers, as if sensing her roiling emotions, but her hands were cold as ice in his firm hold. Meghan wouldn't get her happily ever after until she confronted the nightmare that had stalked her for her entire life.

CHAPTER TWENTY-EIGHT

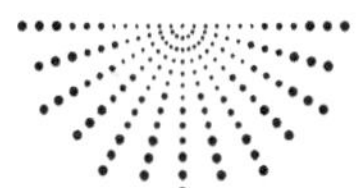

Derrick was impatient to find a cure for Meghan's condition, but his constant questions began to drive Logan crazy. Enough that she banished him from the library.

Connell took pity on him and offered a sparring session, but Derrick had only gotten a few licks in when Douglas came out to watch the two of them going at it.

Technically, Douglas was never out of touch with his son. He could feel Connell through pack bonds, enough to get a general sense of his well-being, but it wasn't the same as seeing for himself that he was all right.

Derrick's relationship with his parents was solid, but he sometimes envied the tight bond Douglas had with his kids. So when the chief drifted out onto the porch, lingering in a way his busy schedule didn't allow, Derrick excused himself to give them some private father-son time.

He ended up freeing himself just in time to take a video call from the chief's other kid. Derrick retreated to the woods to talk to Mara, filling her in on the wild events while trying to hike around to expend some of his restless energy.

"Where is your better half?" he asked after getting a rundown on the honeymoon shenanigans, which included touring a real haunted castle and putting down some killer spooks—Connell had rubbed off on his sister.

"He's passed out, recovering."

"From what?" She'd already told him they had spent a lazy day, wandering around a small village in Italy eating their weight in pasta.

"Oh, you know…"

Derrick cringed then scowled. "Gross." Jackson, Mara's mate was more like a brother than a friend.

"You're one to talk," his cousin smirked. "Three different people texted me to tell me about the 'shower incident.'" Mara held up her fingers, doing air quotes. "And I'm only a little annoyed Connell got to meet your mate before I did."

Derrick blinked, his lips parting. *Oh, shit.*

Mara scowled at him. "She *is* your mate, right? Because if you've gone this apeshit over another fling—"

"I'm pretty sure she's my mate," Derrick said hoarsely, cutting her off.

Mara's head drew back, skeptically. "Pretty sure?"

"More than that. I know she is."

"But you hesitated. I would have thought you'd have nailed that down. She's exactly your type."

"What? Meghan isn't anything like the women I've dated."

"Good," Mara smirked. "Wait, is that bothering you?"

Derrick sighed and scratched his head. "Shouldn't it? Not that I have any doubts about how I feel about Meghan. But once this craziness is over, I'm a little worried about our dynamic."

Mara rolled her eyes. "What the hell is up your butt now? Meghan sounds perfect for you."

He shrugged. "I guess I always saw myself with a different type of woman. Another dominant."

Even his human girlfriends had possessed strong personalities firmly on that end of the scale. Before Meghan, he wouldn't have touched a submissive with a ten-foot pole.

"Yeah, I know," Mara scoffed. "But if I could take you on a guided tour of girlfriends past, you *always* picked the wrong kind of woman. It was almost admirable the way you kept going for the Type A's, had it not been for the fact most of them drifted over the line to straight-out bitch in most cases."

She held up a hand when he opened his mouth to argue. "No offense to my brethren," Mara continued. "Because even a cast-iron bitch like *moi* can find love with the right man, as I have proved."

"But I'm not that man?" He laughed, then scowled. "With an alpha female that isn't related to me, that is."

"Nope. Not even a little bit," Mara said dropping her pearls of wisdom from the safety of the other side of the planet. "You're more overprotective than Connell, and that's saying something. He had to make a lot of compromises to be with Logan, mainly in recognizing she's more of a badass than he is. But you?"

She tsked. "You know I love you man, but you are *gross* as a boyfriend."

Derrick scowled. "What the hell does that mean?"

"Just that you go from sweet and thoughtful to full-on smother, dude."

"Smother? I don't smother," he scoffed. "Just because I like to drive my dates home to make sure they made it home safe? Or making sure their cars have been serviced recently so they are safe to drive? Isn't that the definition of a good boyfriend?"

"Normally, it would be," Mara replied. "But the women you pick are independent to the point of being completely closed off. Their tolerance for constant and conscientious care is naturally low to begin with."

She adjusted a pillow behind her, and Derrick realized she was settling in for a long talk. "Remember Stacy and the Valentine's Day scavenger hunt fiasco?"

Derrick didn't need the reminder. He had been left hanging in the park with all the fixings of a romantic moonlight picnic because his ex had stuck to their earlier agreement that they wouldn't make a big deal of the holiday.

"I'm not trying to crap on all the exes," Mara said. "I liked most of them. But that doesn't change the fact they were one-hundred-percent wrong for you. You need someone who will be happy being taken care of. Not every woman has to be like Logan or even me."

Derrick made a face. "Do me a favor and don't include yourself in that sort of list."

"I was just an example. Don't be a butthead."

"*Fine,*" he groused after a long moment of hard thinking. "Maybe, I see your point."

More than one girlfriend had included the terms "suffocating" and "so extra" when describing his over-protective tendencies.

"I'm just concerned I'm going to steamroll Meghan and not even realize I'm doing it."

"Correct me if I'm wrong, but is this the woman who turned a thirty-foot pine into toothpicks and sent the shards flying at a monster to save the founder of our pack?" Mara smacked her lips. "Pretty weird for a submissive to pack that kind of punch, but witch stuff gets weird. Magic jumbles the spectrum and can turn it inside out."

He pursed his lips. "You may have a point."

"Then why haven't you initiated the mating bond? I would have thought with all this anchoring-her-to-the-here-and-now business that would have been the first thing you'd have done."

"I have considered it," Derrick snapped. "But you're forgetting one of the drawbacks of the mating bond—the one only a handful of dominants, your dad included, have actually overcome."

Mara's mouth pressed into a thin line. "Why the hell are you bringing up my da—"

She broke off, the light dawning. "Oh."

"Exactly."

He felt more than heard someone watching him.

Derrick turned to see Meghan was standing around six yards away. His grim expression fell away when he saw the hurt in her expression.

"I've got to go," he said quickly, hanging up on Mara.

But Meghan was already out of sight. Derrick ran, catching her walking back to the house, her hands in her pockets.

"Hey!" He stopped her with a hand to her shoulder but immediately snatched it back. This was the sort of behavior he had to keep in check if they ever got to make a life together.

When Derrick, you idiot, he berated himself. *Not if.*

"What?" Meghan turned, trying to hide her suspiciously moist eyes.

"I'm just being a fucking idiot, baby. You'll have to get used to that. But no matter what you just heard, I do believe we belong together, and I am not letting you go."

She frowned. "Even though I'm not the kind of woman you think you should be with?"

Derrick swore, pulling her close until she was plastered to his chest. "You don't know her enough to appreciate how annoying it is for me to admit this—but Mara was right. She usually is."

Meghan still wouldn't look at him, engendering a sensation that felt like his insides were being grated with a lemon zester. "What was she right about?"

"That you are the woman I *need*," he said, letting his possessiveness bleed into his voice. "Because I am an insufferable son of a bitch who will try to feed you four times a day and would much rather drive you someplace than let you drive yourself."

"I don't know how to drive," Meghan said, blinking to ease the sting in her eyes.

Derrick threw his arms out. "Perfect."

"But I want to learn," she sniffed. "I don't want to be needy and helpless."

He wrapped his arms around her, tilting her chin up to look at him. "Yeah, that's the last thing you are. I'm an asshole for implying otherwise. I'll even teach you how to drive once we get your traveling under control."

He could still smell her hurt and distress. "But you still don't want to bond with me."

Shit. This was so fucked up. "Only because it's dangerous—for you."

Her pain turned to irritation. "You don't have to lie to me. I know what a wolf mating bond is. It's about commitment and love."

Jaw set, she pushed at him, but she couldn't break his hold. Growling despite the tears in her eyes, she kicked him in the shins.

"I *love* you," he said, trying not to burst with pride that she, the gentlest of submissives, felt free to hit him with impunity.

"I just kicked you," she said, raising her voice as her temper began to fray.

"And it was adorable. You can do it again if it makes you feel better."

Meghan threw up her hands. "Wolves are so frustrating."

"I know," he said, sympathetically.

Derrick meant it too. Yeah, he had a lot to offer a mate, but he was honest enough to admit that he was going to be a handful. And not just because he got furry on a regular basis and hunted rabbits in the woods.

He took her shoulders and held her a little away, so she'd meet his eyes. "Meghan, I know you're my mate. I *know* it. But there is something you should be aware of before we bond—at least until after your traveling is fixed."

Meghan contemplated him, chewing her lip in consternation. Slowly her hand crept up to take hold of his fingers.

Relaxing, he gently tugged her until she willingly walked into his embrace. "The bond between true mates is a powerful force. Not every wolf gets to experience it, which is why I'm happy as hell that you've turned up."

The moonlight and shadows on her face shifted as her head pulled back. "But?"

"But the bond can be severed. If something were to happen to one of us, it would be a severe shock. A lot of wolves don't survive the loss."

"Oh." She sucked in a breath. "So it would hurt you if I died?"

"No—I mean yes. I would be destroyed." Derrick scrubbed his face before putting his hands on her shoulders. "Shit, I'm explaining this so badly."

He stooped so they were at eye level. "Most wolves don't survive the loss of a mate. Sometimes if they have kids they soldier on, but that's not a given."

"You're thinking of the chief."

"Yeah, but in his case he also had his responsibilities to the pack and the coalition to keep him going. But most of the time when one bonded partner dies, the other follows. It's just a fact of life."

He took a deep breath. "And if one of those partners is a submissive..."

Understanding dawned. "Then they definitely die."

"Almost always." Derrick squeezed her shoulders. "If the opposite were true, I would risk it. I would risk anything for you. To have that kind of bond with such a fucking amazing person would be everything to me. But I don't know what would happen to our connection if you went through a bubble to a time when I don't exist."

Meghan inhaled sharply. "Would it break?"

He shrugged helplessly. "I have no idea."

A little wheeze escaped her lips. She staggered to the nearest place to sit, a small boulder with a flat ledge wide enough for her to sit.

"So even if we want to be together we could never have that bond?" she asked, those big amber eyes holding a lifetime's worth of loneliness and pain.

Derrick crouched, sitting cross-legged in front of her. He took her hands in his. "I won't initiate the mating bond. I can't risk you that way. But we can still make a life together—a good one."

"What if you do it on accident?"

"It's a hard thing to do unintentionally," he said, explaining about the bite to the base of the neck that initiated the chemical reaction to connect a couple, or less frequently a throuple.

Derrick decided not to tell her about the part where the bond failed to take. He already knew he wasn't in danger of misidentifying his mate. The pull to claim her was there. It was even stronger now, as if saying she was his mate aloud had dialed those instincts to full throttle.

Yeah, he could see himself biting her in the heat of the moment. *But you won't.*

Derrick wanted to believe a mating bond would survive one partner traveling in time, but he wasn't about to bet her life on it. Not even to assuage the pain he could smell coming off her now.

CHAPTER TWENTY-NINE

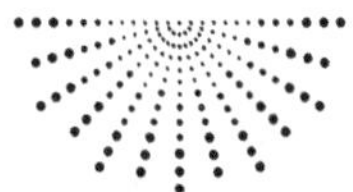

"You are not traveling through time."

"What?" Meghan stared at Logan.

She and Derrick had been sitting in the library with Douglas and Connell when the Air Elemental burst in, holding a cell phone in one hand and an ancient-looking scroll in the other.

"Because we already know she did," Connell pointed out. "Her appearance is recorded in the pack annals and probably a dozen other places."

Logan held up a hand. "Let me explain. I've gone over the results of our diagnostic spells like five times since I did not understand what I was seeing."

She tugged a side table in front of her and perched on it, the delicate spindly legs miraculously holding her weight.

"Most of my findings contradicted the others, coming up with seemingly impossible combinations, including trying to find the signature of time travel in your aura."

Logan leaned forward, a move that should have caused her to topple over, but the table stayed upright, defying gravity. "That signature is missing."

"Wait," Douglas said. "There's a signature to time travel?"

"Natural passages between different points in time do occur," Logan explained. "They're rarer than ice cubes in hell, but they do happen. We've recorded them in the T'Kaierian annals. Passing through one leaves a mark."

"Which I don't have?" Meghan asked. Her stomach sank at this further proof of her otherness.

"Is that so surprising? If Meghan was going through some fixed passage, anyone could follow her," Derrick said. "But it's unique to her. She's traveling without using a door."

"Which is impossible." Logan grinned. "Because—again—she's not traveling in time. She's breaking reality."

Meghan's lips parted. "I don't understand."

"I don't either!" The Elemental laughed, tossing the scroll in the air. It disappeared, and Logan didn't bother to explain where the vellum had gone. "Or at least I didn't until I realized that Meghan is generating so much energy it doesn't register on most instruments—even the magical ones."

Too much energy? "Am I dangerous?"

Was she giving off some sort of supernatural radiation right now? Could Derrick get cancer just sitting next to her? She started to edge away from him, but he held her fast.

"No…but also yes," Logan hedged.

"Seriously?" Derrick snapped, a growl in his voice.

Logan was unimpressed with the tone. "Slow your roll, lover boy. I'm trying to explain an exception to the laws of the reality here."

She turned back to Meghan. "You are generating your own pocket universe."

"I'm *what?*"

Logan was almost making the table hop, she was so excited. "It's fucking amazing. The bubbles you keep falling into are a whole separate universe within ours. You don't attract them. You *generate* them."

She lifted her hands and mashed them together. "But two realities can't occupy the same space. So wherever Meghan goes, reality begins to fragment. My guess is that the broken-off bit tries to heal itself. It naturally reforms, and the easiest shape for it to take is spherical. *Voila* —a bubble."

"And this broken bit of the current reality connects to another randomly?" she asked.

"With you in it. Then it spits you out into that second reality. Usually in another time and place," Logan finished.

"That's…a lot to take in," Meghan murmured.

"Yeah, I know, kiddo," Logan grimaced. "It's also not the worst part."

Derrick groaned, rubbing his forehead. Unable to help himself, he picked Meghan up and put her in his lap. He let his breath out with a whoosh as his body released some of the tension it was holding.

"Okay," he said, breathing a little easier. "Go ahead and tell us."

Logan started and stopped, then started again. "So, as far as I can tell the universe self-heals after you move on, but its capacity to do so might be limited."

Her slow mind processed that. "I could permanently damage the universe," she said, sinking into him like a deflated balloon.

But the Elemental did not have any words of reassurance for her. "The longer you stay in one place, the greater the risk of permanently undoing the fabric of reality past the point where it can self-heal. Traveling in time was one way for the universe to minimize the damage."

"So the shorter my stay in one place, the less damage I did," Meghan finished despondently. "Any longer and I start damaging *everything*."

There was a long silence.

DERRICK GRIPPED MEGHAN'S WAIST. She hadn't moved, but it was as if he could read her mind. "I know what you're thinking, and, no, you can't leave."

Logan's announcement was messing with his mind, but that was nothing compared to what his mate was going through. He didn't need the damn mating bond to feel her pain and distress.

Derrick took her ice-cold fingers. "Don't even *think* about it."

"Even if by staying I break the world?" A more heartbroken sentence was never spoken.

He looked at Logan, giving her a "do something" glare.

The Elemental stepped up. "Derrick is right. You shouldn't consider leaving. That would just postpone the inevitable. Or worse it would play right into that shadow creep's plan."

"Is he like me? Is he afflicted with the same condition?" Meghan's face fell as a new thought occurred to her. "What if all his attempts to capture me were his way of asking for help?"

"Don't go feeling sorry for that crap-bag," Derrick groused. "If he was so desperate for help, he could have found a way to ask for it without terrorizing a small child. And let's not forget his touch kills."

"But is that intentional?" Connell asked, playing devil's advocate.

"It is now," Derrick scoffed. "I don't care if he started as Father freaking Christmas himself. He uses that ability to kill. The asshole has to go."

"Agreed," the chief said. "Once we figure out how."

"Can't Logan…" Connell held up his hands, twisting them as he made a clicking sound with his tongue.

"I would love to," Logan said. "But from what I can tell his weird-ass composition may make him immune to my Mother-given talents. Not that I'm taking that lying down. I'll find a way to ax the asshole. To do that we need to know more about him and Meghan and their connection. There are a few more things I want to try, more diagnostic spells to give us a better idea of what we're dealing with."

"Whatever I can do to help."

"Meghan's affliction can't be some random mutation in witch kind," Douglas added before a pause, scratching his chin.

"No, I don't see how it can be." Logan rocked a little, sending the table teetering. But it stayed upright, improbably balanced on the tip of one leg.

Even more improbably, none of the wolves made a move to right the table, saving Logan from a fall. *Freaky.*

"It's more important than ever that we figure out where you are from. Magic has a foundation and can be strongly influenced by its region of origin," she said, shifting her hips so the table was balanced on another leg. "The verbal description was a decent start, but a visual one would be even better. I don't suppose you can draw?"

Meghan shook her head. "Not even stick figures."

"Don't worry. There is something else we can try. It'll require some rare ingredients, but it's really cool and I'm super excited to try it."

Meghan raised her brows.

"You'll understand once we do it," Logan said with a sheepish grin.

"Hey, I hate to point out the obvious, but why don't you just strip her?" Connell asked.

Derrick scowled. "Hey, he's right. Can't you do that?"

"From context, I assume you don't mean undressing me." Meghan's head was whirling. "What is stripping?"

"Logan can remove magic from any type of Supernatural. It's part of her skill set as an Elemental."

Derrick adjusted her in his lap so he could meet her eyes. "If she stripped you, you'd be magically inert. The bubbles would disappear. That wouldn't be so bad, would it?"

"No, it would be good. That's what I want," she breathed. "I know I should want to keep it, so I can keep helping, but I...I'm so tired. I know that's selfish."

She hung her head.

Logan set all four chair legs on the floor. She got up and squeezed onto the couch by Meghan's other side. "No, it's not. You don't have to apologize for anything. But I'm going to be honest."

"Like you know any other way to be."

The Elemental scowled at her mate's interruption.

"Anyway," she continued. "We're assuming the bubbles would disappear if you weren't magical, or that the shadow man wouldn't keep pursuing you if your ability was gone. But for all we know you could have been targeted because you were the seventh daughter of a seventh daughter, or you were born at a key moment during a rare planetary alignment."

She gave Meghan a commiserating look. "I admit those aren't all that likely given what you've experienced. But it doesn't change the fact I'd be inflicting one of the most brutal punishments at my disposal on an innocent person, one who has only used their ability to do good."

"Can't we take my ability away for a little while? You could always bring it back once we figure out how to deal with the shadow man."

Logan shook her head. "The stripping process changes you on the most fundamental level. Once your magic is gone, it can't be returned."

Derrick grunted. "But you returned Connell's wolf to him when it was stolen."

Meghan blinked, confused. Belatedly she recalled the story Derrick had told her of how Logan and Connell had met. It had been a case of enemies at first sight...

"His wolf was removed with a blunt instrument," Logan explained. "Elemental abilities have evolved since then. I'd be removing all the little bits of her aura where magic could anchor, rendering her inert. She'd even be less adept than your average human. Many of them can access small magics. It might manifest as finely honed intuition or preternatural luck, but that's already something."

Her phone chimed. Logan paused to read the incoming message.

"There is also the fact stripping her would leave her defenseless," Douglas pointed out when she was done reading. "Meghan was able to fight off the creature because of her offensive skill. It was raw and uncontrolled, but she succeeded."

"Another good point," Logan acknowledged. "And the time may come when stripping becomes the only option. First, let's do my other tests. They need to be conducted while she is in full possession of her abilities."

She hopped off the table and turned to Douglas. "I also need you to put the word out to the pack. We're going to need them to gather here."

Meghan had the impression that the chief liked his daughter-in-law, but he still frowned at her. "Why?"

"Because Mom and Hope just found a solution to the time-traveling—one that doesn't involve stripping Meghan."

Douglas straightened, looking less than pleased in that subdued way of this. "What will you need from my wolves?"

"The usual." She clicked her tongue. "Which means you may have to talk some of the hardline anti-witch folks into complying. The more donors the better."

"*Ah*." He inclined his head. "But I don't foresee a problem. This is for a mate."

Meghan was back to feeling lost. "I missed something. What's the usual?"

Logan turned back to her. "Blood," she said. "When magic is involved, remember that the answer is always blood."

CHAPTER THIRTY

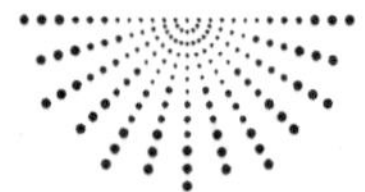

Meghan leaned forward, fascinated by the intricate spell Logan was constructing to help her visualize her memories.

She was sitting in the middle of the library, the focal point of the pyramid made of runes, where the tip was like an arrow pointing at her. The flared base was where Logan would sit, but she had explained that anyone in the room would be able to see the images in her mind. She could even rewind and zoom in and out like an arcane version of VLC.

"Now normally I'd insist on doing the binding spell first given the extreme nature of your affliction," Logan was saying as she wrote on the hardwood floor with a piece of chalk. "But we're going to try and figure out where you're from first, because that binding spell will be more effective if multiple wolves of different bloodlines are donating blood. The more, the better. Gathering that much of the pack together will take some time."

"How will the binding help?" she asked, craning her neck to see the shape Logan was drawing.

"Well, that spell has two layers. First, that shady bastard isn't going to be able to rip you out of this time because you're going to be physically anchored to the pack, in this time and in this place."

"Kind of like she was doing with the soil hand washing, but stronger," Derrick observed. He was sitting cross-legged a few feet away, the closest Logan would allow him to be.

Derrick was also not allowed to touch her for the duration of the spell or its preparation, a detail he did not like one bit.

"Pretty much," Logan said, frowning at a complicated rune in the shape of a sunburst with small specific embellishments within each ray. It did not pass muster. She wiped it away with her palm and began to redo it.

"Derrick thought a tree would do," Meghan shared, eyeing one of the potted palms near the window. It seemed that Douglas had a fondness for that type of plant.

"And he's right. We could use tree sap in a pinch and anchor her to the forest." The rune took shape more decisively the second time around. Logan moved on to the next one.

"Oh, that sounds much better than asking a bunch of strangers for their blood." The idea of being in front of such a group, asking for their help was nerve-wracking—even if she knew they would be doing it to help Derrick, not her.

Because he loves you. Meghan sucked in a breath. Sometimes that felt like the most unbelievable part of her new life.

"And it would be except for the fact fire can wipe out the trees like that," she said snapping her fingers. "At least the wolves would run if there was another big one in this state."

She rocked back, balancing on her heels. "Also, human blood is more potent than sap."

"Why?"

Logan grimaced. "There's a lot of theories on that, but I've always believed in the shittiest because it makes the most sense. Blood is life, but for humans it also usually means pain. Sacrifice and suffering is kind of a coin of the witching realm."

"Oh." That made a terrible kind of sense. "I don't think I like that part of being a witch."

"I didn't mean to make it sound all bad. Most spells don't need blood. And the ones that do are often satisfied with a symbolic amount."

"Then why don't you just anchor her to me? Why do we need so many other donors?" Derrick asked.

Logan's lips pressed together. "Not to be Betty Buzzkill, but what if something happened to you, bud?"

Scowling he grunted something under his breath. "So how many people is safe?"

"A dozen full-grown wolves should be more than enough, but Douglas doesn't want to take any chances. He's called an all-hands. Everyone of age who is willing donates a drop. That should ensure the anchor is spread wide and won't be affected by wolves going on vacation or moving out of state. At the numbers we're talking about, the spell becomes about the *pack* and not the wolves, if you know what I mean."

Meghan nodded. "It's a good idea to exclude the children," she added in a murmur. If the shadow man broke through, she wouldn't want it to happen anywhere near the children.

Not that she could control that, but she could try.

"A lot of them are coming regardless," Derrick shared. "That's what all-hands means. We're also making participation voluntary. Most wolves are leery of spells and witchcraft."

"How leery?" What if they didn't get the numbers they needed?

"I'm not worried. Our pack is the largest in the states. And everyone knows Logan. More importantly, they trust the chief. We'll get what we need and then some."

He leaned over, reaching for her.

"No touching." Logan had appeared between them, crouching at their level so she could smack his hand. With a gust of wind, she disappeared, assuming her former position to continue drawing.

Meghan blinked. She'd seen the way Logan moved a few times now, but it hadn't gotten any more normal.

Focusing on Derrick, she gave him a commiserating smile. "I can't wait to touch you too."

"That's so cute. And gross."

Blushing, she looked at Logan. "Sorry."

She chortled. "Don't be. I'm happy for Derrick. I'm even happier he has to stop giving Connell shit for cradle robbing."

On her left, Derrick straightened. "Why do you say that?"

"For the obvious reason."

Meghan's lips twitched. Logan was enjoying this.

Derrick cleared his throat. "Meghan, baby—I mean sweetheart—I don't suppose you know how old you are?"

"No," she said, concerned because he seemed worried.

Logan's smile was downright smug. "Don't worry. She's of consenting age…in most states."

The strangled noise that Derrick made would have been funny in other circumstances. He dropped his head into his hands.

"I'm *kidding*. She's at least twenty. Still younger than me, but legal in all fifty states."

He lifted his head to glare at her. "That wasn't nice."

Logan ignored him, smiling sweetly at Meghan. "His nickname for me used to be jailbait."

"Oh, I see." She turned to Derrick. "If it makes a difference, I *feel* like I'm a million years old."

The look he gave her was almost as comforting as a hug. Until he turned to Logan with barely concealed impatience. "How much longer is this going to take? I don't like not being able to touch her."

"Aww, you really are adorable." Logan rose to her knees, putting one hand on the side of the pyramid so she could add the flourish to the rune on top. "But I told you before that you have to keep your distance. If you're touching her, you'll interfere with the visualization of her memories."

Logan had explained that the spell triangle was a mystical magnifying lens. It would take the memories she saw in her mind's eye and visualize them like a projector. Everyone in the room would be able to see them, overcoming her limitations to accurately describe them.

The spell would also take her hazier memories, the fragments, and attempt to nudge them into a more coherent narrative.

That part was going to be difficult. Meghan didn't want to see her mother lying dead in the reeds, but she knew hiding or burying those memories was no longer an option.

She needed to know where she was from, *why* she was the way she was.

Logan turned back to Meghan, reaching behind her for a collection of tiny vials nestled in a box. Then she spoke a few words in a language Meghan didn't recognize.

"The spell is now primed. Some memories may come to the surface on their own, but others will have to be coaxed. Open these vials one at a time," she said, handing Meghan the box.

"What's inside them?"

"Spices, soil, minerals, motor oil, different metals, and samples from every major body of water in the world. It's not exhaustive but is hopefully a fair representation of different substances, a grab bag of scents meant to stimulate your brain's memory centers."

"Oh." Meghan picked up a vial that held a downy feather. She opened it and took a deep whiff. She flicked her eyes up, checking to see what memory it triggered, but the air around her was normal.

"We can start with your clearest memories and use them as a jumping-off point."

Meghan gasped as Derrick's face flickered above them. He was in the shower. It was her memory of their first lovemaking encounter.

Don't look down, she ordered herself sternly. But her point of view captured enough of his naked upper torso for her cheeks to flame. Then his mouth zoomed in, closing in for a kiss.

The image froze there with a close-up shot of Derrick; his lips were puckered but also open as he leaned down to kiss her.

Logan started howling with laughter, choking it back and then trying to cover it with a coughing fit. "Maybe not the freshest memories. Try and focus on your city of spires. Grab any vial you think might help you."

"Okay." Still mortified, Meghan closed her eyes and tried to bring up the image. It was more difficult than she would have imagined, but eventually a hazy image flickered to life in her mind.

"That's it." A vial was pressed into her hand. "Try uncorking that one and giving it a whiff."

Obeying without looking she lifted the little bottle and took a deep sniff. She smelled dry grass, sun, and soil with a hint of decay—all the scents of high summer.

There was a click. "I think that's good."

She opened her eyes to find Logan holding a cell phone. In the air between them was a shimmering vista, one she had just taken a picture of.

The city of spires was beautiful. Glowing gold in the setting sun it stood tall and proud, dominating an entire mountain ridge. Turrets and conical towers were highlighted against a clear blue sky. The elevation must have been high, because clouds wreathed the tops of many of them.

Thanks to Logan's trick with the scents and the power of the spell, this vision was sharper and brighter than any she had ever recalled.

Over time the city had become blurry, faded like a sepia photograph. But the spell had brought it forward from the depths of her mind as it was when she last glimpsed it in life.

The reality of her birthplace—the meld of ancient and awesome— took her breath away. No wonder she hadn't been able to find the words to describe it.

Logan snapped more pictures before letting out a low whistle. "Bitchin' city."

"Do you know when it existed?" Meghan asked. "Or where?"

"I'm afraid not, but that's no cause for concern. Even I can't hold pictures of every city in Earth's history in my mind. I'll send this image to my mom and aunt. It should speed up their search in the archives considerably."

"That's good."

Logan gave her a thumbs up, studying the photo version of the city on her smartphone screen. Tapping on the image she squinted as if trying to make out a specific detail.

"What is it?"

"A bird, I think." Logan lowered the phone. "Let's keep digging around that noggin and see what shakes out."

They resumed their work. Meghan would open each vial and smell, letting her mind wander. The spell seemed to work best that way.

Inevitably it led them to the one memory she didn't want to recall. She knew exactly when Logan and Derrick saw her mother dead in the tall grass and what preceded it, because it got very quiet as if they had stopped breathing.

The click told her Logan had recorded the image. "Why don't you try another vial?" she suggested in a gentle voice.

Taking a deep breath, Meghan opened her eyes and took another bottle out of the box. But she didn't have the chance to open it before there was a knock at the library door.

Nathan waited a beat before poking his head inside. "Sorry to disturb, but could I borrow Derrick?"

"What's wrong?" he asked.

"A few things. A crowd of kids just ran in, claiming the ghost from the Hollow showed up again and is chasing them...and Edgar answered the all hands on deck."

Derrick got to his feet. "That last part is good, right?"

"It was until he saw Connell."

His face transformed, sobering "*Oh.*"

Hustling to the door, Derrick looked back at them and winced. "Sorry. But I better get out there."

"Go," Meghan murmured. She looked back to find Logan unnaturally grave.

"I guess you know the background better than I do."

Logan nodded. "I do. Edgar has been grieving since his son's death. Leeland sacrificed himself to save Connell from a traitor to the pack. It makes it painful for him to see him. Derrick too, because he was there during the firefight, but Connell is the one Lee died to save. We've been hoping time will blunt some of his pain—all their pain. Lee was like a brother to Derrick and Connell both. They were thick as thieves as children and became even closer when they did their tours of duty together."

"Yes, Derrick told me some stories about him." Her wolf hadn't spoken of his sense of loss, dwelling on the happy moments with his childhood friend Leeland. But Meghan had felt his pain in the quiet moments after he shared those stories.

"It must be a thousand times worse to lose a child." Meghan could barely handle the murky memory of her mother in the grass, and she *did* have the blessing of the blunting effects of the passage of time.

As if on cue, another image appeared in the air. It was of a large room with a high vaulted ceiling. At least half a dozen robed people were milling about, flash-frozen in the amber of her memory. One of them was her mother.

The curly-haired woman was reaching down as Meghan looked up, her face serene but animated with life.

"I don't remember this." At least she hadn't before this moment.

"The spell digs deep. From the angle we're seeing it looks like you were very small, a toddler perhaps. Or you were sitting on the floor, five or six years old tops."

Logan snapped a picture as Meghan studied the faces of the others. Had this gathering been some sort of meeting? The robes gave it a formal air, but she knew next to nothing about her own civilization. This could be their version of casual Friday for all she knew.

Then she saw him. Shuddering, she pointed to the robed figure on the left. "Do you see?"

Logan stood, leaning closer to the luminous snapshot. "I'll be damned. It's our bogeyman."

The shadow man was just a normal human in this memory. But his bone structure—the width of his face and the angular lines that made up his cheeks and sloping forehead were unmistakable.

In life her nemesis had been thin and tall, his pale, sallow skin paired with a receding hairline. His hair had been a dirty dishwater blonde.

"Why is he there?" she asked, failing to hide the horror in her voice. "Is he? He couldn't be...my father?"

The very idea made her sick to her stomach.

Logan held up a hand. *"Hey,"* she said. "Slow down. There's no way to know who he was to you from this snippet."

She gestured to the now-flickering image. "We can't tell anything from…"

The words trailed off. Logan was quiet so long Meghan began to panic. "What do you see that I don't?" she asked, peering at the image.

Shaking her head, the Elemental refocused on her. "There's a lot of lab equipment in there."

Meghan tilted her head. "So my civilization was advanced?" She broke off excitedly. "Maybe I'm from Atlantis?"

That would be something.

"Nah, I know where that is," Logan said absently. Her head had turned to the door.

The muffled sound of an argument filtered through the thick oak of the door. It grew louder until it sounded as if it was coming from the hall on the other side. Then came a thump that rattled the heavy wood.

Meghan and Logan exchanged a look. By mutual silent agreement, they both stood.

The door burst open, dumping a tangle of big bodies on the floor. Derrick and Nathan were struggling with a third man while Connell appeared at the door, his face set and pale.

It was Edgar at the bottom of the pile. She knew it before Nathan rolled to the side, trying to haul him up.

The older Were's face was bloody, and he was shouting loud enough to make her ears ring. Sucking in a sharp breath at the ferocity in his expression she took a big step to the side, away from him.

That just set him off. *"You have to go back,"* he screamed, reaching out for her with bloody hands.

"Go where?" she asked bewildered, her heart squeezing and contracting painfully.

Meghan didn't understand what was happening. What had set

Edgar off? The older wolf's pain and desperation made the air in her lungs freeze like sharp blades of ice.

Derrick turned, still grappling with Edgar. His face was bloody, a trickle coming from his nose.

It was a measure of Edgar's ferocity that he'd bloodied the younger warrior. The Were was fit, big, and muscular in the ways only shifters could be at that age. But he was no match for Derrick or Nathan, shifters in their prime.

The grieving father hit the wooden floor with a meaty thud that her mind transformed into another fight with high-pitched screams that made her ears rang.

The room swam. Dark brown curls tipped with lighter brown fell in the tall grass. There had been blood then too.

Crying, Meghan covered her ears with trembling hands, her breath coming in short pants.

Derrick's hand knocked into her on accident, leaving a thick blood smear on her arm.

"Meghan," Logan reached out for her, but Derrick was calling out to Connell for help.

The smell of blood filled her nose. Edgar's hands went clawed. They dug into Derrick's chest despite Nathan's attempt to restrain him.

Connell ran into her field of view, but Logan intercepted him, pushing him toward Meghan. She waded into the fight instead while her mate looked on helplessly.

"Fuck," Connell said. His hands pushed into his hair roughly and then he turned to her, his eyes wolf gold.

"Hey, are you bleed—" His hand touched her arm, searching for a wound that wasn't there.

Then his hand was gone as she fell away, spinning into the darkness...and into the path of a bullet.

CHAPTER THIRTY-ONE

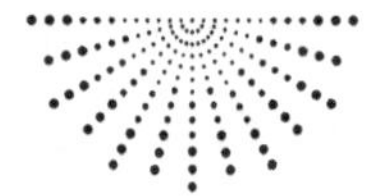

Meghan howled as the bullet pierced the back of her shoulder. She was no longer in the room but the woods—and she wasn't alone.

Connell was there. He landed on the ground, bleeding from the chest. He'd been shot multiple times.

Meghan experienced a split second of true horror. Somehow, she had brought a person through her bubble *alive*. By some miracle, Connell had survived her pocket universe, but she had dragged him into the middle of a firefight.

Except...he was wearing different clothes. Connell's cargo pants and lightweight sweater were gone. Now he was in jeans and a bloody t-shirt. His hair was shorter too.

And then she was taken down as a heavy wolf landed on her. A blue glow danced before her eyes, and suddenly there was a naked man bleeding all over her.

"On the ridge," he gasped, and she realized the bullets that had stopped with her appearance had resumed flying. Another hit him in the arm, spraying her face with blood.

Megan screamed so loud her throat ached as if the muscles were going to rip apart.

"*Witch.*" Meghan jerked her head to Connell, his growl barely intelligible.

Acting on instinct, she thrust out her hand, and he went flying back, dirt and leaves kicking up as he went. He came to rest behind a rock, out of the line of fire.

And then the strange shifter collapsed on her back, sending her to her knees. But they had no sooner touched the ground than she went spinning back into the darkness.

And this time she did take a passenger with her.

CHAPTER THIRTY-TWO

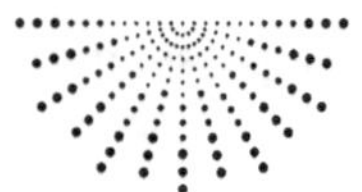

D errick pushed away Connell's hand when it reached for the cut on his face. "What the fuck happened?"

Edgar was sprawled on the floor, unconscious. Nathan had been forced to cold-cock his elder over the head to get him to stop going after Meghan.

But even though Edgar hadn't laid a hand on her, Meghan had still disappeared.

One second she had been there, crying. Edgar's maddened struggle had triggered what looked like a bad flashback. Derrick had seen his fair share during his many tours of duty. He knew what one looked like.

Meghan had been a few feet away, thrust into the nightmare of some PTSD episode as Edgar, acting insane, tried to rip open his chest.

Watching Meghan shaking like a leaf because of Edgar's fit had been hell, especially since his formerly placid packmate had suddenly turned into a foaming-at-the-mouth madman.

Ignoring the unconscious werewolf, he turned on Connell. "What the hell did you do?"

"*Nothing*." Connell was scowling, his confusion and concern tempering the sharp edge of anger in his scent.

"I just touched her arm, because I thought she was bleeding, but the second I did she went poof—in an entirely different way than Logan goes poof," he added. "It was like she just slid away through a crack in reality."

"Fuck," Derrick spat, turning to Logan. "I thought that wasn't supposed to happen here. Wasn't the purpose of restarting your mother's protection spell to keep her in this time and place?"

Logan's frown wasn't as deep or as ferocious as Connell's, but it should have been more than enough to make him back off. Elementals were dangerous things when riled.

But Derrick didn't back down. Logan's irritation wasn't with him.

"The spell around the property is a deterrent against invasion by an enemy," she said pointedly, gesturing to the room around them. "As you can see, the shadow man did not make an appearance. Meghan left on her own steam."

She looked down at the broken wolf lying still on the floor. "I think Edgar's hysteria activated her ability and sent her jettisoning off into parts unknown."

Nathan winced as she knelt to check Edgar's pulse and the bump on his head. "I'm so sorry, but I had to hit him hard enough to knock him out," he apologized, the guilt over striking an elder all over his face. "I didn't know what else to do. I've never seen him like that."

"It's not your fault, Nate," Connell muttered, his tension betrayed by the way he hovered over the unconscious wolf. "If I'd known he was going to be here, I would have stayed out of sight until the ceremony."

"That might not have been enough," Derrick admitted. "He was railing against binding Meghan."

"Well, he's not going to be able to tell us why until he wakes up," Logan said. But her eyes met his, the knowledge of what Edgar had likely been trying to do clear in them. "But that won't happen for several hours."

Nathan sucked in a breath. "Is he permanently damaged?"

"I don't think so—you wolves have very hard heads. But he is going to wake up with a bitch of a headache."

It was on the tip of his tongue to ask her for her opinion of Edgar's motive when Douglas came in.

He knelt by the fallen wolf, touching his head with two fingers, a resigned expression on his face. "What have you done, old friend?" he sighed.

Rising, Douglas scrubbed his face. "What happened?"

Connell gave him a concise summary. Grim-faced, he nodded. "No sign of the girl?"

"Not yet."

The attention turned to Edgar and what to do with him. They debated carrying the old wolf upstairs, but his lack of control meant only the most dominant wolves could restrain him. However, with the entire pack coming Douglas would be needed elsewhere. And the next strongest wolves in line—Connell and Derrick, were the ones Edgar would have the strongest emotional reaction against.

Nathan might have been able to keep him subdued, but that might have involved physically restraining him, something Douglas wasn't willing to do.

After a brief conversation, Edgar was taken to the hospital. They had intended to send Kiera with him, but she wasn't there yet. A few of the calmer teens—too young to volunteer but old enough to have driver's licenses volunteered to take him.

The clinic staff was exempt from the all-hands. There were enough shifters on duty to handle Edgar if he woke up before they could secure him in the silver room.

The special convalescence suite was designed specifically for their kind. Sometimes injured werewolves were not rational, and though they healed fast from most injuries and suffered very few illnesses there were enough exceptions to make such a room a practical addition.

The "wolf room" did not have bars on the door. Instead, silver had been worked around the steel beams and into the reinforced door. It was not meant to be a prison, but they had used it in a pinch as one before when a rogue shifter had stumbled into their territory. The woman had been intent on picking a fight until someone put her out of her misery.

Instead, Douglas had talked that suicidal wolf down, sobering her up and after a long stay at the lake finally letting her go home.

Once Edgar had been packed off, Derrick scoured the house and the ground immediately around it, searching for any sign of Meghan's return. When he didn't find any, he went back to Logan.

The Elemental was alone with Connell in the library, one hand out in a mage pose—the tip of her index finger and thumb touching. A gentle gust of wind was circling the room. It almost looked like she was meditating. Frustrated, he demanded she try a spell to bring Meghan back.

"What do you think I've been doing?" Logan made a fist with her free hand, then released it quickly.

"Damn it," she swore with a growl that rivaled Connell's as a rain of powdered chalk fell to the floor.

She grabbed another stick out of her pocket, bending to add a flourish to the rune at her feet. "I've been looking for cracks in reality —I would feel it if the air bled off into the aether. But there's nothing. Whatever door she opened closed right after she went through."

Scrubbing her hand on her pants, leaving a streak of chalk residue. "As for bringing her back, nothing I try is working. It doesn't help that she went of her own volition."

"The hell she did," he interrupted.

The look she gave him forced him to clamp his mouth shut.

"You know what I mean," Logan said. "It was her own magic that carried her off, covered in your blood I might add."

"His and Edgar's," Connell pointed out.

His mate considered that, worrying her lip. "Well, if that's the case she's got a better chance of making it back here than she would otherwise."

She frowned as the background hum of conversation behind the doors rose and crested. A human wouldn't have noticed, but an Elemental's hearing was as sharp as a wolf's.

"What the hell is going on out there?"

"The kids are still going on about the ghost in the Hollow," Connell explained. "There's been another sighting."

He flicked a hand through the air, dismissing the pre-teen drama.

Only half-paying attention, Derrick sat on the couch's arm. Then the words penetrated through his thick skull.

"The ghost," he mouthed. He stumbled to his feet, whirling around like a drunk.

Derrick grabbed Connell's arm. His cousin frowned. "What?"

"The ghost—*the god-damned ghost.*"

His cousin's mate was far quicker on the uptake. "You think the ghost is Meghan?"

"That makes no sense." He recognized the expression on Connell's face. It was the one he wore whenever he was trying to talk sense into him. Derrick had gotten very familiar with it as a child and teenager.

"The ghost isn't real. It's a trick of the acoustics in the Hollow," his cousin said.

But Derrick wasn't ready to dismiss his new theory. Not when it made so much sense. He walked out, gesturing for the others to follow. The Haunted Hollow wasn't that far on foot.

"*Derrick.*" Connell and Logan were right behind him. They weaved through the crowd that had gathered in answer to the all-hands call.

"It's the only thing that *does* make sense," he argued. "The ghost has been part of our history for so long we stopped thinking about it."

"But that's just it," Connell argued. "There have been rumors and supposed sightings of the ghost since our earliest history. Meghan just left."

He threw up his hands, not bothering to turn or stop. "Meghan is a freaking time-traveler. None of the rules apply."

Logan drew level with them, choosing to jog alongside them instead of going on ahead with her ability. "But if she fell backward in time, would she have ended up that far? And why is she having trouble breaking back through?"

That did slow him down enough to exchange a worried glance with her.

"Something has gone wrong."

The truth sank into his stomach like a lead weight. He had seen the ghost in the woods that night he took the dare as a child. Meghan had appeared twice, first at the far end of the clearing and then closer to the middle.

And she keeps moving. Putting the pieces together, what the old-timers had said versus what the children were saying now, the answer was obvious.

"We're going too far," he said, stopping.

"But we're not at the Hollow yet," Connell protested.

He shook his head, scenting the air. "No, *she's* trying to get back to us. And she saw us last at the house. That's where we have to wait."

Logan made a face. "Yes, but for how long? If she's been trying to get back for hundreds of our years, it could be months—even years before she manages to break through."

Her words should have scared him, but Derrick shook his head. The blood. He had to believe in the blood.

"It's this time and place," he said. "This is when and where she's fighting to get back to."

With that, he started running, choosing a route that was a straight shot from the Haunted Hollow to the house, even if it wasn't the fastest. After all, Meghan didn't know the terrain. She would choose the direct route, as the crow flew, despite the obstacles that made it longer than going around to the established paths.

He had just scrambled over one of these obstacles—a cluster of jagged rocks surrounding unstable pebbly ground that had turned more than one ankle when he heard her.

"Which direction?" he shouted behind him.

"Dead ahead," Logan answered. Connell was right behind her.

His cousin swore, then whistled. "*Fuck.* I think I see her."

Derrick didn't, but he believed him. They were only half a klick from the house, close enough to hear the crowd milling around outside.

It should have warmed his heart that Douglas hadn't sent them home, but right now he wanted to yell at them all to shut up. But soon they didn't have to. Derrick was right next to the ghost when it flickered to life next to him. The scream caught him off guard.

It was only a few seconds, but it was a longer snatch than the fragment he'd heard as a child—more than enough to recognize Meghan's voice. How could he not?

It was burned into his soul now.

The next time she flickered to life she was three feet away. He tried to grab her, but she disappeared in a blink. Swearing, they spotted the house and continued on.

The sun had started to go down, pulling the shadows down under the trees surrounding the Maitland home. The house itself glowed in the setting sun.

Meghan kept pace with the dying light. The darker it got, the closer she came, her image becoming clearer and more distinct with each appearance.

The crowd gathered thick at the door, alert to the bizarre phenomenon happening before their eyes. Watching in perplexed fascination and horror, they had fallen deathly silent.

Derrick pushed his way onto the front steps of the house, exchanging a wordless glance with Douglas, who waited at the top with his arms crossed. The naked concern on the chief's face was disturbing. Douglas normally had the best poker face in the world.

Meghan was almost on top of them, her appearances coming in faster and faster. Her lovely face was recognizable but flickering in and out like a strobe light as she approached.

He was so focused on her face that he didn't notice she wasn't alone.

Logan grabbed his arm. "She's towing something."

"What?" He ran down the steps, almost dancing in his impatience for another glimpse. Then she was there right in front of him. His eyes barely registered the moving blur on her back.

"Oh my God," he breathed, staggering back. "It's a body."

The form Meghan was dragging was big and *bloody*. He couldn't make out a face, but the red stains were unmistakable.

She didn't...did she?

"Bad. This is fucking bad," he breathed. He suspected he knew who it was. Fucking Edgar. But the father wouldn't get his wish. Because no one could travel with Meghan and live.

He watched, the breath trapped in his lungs so long they started to burn. But he couldn't make his chest obey him. Breathing should be automatic, shouldn't it?

But Derrick was frozen in cold amber. Meghan's screams had that effect on him.

This is wrong. It wasn't just that she wasn't traveling alone. He could hear it in her voice. Meghan was in pain. And there was nothing he could do to help her.

All his attention was fixed on the pair. They were on the stairs now—a horror in stop-motion animation with too many gaps in between.

The smell of blood filled his nose.

"C'mon." Logan grabbed his hand. "She'll head back to the library."

They didn't have to push through the crowd. It parted on its own.

Sammy was there, edging away from the apparition. Jeannie skittered aside too, crossing herself. George put his arms around her, but that was all he saw because he was chasing after Meghan.

He threw open the library door to find Logan ahead of him. Connell and Douglas were at his back, letting him take the lead.

His feet skid across the wooden floor, his speed unchecked. He lost his balance and hit the floor.

He rolled to his feet with a grunt. No one else said anything because Meghan was coming in loud and clear now. Her scream was coming in and out too, a staccato assault on their sensitive hearing.

He knew the instant Connell recognized the body Meghan was dragging. Derrick spared a second to thank the fucking stars that they'd moved Edgar to the hospital.

"Is that...?" Douglas began, his face ashen. His voice trailed off. There was no need for questions. The chief knew all his wolves. Even the ones who had crossed the veil.

Especially those.

Then Meghan spilled out of the tear in the air that wasn't there before. A heavy bloody body landed on top of her.

"It's Leeland." Logan's shocked voice. "But I thought no one could travel through one of Meghan's bubbles.

He rolled Leeland's body off his mate, gathering her in his arms while avoiding the sight of his cousin's corpse. He'd already seen it before, two years ago when he'd died. That was enough for one lifetime.

Meghan whimpered. His mate was breathing shallowly. Warm blood covered his hand.

"Baby," he breathed. "Talk to me, please, baby. *Talk to me.*"

"I guess they can travel the bubbles with her if they're dead." That was Connell, his voice both hoarse and flat.

"Connell, he's *not dead.*"

Derrick didn't register anything after that because he had just found the bullet hole in his mate's back. It wasn't Lee's blood she was covered in. It was her own, and she was losing it fast.

CHAPTER THIRTY-THREE

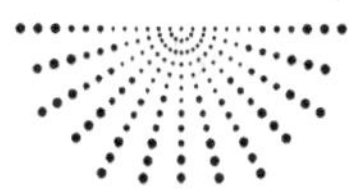

Meghan wheezed, fighting to draw breath, but the fire in her shoulder made it next to impossible.

Her entire back and chest burned, but her pain meant nothing in the face of the chaos that broke out when she landed on the library floor...because she wasn't alone. The man who had fallen on her in the clearing, the strange wolf, he was here too. Or at least his corpse was.

She had dragged a dead body through her bubble, displacing it in time.

And then it got worse. Because the dead man was no stranger to the wolves.

"Lee. It's fucking *Leeland*," Derrick shouted.

"Oh no, no, no..." Meghan cried, tears blinding her as footsteps pounded all around her. "I didn't mean to. I didn't mean..."

Sobbing, she tried to turn but the bleeding man was surrounded, hidden from her blurred vision by a wall of legs.

"*Baby.*" Strong arms pulled her into a warm embrace.

"I'm sorry," she whispered, feeling faint. "I didn't mean to—he should not be here. It's wrong. I didn't mean to. You shouldn't have to see him like this. Not again."

"They're trying to revive him. He's not gone yet."

His voice was a mix of disbelief and concern. Her lips parted, and she started to turn.

"*Don't.*" Derrick turned her to face him. "Don't look."

His voice was hoarse. Because he knew he and the others were going to have to watch the brother they loved die all over again.

The sight must have been a terrible one, because he hugged her close—the comforting gesture made her scream, her body convulsing.

"*Fuck.* You've been shot." Derrick ripped his shirt off, folding it up to make a pad he pressed to her back.

It hurt, but not nearly as much as it should have. Her whole body felt cold. *No. I hate the cold. I hate it so much.* Meghan craved Derrick's heat. She needed it.

Fortunately, he gave it to her without the need to ask, gathering her close as he picked her up and began to run, keeping the compress pressed into her back as he went.

"I didn't mean to do it," she repeated, much more weakly this time. The world spun as they moved out of the library and then there was the night sky.

She knew it was the one she sought. Meghan had been under so many different skies—the constellations shifting overhead between one bubble and the next.

"*Meghan.*" Derrick sounded panicked. His grip on her tightened, but she couldn't tell him everything was going to be all right. It all felt so distant now.

"Don't you quit on me, Meghan."

But she couldn't help it. She was going to let him down. "S-s-sorry...again about him. Shouldn't have...brought him...but Edgar was shouting...and the blood..."

Lifting one hand with great effort, she fisted a hand in his shirt. "Tell Logan...she was right about...the blood..."

Then she lost her grip, and the world slipped away.

CHAPTER THIRTY-FOUR

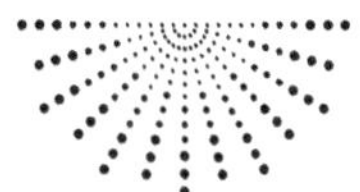

Kiera slipped her surgical gloves off and stared at the front of her gown. She closed her eyes, but when she opened them the blood covering the usually pristine teal scrubs was still there.

The only other time they had been this badly stained was when Connell had been shot. When Leeland died the first time.

Her eyes looked down at her hands and beyond them to Leeland's still form. She had removed over half a dozen bullets from his body... but it was one less than had been there at his autopsy.

The bullet through the heart was missing—one of the few non-silver-bullet related wounds a wolf as strong as Leeland McGill couldn't heal on his own.

Tellingly, there was a bullet in Meghan's back, a wound high up on her shoulder. Dr. Ratner, the semi-retired doctor on staff had been called in while they were *en route*. Rainer had removed that bullet and relayed the relevant information about it to her in the surgical suite.

She took the hit. Somehow Derrick's witch had traveled back in time to the moment when Bishop Kane had sprayed over a hundred bullets into a clearing to kill Connell, the chief's son. Leeland had saved Connell's life at the cost of his own. He'd taken a bullet in the heart. And now that bullet wasn't there. Her mind couldn't wrap itself around that.

Leeland McGill had died a hero. Everyone had mourned him. And now he was here, lying in her surgical suite in a medically induced coma.

Douglas had accompanied her in the ambulance. He'd used his power as pack alpha to pour healing energy into her and the fragile connection to Leeland that had suddenly revived when Meghan had crossed over with him.

Logan had added her magic as well, giving it without hesitation despite Meghan's cries that it was wrong and she was sorry. The Elemental wasn't a healer, but she had magic coming out of her ears. Between her and the chief, they had somehow managed to stabilize Leeland, despite the catastrophic damage done to his body.

It had been a very different story two years ago. The young warrior had died miles away from help. They had barely been able to save Connell.

"Kiera."

Startled, she turned to face her alpha, suddenly realizing he had been speaking to her for some time.

"Is there anything else we can do?"

"I don't think so." Gesturing to her nurse she ordered Leeland be taken to their one recovery suite.

Kiera looked around and frowned. "Where did Logan go?"

The Air Elemental had been there just a minute ago.

"She was concerned about the blood in the library—Meghan's blood specifically. I left Nate there to stand guard over the scene, but Logan wanted to go back and deal with it personally. Blood from a witch of Meghan's strength can't be left lying around. Logan will burn all traces of it away."

There was an undercurrent in his tone, a hint of disappointment, pain, and resignation. It hurt him to think that any member of his pack couldn't be trusted to steer clear the blood in the library, but she of all people knew and understood. Kiera had been here when Bishop

Kane had blown up all her preconceived notions of the infallibility of pack loyalty.

We've come full circle.

"Has Edgar been told?" she asked tentatively.

"Yes," the nurse answered, giving the chief a nervous glance. As a rule, submissives were calm around Douglas, but their alpha was giving off some powerful and conflicted vibes.

"Connell took him aside and explained the situation. We also cleaned out the suite so it could be ready for Leeland," the nurse added.

"Thank you," Kiera told her, touching the woman's shoulder in appreciation for her flawless work in the OR. She ended by rattling a few instructions for the patient's post-op care.

Douglas helped wheel Leeland to the recovery suite. He spent a long time standing over him, his face inscrutable. She turned to sneak away when he stopped her.

"What is his prognosis?"

Kiera lifted her hands helplessly.

"I wish I knew. Even with the fatal bullet missing, he still took a lot of damage. A major artery was severed. I repaired the damage as best I could, but without the magic you and Logan poured into him Leeland would be dead...again. We could lose him a second time," she admitted. "If that happens we'll lose Edgar too, won't we?"

The chief closed his eyes, but he didn't reply to that. "Tell Connell to stay with him."

"Are you..." she trailed off, gesturing at Leeland.

"Yes." Douglas settled in the chair next to the bed. "I will stay and do what I can to hold him."

Nodding, she excused herself to relay his message to Connell.

She found the chief's son deep in conversation with Edgar. The hope in the older wolf's face was like a knife to the heart. But she was the surgeon in charge of this facility. It was her responsibility to prepare the family for the worst.

So she took Edgar's hands and explained what he could expect in the next few hours. Kiera tried to dance the line between giving him false hope and completely taking it away. She ended her short speech by asking him to change into scrubs, sit quietly with the chief, and not disturb Douglas's concentration as he did what he could to help Leeland heal.

Edgar was only too eager to obey whatever instructions she gave. It was a marked change from the nearly rabid wolf who had to be sedated just hours before. He would have done cartwheels if she asked.

She and the nurses helped him wash up and change before leading him to the recovery suite. By the time he was ready, Logan was back. Her grave expression as she spoke to Connell was enough to make Kiera steer clear of the pair.

She simply couldn't take any more shocks or bad news today.

MEGHAN ROUSED SLUGGISHLY, the warmth of Derrick's body at odds with the strong astringent smell in the air.

She felt more than heard him suck in a deep breath. "Baby, are you awake?"

"Hmm," she hummed, trying to force her eyelids to open.

There was a softly spoken swear word, but as far as she was concerned it may as well have been the tenderest of endearments. Because she was warm and safe in Derrick's arms.

Then she remembered what she had done. Meghan jerked up, making the skin on her back stretch tight. It hurt, but not nearly as bad as it should have.

She took in the hospital room around them with a gasp. She was on the narrow bed, Derrick crammed in next to her. He was trying to make himself as small as possible and failing miserably.

"How did we get here?"

"You passed out in the library—blood loss." His hand cupped her cheek and he kissed her gently.

"Douglas can't heal you because you're not pack yet," he said. "But Logan was able to work on you a little bit after she was done with Lee.

She also put a portable version of her mom's spell on you so the shadow man can't break into the hospital."

He gestured at the sterile hospital room. "This version she rigged up is not as stable as the one on the chief's house, so we'll be going back there as soon as Kiera gives you the all-clear. But Kiera's been busy. With Leeland."

Her stomach dipped, twisting. "Is he...?" Meghan was afraid to finish the question.

"He lives."

She couldn't have been more shocked if he slapped her in the face. "But he *can't* be. It's not possible. My bubbles, or doors, they kill everything."

Derrick's expression was hard to read. "Except Leeland was dead. Or close enough as to make no difference."

He passed a hand over his face. Meghan noted his paleness and the circles under his eyes that were almost blue-black. "I had a chance to speak with Logan while you were asleep. Leeland came back with you, shot up all to hell, but he was missing the bullet that pierced his heart —the one that killed him."

His hand hovered over the wound on her back. "I'm pretty sure that bullet is the one Kiera dug out of your back."

Meghan shuddered. "I don't know how that's possible. Any of it."

He pressed his forehead to hers. "I think we've pieced it together. You see, when Connell, Lee, and I were ambushed, we were miles from anyone. He died before help arrived. You cut across time and were shot in his place. Lee was still dying from the other bullet wounds. When he got caught in your bubble, he wasn't breathing, so he couldn't suffocate. I don't know how else your bubbles kill people. This is speculation, but I thought he might have survived because it registered him as already dead. You towed a corpse. One that could be brought back...."

Derrick had loved Leeland like a brother. He should have been rejoicing, but his grim expression remained.

"Will he make it?"

He closed his eyes. "His body might. But we have no way of

knowing how long his brain was deprived of oxygen. He's a wolf, and that means healing on a supernatural scale, but he took a lot of damage. Lee might never wake up, but he does have a chance now. Thanks to you."

He was stroking down her hip when her face fell. "That was supposed to be comforting," he said, hesitating.

She closed her eyes, terrified to speak the truth. But she had to tell Derrick. He was her mate. There were no secrets between them.

"Even if he lives, he's not supposed to be here." She was crying now. "Saving the cubs was different. I was able to intercede *before* they died of exposure. But you all lived a reality where Lee died."

Her cheeks tightened. "You buried him. Bringing him back this way was wrong. What if I broke something?"

His touch attempted to soothe her, but the warmth couldn't penetrate the icy chill of panic spreading over her skin. "I told you. Lee is breathing. So long as that is true, he has a chance. What you did helped him get that."

"I wasn't talking about Leeland," she said, eyes wide. "I meant the *world*. What if I broke the world?"

CHAPTER THIRTY-FIVE

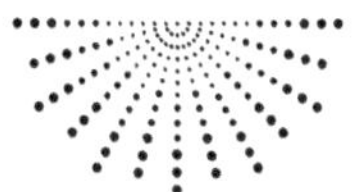

Douglas did not take the news well. "What the hell do you mean that the fabric of reality might be unraveling?"

"That's what she said." Derrick scrubbed his face. The last ten hours had aged him ten years. "Meghan is passed out now—the shot took a lot out of her, despite what Logan did to help her."

He nodded at Connell's mate, who had come back from the Maitland house a half-hour before.

Logan's face was hard. She answered the chief's unspoken question. "I don't know if she's right. I can't feel time the way she can. All I can say is that the aether appears to be intact. If bringing back Leeland affected reality, there should have been a ripple there. I don't feel one."

The chief raised a brow. "But?"

She lifted a shoulder. "If there is a tear, it could be small. There could be a slow bleed that I can't detect."

"What can we do?" Derrick asked.

"I've been in touch with my sisters. I asked them to do certain rituals to assess the aether in their area."

"What good will that do? They're scattered all over the world, aren't they?"

Logan lifted a shoulder. "We don't know how Meghan's ability works. What we do know is that her bubbles can open anywhere. I assume a tear could too. The others are doing what they can to assess the aether in their current locations."

She scratched her eyebrow. "We have a long reach, but I'll need Meghan to do a real assessment. This is her magic and it's unique."

"And what happens if there is a tear?" Douglas asked.

"Hell if I know." Logan rubbed her forehead.

Edgar grabbed Douglas's shirt. "You won't send him back, will you?"

"*What?*" The chief covered Edgar's hand with his own. "No. That's not what we're talking about."

"I know that look on her face." He pointed an accusing finger at Logan. "If there's a hole, she will plug it with my boy."

His voice was a rasp like sandpaper over his skin. Edgar was crying and getting all worked up and red-faced again. "You make her promise—make her swear she won't put my Lee back in the ground."

Douglas drew himself up. "That will not be necessary," he said with finality, giving his witch-in-law a significant glance. "But don't forget at this point Lee's prognosis is uncertain. Even Logan can't tell you whether or not he will pull through. And neither can Meghan, despite her ability."

"Well..." Logan began.

"*No,*" Derrick spat. "We're not going to send her to a future that might not exist. She's not immortal, and she doesn't know how to control her abilities the way you can."

"But what if she can summon a window and take a peek?" Connell asked.

Derrick gritted his teeth. The idea of Meghan willingly summoning a window was a lot less threatening than opening a door. "You assume she can control it. I don't think she can learn how in the space of a day. Her ability is too wild. I'm not sure she can learn to direct it at all. It may take a lifetime. That and she wants to stop traveling—she just got shot for fuck's sake. Better to bind her here once and for all and figure out the rest later. Do the spell your sisters are doing with her instead. I'm sure it will be more informative with her input."

"What if her spell says Lee has to go?" Edgar's voice was edging into hysteria.

"If there's a problem, we will do everything in our power to avoid involving Lee."

"*That's not an answer!*" Edgar was shouting now. "Douglas, tell her that's not an answer."

"It is," Logan said softly. "It's just not the one you want to hear."

"*Babe,*" Connell whispered, putting a restraining hand on her shoulder. Hurting Edgar was ripping him to shreds.

"I know how it sounds, but what do you think Lee would do if he discovered we kept him here at the cost of everyone else?" She pivoted to face her mate. "He died to save *you*. How would he feel if his presence here threatened the rest of the pack—possibly the world?"

Even Edgar grew quiet then. With a silent sob, he closed his eyes and turned his back. After a moment, he shuffled off to the recovery suite.

Douglas cleared his throat. "We don't know the repercussions of Lee's return yet. Do whatever you have to do to discover them as soon as Meghan is able to assist you. In the meantime, my place is at his side."

The world might be ending, but the chief knew that if that were the case there was little he could do to prevent it. His priorities were his wolves.

Turning, he followed the trail of Edgar's sorrow, its thick perfume strong enough to overpower the normal disinfectant hospital smell.

Logan put her hands on her hips, kicking the shiny linoleum with one booted foot. "Look, this is all worst-case scenario. My gut says Lee is here to stay. Meghan's ability does more damage to the fabric of reality with her bubbles than bringing one wolf back through one."

Derrick grunted. "She needs to rest."

"Can't we wake her, just this once?" Connell asked.

He bristled, ready to launch into a speech about looking after a mate's best interest—something he'd heard from his cousin more than once.

Well, the shoe was on the other foot now. But instead of getting to gloat about it, he wanted to deck Connell.

"She can rest," Logan said, cutting him off before he did something he regretted. "We're obviously not being sucked into the seventh dimension of hell as we speak, so we have a little time. It's best to take some of it to figure out how to do this ritual right the first try. I'll need to figure out how to best tweak the scan spell anyway, to incorporate Meghan's ability."

Derrick put his hands in his pockets. "Okay," he agreed with a grunt, standing down.

They stood there another minute while he fought the urge to return to Meghan's room.

Logan's lips twitched. "We're good here. Go back and watch your girl sleep—you know you want to."

He scowled. "I don't need to watch her sleep."

"Sure, you do. You're all stalkers." She dismissed him with a flick of her hand.

"It's called being in love," he sniffed. Derrick was done pretending otherwise. "And you two are no better."

"Hey, we save the mushy stuff for the bedroom," Logan called after him.

Connell snickered, looking smug. "Or the woods, or the kitchen counter. Sometimes the nearest closet…"

"Shush, you," she scolded. "And don't wag those eyebrows at me like that. I have a spell to rework."

CHAPTER THIRTY-SIX

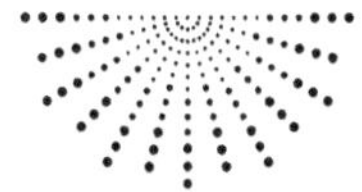

Meghan could feel the power running through Logan the moment she touched her fingers.

"Woah," she said, jerking her hands away. Her head swirled, and she let herself fall back on the pillows of the raised hospital bed.

Logan was sitting there too, cross-legged in the center of the bed.

Derrick stepped forward, hovering next to the bed. "Are you okay?"

"Yes, I'm fine. Just a head rush."

"Sorry," Logan said, a calculating expression on her face. "Some of the gifted are affected by an Elemental's touch. You're highly sensitive."

"Or she's still weak from the gunshot wound," Connell pointed out from a spot against the wall.

"Probably both," Logan acknowledged. "Do you need more time?"

"No." She took a deep breath. Meghan was determined not to be a weakling. "Although I could use a juice box."

Logan looked startled. "Oh, of course."

"I'll get it." Connell peeled himself off the wall, excusing himself as he went. He came back a few minutes later with a bottle of apple juice from the vending machine, an orange, and a bag of maple bacon jerky that he didn't share.

Once she had eaten her fill, she and Logan tried again. Touching the Elemental's skin was still challenging, but she didn't feel the need to keel over immediately.

"Don't we need a circle?" she asked, cataloging the different sensations Logan's touch engendered. She felt dizzy but also charged, as if she were touching one of those static electricity balls at a science museum.

"Not for this. I'm built to check nature's balance. It's sort of an Elemental's *raison d'être*," Logan explained. "That usually means targeting individuals who threaten it. But I can check the balance itself via the aether—which in a nutshell is pure magic and the life-force of every living thing on earth woven together."

Her lower lip jutted out and to the side as she studied Meghan. "It's not the same as being able to check the integrity of reality, except it sort of is."

"Uh-huh." This was over her head, but she was going to smile and nod because she half-suspected Logan didn't entirely understand it either. Some things just had to be accepted , like the Internet. Tearing apart a computer wouldn't help her understand how it worked any better.

Just click and surf. That was what she had to do now. Click and surf.

Logan began to speak—a mix of Latin and another language Meghan had never heard. The tingle that began in her fingers got stronger and then something rushed out of her.

Refueling had been smart because it felt as if a thread of energy was being pulled from her very core. It stretched out, like a hair being tugged out of her head except without the pain.

In her mind's eye, the string passed from her through Logan's fingers and into the air beyond. Then it spread out long and far until it covered the world.

Gasping, she held on, the sensation of being gossamer-thin but *huge* disorienting.

"*Meghan*, baby."

She could hear the concern in Derrick's voice. But sound was all she had. Unnervingly she could not see him, although her eyes were wide open.

You don't just have sound. You have touch. "I can feel something. Like a spiderweb." Her throat tightened. She didn't mean to sound frightened, but it came out that way. "It's everywhere."

"That's the aether," Logan said. "It's a little jarring to feel it, especially the first time. Which is why it's a good thing most witches can't."

Meghan frowned. "So I'm special?" she asked despondently.

"Try not to sound so happy about it," Logan deadpanned.

"I don't like being special."

"I know, sweets," Logan said, not unsympathetically. "Sometimes being special hurts more than it helps, but we are going to make you a little less special soon. Then you'll get to decide to be whatever you want."

She sucked in a breath. "That would be nice. Um, can *you* see the aether?"

"If I dug through my subconscious perception deeply enough, but I try not to do that. Gives you a hell of a migraine if you focus on it too long."

"When will you start scanning?"

"I already did. Halfway done actually."

"*Oh.*" Logan didn't appear to be doing much of anything, but that meant little. Meghan was wading in deep waters here. "Really?"

"You're the perception filter. I'm the battery," Logan grinned suddenly. "And I've got juice to spare."

"I do enjoy my energizer bunny," Connell chimed in. Meghan decided from his tone that it was meant to be sexual innuendo. She blushed.

"Connell, don't be gross." But Logan smiled as she said it.

Derrick laughed, a smacking thud indicating he had punched his cousin the way men did. "My mate's ears are relatively innocent, so try not to embarrass her."

"Yeah, I don't think that's going to be a problem long with you as a partner," Connell shot back. "You'll desensitize her soon enough."

"What are you implying?" Derrick growled. "That I should be a jackass like you?"

"Not implying. I'm saying flat out—you're an embarrassment. Meghan better get used to that now. The sooner the better."

The cousins continued to tease each other, adding the odd push and shove here and there. Their behavior didn't seem to distract Logan from her task. Whatever she was doing appeared to be autonomic now that she'd begun.

It took far less time for their thread to cover the world than she would have imagined.

"I'm done," Logan announced a good twenty minutes later. Meghan blinked, belatedly aware that her vision had returned.

Connell and Derrick stopped messing around, their postures shifting to what she now recognized was combat readiness.

"What's the verdict?" Derrick asked.

"The only disturbances are the ones I sensed before, around Meghan herself. Nothing around Lee. As far as I can tell the bubbles are self-healing. They pinch off from the aether in her presence and remelt into the larger whole once she's gone."

"But what if I'm here too long?" Meghan couldn't go on shaving off bits of time or reality wily-nilly.

"Long term it's bad," Logan acknowledged. "But if we close the doors, the floating bubbles that exist now will be reabsorbed. That appears to have been what happened around Vicky's cabin at the lake."

The relief almost made her fall back a second time. A second later she did just that—because Logan pushed her.

It was a gentle shove, using a fraction of the Elemental's strength, but it was necessary to break off the connection, which had locked them together as if their fingertips were super magnets.

"I hadn't realized it would get so sticky," Meghan said, grateful to be lying down after. Her fingertips felt raw as if the top layer of skin had been taken off. But it didn't hurt. Not much anyway.

"So Lee—" Connell broke off, clearing his throat with a harsh sound. "Leeland, he gets to stay?"

Logan sighed, her eyes meeting his and holding. "I keep telling you that is not up to me. He has to pull through his injuries on his own. I've done all I can to help the healing process. As for Edgar's fears, we can lay those to rest. There is no Lee-shaped hole we need to plug."

Both wolves relaxed, but neither looked happy.

The air was thick with unacknowledged sorrow and regret. *They had to learn to live without him.* It was only natural that they would be afraid to hope.

Logan was also looking uncharacteristically gloomy. But Meghan didn't think it had anything to do with Lee. Not with the way she was looking at her.

"What is it?" she asked.

The Elemental bit her lip, and Meghan knew that whatever she was holding back was bad.

"Is there a me-shaped hole that needs to be plugged?" she asked.

"No." Logan's face softened. "It's nothing like that. But there is something."

Meghan braced herself. "What aren't you telling me?"

"Something I'm not sure you need to hear." Logan gestured to Derrick. "Your life is here now. And I want you to be happy."

Meghan put two and two together. "It's about my past, isn't it?"

The Elemental's thick lashes screened her eyes.

"Please just tell me."

But Logan continued to hesitate.

"If there's something you're not telling her, just spit it out," Derrick said with a scowl. "Even if it's to confirm that shit shadow man's real identity."

Logan's head drew back. "What?"

"Meghan thinks the shadow man is her father." He said it calmly, but Meghan knew he was hiding his distaste.

"Is that what you believe?"

She raised her hands in a broken gesture. "I don't see how we have such similar abilities without a tie."

Logan dropped her eyes to the bed and considered that. "Based on the memories we visualized, it's not likely he is your father...but he may have contributed some genetic material."

It wasn't like Logan to talk in riddles. "I don't understand the difference."

"The difference is that you have the shadow man's nose. But you don't have his ears." She took out her phone and pulled up a picture—the one of the group of scholars standing over her as a child.

"You have this man's ears," she said, zooming in on a figure frozen in time forever coming down the stairs. Then she pointed to the woman Meghan secretly thought of as *mama*. "And while you most strongly resemble this woman, in terms of hair and skin tone, you have the cheekbones of the blonde on the left."

Logan put down the phone in the sudden silence.

Meghan fought to keep her voice steady. "That's too many parents."

"I can't see the others in the hoods in the back, but I suspect they also contributed their genetic material, splicing it together to make you."

It took some time for the words to break through her numb confusion. "I'm an experiment?" she asked slowly.

Logan's posture was very straight for someone sitting cross-legged on a bed. "One made to maximize your magical potential. I suspect they were trying to create a being who could manipulate reality to their ends. You couldn't have known what they were doing because you saw everything from a child's perspective, but the results speak for themselves."

"And they failed?" Meghan whispered.

Logan shook her head, a mix of sympathy and something else in her expression. Anger maybe. "On the contrary, they succeeded beyond their wildest dreams. But you can't bottle that kind of power. Once they did what they did, you slipped away—possibly with help."

"My moth—the woman whose hair I have."

Logan held up her phone, indicating she had captured other memories Meghan wasn't consciously aware of. "From what I saw, she was trying to get you away from the lab. Something may have scared her, or they had a falling out. It's also possible your physical similarity to her may have played a role. She came to care for you as her child and no longer wanted you treated as…"

"A lab rat?" Meghan supplied.

Logan reached out and took her hand, her grip firm. "We are all more than the sum of our parts. And God knows you are *much* more."

Meghan nodded because she couldn't speak. "Is there anything else?"

The Elemental shrugged. "The shadow man was normal in your last memories of the city with spires. Again, this is speculation, but I suspect he was trying to recreate what they did to you on himself—but without the groundwork that made it work. The end result was an unstable shadow man who rips apart time instead of sliding through it."

"Wait, how did people in the city even know how to do all this gene splicing and magic manipulation? Shouldn't it be beyond their technological abilities?"

Just how advanced had her civilization been?

Logan and Connell exchange a loaded glance. "Actually, my guess is that by their time, gene splicing an entire person together was likely child's play."

"Their time?" Meghan echoed. For some reason, these words had penetrated the ringing that had begun in her head.

Logan sucked some air between her teeth. "That's the other thing. I know you've been operating under the assumption that you've been moving randomly in time. The robes the people wore and architecture in certain memories certainly suggested they were from another era. But it's become clear to me at least that you're not from the past. You're from the future. And you've been falling *back* in time—well mostly backward."

Derrick scowled. "Backward?"

"Falling back makes a lot more sense than springing forward," Logan said. "It would take a lot more oomph to break into a future that hasn't happened yet. So, in a quantum kind of way, back is easier, more in line with the forces of entropy."

Meghan turned to look at them all in turn. "But I can move forward too."

"Yeah, that was a puzzler. Best I can figure there are hard spots in time." The Elemental held up her hands and bobbed them up and down. "You might be able to bounce back within certain limits, like a sphere in a pinball game. But overall, the general trajectory is backward, relatively speaking. And you've come from a long way off."

Connell snickered suddenly. It was jarring. "Sorry," he apologized, holding up a hand. "I uh, it just occurred to me that Derrick would make a hell of a hard spot."

"Because he's so muscular?" Her eyes drifted to her man. Connell might have rivaled him physically, but he was nowhere near as handsome as her Derrick.

Her mate preened.

"Actually, it's because his head is so hard."

Derrick lunged for his cousin, grabbing him in a headlock.

"Boys," Logan scolded. "There will be time to play later."

She climbed off the bed, pausing to pull Meghan into a hug. "I know you have a lot to process, but we can't count on Derrick's hardness—"

Breaking off, she closed her eyes, her mouth squirming as if holding back a laugh. "I mean his apparent sustainability as a landing place. We still need to prepare the binding spell."

Meghan nodded. "The sooner the better," she agreed.

CHAPTER THIRTY-SEVEN

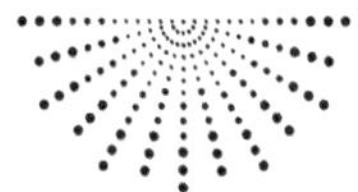

The woods were cold, but with Derrick pressed against her back she hardly felt it.

Meghan had been discharged from the hospital a mere hour ago, but Logan had worked quickly. At least a hundred wolves were ready to donate a drop of blood to bind her to the pack.

Technically, the shifters didn't need the little bonfires that dotted the clearing edges a few hundred yards behind the Maitland home, but Meghan was glad they had lit them. It made this seem more like a party she had seen on television once—a kegger, they had called it.

Of course, the people who had organized that in the movie were teenagers, and there were people of all ages here, chatting and drinking from bottles of beers or flasks. There were even small children, including one or two babies being passed around like party favors.

"What's wrong?" Derrick asked, his deep voice a pleasant rumble at her back.

"I was thinking about babies."

"How many you want?" he asked in a teasing tone

"More like how I was grown, not born." She dropped her voice to a whisper, aware that wolves had superior hearing. "How I'm not a real person."

His arms wrapped around her, pressing her to him higher. "Hey, you might have been designed, but you are as real as everyone else here. You took your first breath and crawled before you could walk, just like us. You are as real as it gets. And you won yourself a hell of a wolf as a mate if I do say so myself."

Meghan's lips quirked despite her lingering confusion and pain. She wasn't a human born. She was *witch-made*.

Her wolf must have read her conflict in her scent because he held her very close before tugging her in the direction of the house. "Come with me."

"Don't we have to stay?" she asked, looking back over her shoulder at the waiting crowd. "Logan is almost done setting up."

The Elemental and Connell were drawing a huge circle in the center of the clearing, one made with salt, not chalk.

"She's not done yet. We can spare a few minutes for this."

Her cheeks flushed. "Derrick, I'm not sure we should do *that* with everyone here."

Facing everyone after the incident at his home had been embarrassing enough, but there were at least twenty times more people gathered here tonight. Probably more.

"I wasn't thinking of *that*," Derrick laughed. "Although nobody in this crowd would begrudge us some alone time. We're wolves, not bear shifters."

Her brows drew together. "Are bear shifters less amorous?"

"Compared to us, yeah." Derrick led her inside through the back, not stopping until they were upstairs. "But I brought you here for something else."

They entered the third bedroom on the right. Judging from the fine layer of dust on the oak bureau, the room was unoccupied, but it was by no means empty.

She pivoted on her heel, studying the mix of feminine and martial decor. A collection of Japanese swords hung on the wall over a bed covered with a duvet in dusty rose pink.

"This is Mara's room. You'll meet her after she and Jack get back from their honeymoon."

"Your other cousin has interesting taste," she said, reaching out to touch one of the swords.

"We can blame Logan's aunt Mai for starting the weapon fetish. She gave her the first one for Christmas last year and Mara being Mara, she soon acquired over a dozen."

"I would have thought weapons of any kind would be of interest to a wolf who had been a soldier."

He opened the closet and started rummaging through it. He tossed a few things from the top shelf out onto the bed. "Guns yes, but only during open warfare with humans. It's frowned upon to use tech in normal conflicts with other wolves. But swords—they aren't a common interest for our kind."

"I suppose they are kind of redundant when you can sprout claws and fangs."

"Exactly." He turned around to find Meghan holding a battered black velvet witch hat with a purple band. Mara had used it as part of her costume for Halloween in high school.

The corner of his mouth lifted as she placed it on her head. "How do I look?" she asked, striking a pose for him.

The way he stared at her made her heart skip a beat.

"You're so freaking adorable we're coming to steal that come October, but it's not actually what I was looking for."

Derrick dived back into the closet, pulling out a garment bag from the back of the closet with an air of triumph. "Pretty sure this is it— why I wanted to come back to the house."

Unzipping the bag, he pulled out a beautiful white dress. It had a very little adornment—the style was in the cut, a retro-looking piece reminiscent of a fifties gown, but with a longer hemline.

He held it against her, measuring the potential fit. "I think you should wear this tonight."

Meghan's lips parted. Her hand reached out to the silky cloth almost without her volition. "But isn't this Mara's wedding dress?"

She didn't know much about weddings, but she'd seen enough

about them on the computer to recognize that most brides wouldn't lend their gowns to anyone. They were meant to be worn once, a prized souvenir of their most memorable day.

"This was sent to Mara on accident. She was pretty upset about it at the time too. She ordered a gown from her favorite designer and got this a week before the wedding."

Meghan stroked the gown's gossamer sleeve. "Why didn't she wear it? It's beautiful."

"Yes, it is, but it's also three sizes too small. Mara is about ten inches taller and has about forty pounds more muscle than you. Fortunately, the designer sent the right dress via express mail as soon as she called them. It got here in the nick of time. They never asked for this one back."

He held the dress out to her. "Mara won't mind if you use it. The only reason it's still here is that she said it was too beautiful to give away. She wanted to find the right person to give it to."

Derrick cupped her cheek with his hand, his smile melting her insides into molten butter. "You haven't met her yet, but you already have her stamp of approval. Trust me, she won't mind if this becomes your wedding gown."

Meghan sucked in a breath. "So you want me to wear this because you want to marry me? Tonight?"

"Well, we call it a mating ceremony. And yes—everyone is here anyway. I want to claim you the minute you are bound to this time and place. Why wait?"

A sob caught in her throat. It was so sudden and unexpected that it shocked even her.

Derrick took her outburst for a negative. "Or we can wait. No rush," he said with sudden hoarseness, his hands hovering over her arms as if he were afraid to touch her.

Meghan threw herself in his arms, knocking the hat off her head when the brim hit his chest. It fell to the floor, forgotten.

"It's not that. I want to be yours. Forever. I just never thought I would belong anywhere, to anyone..." She looked up at his blurry visage. "And I never believed I would find someone like you—and it's not because you're so strong and protective or that you're stupidly handsome.

"It's because you *care*. You worry about children you don't know and your pack elders, always making time for them. But you also help complete strangers. You're so *kind*, deep inside where people usually aren't."

Sniffing, she wiped her cheek with the heel of her hand. Derrick gathered her in his arms, wiping the last traces of her tears before holding her for a long minute.

"I don't mean to talk you into a lesser opinion of me, but it's very easy to be kind to you. You're a fucking hero, sweeter than honey, and more beautiful than anyone has a right to be. You deserve way better than me as a mate, which is why I want to lock this down before you can meet anyone else. I'm being entirely selfish asking you to commit so soon."

Meghan smacked his back with a closed fist, not too hard. "There is no one better than you. And I want to do this too. Tonight."

"Good." He squeezed her closer to him choosing that time to explain a few things about the mating ceremony. "Normally it takes place after the actual mating bond is initiated, but we're not a conventional couple and also because we don't have time now."

"Because that part usually happens during special adult private time?" she interrupted.

He laughed. "Usually yes, but it doesn't have to."

Derrick put two fingers in the crook of her neck. "It'll just be a little nip. But I should warn you that Logan isn't willing to say you'll be completely protected by the spell. She's as annoying as a scientist—they never want to go on the record that something is one-hundred-percent sure. There's still a chance you might keep traveling after we do this. It's small but not zero."

His fingers stroked her neck, the touch gentle and hot at the same time. "But Logan knows what she's doing. I would never risk you if I didn't think the binding spell would work. But the possibility exists. You could fall into another bubble. Our bond might be damaged. We can wait and see."

"No." Her heart was pounding. "I don't want to wait."

Derrick's cheek twitched, and she could tell he was rethinking the mating ceremony, talking himself out of doing it tonight.

"You said it yourself," she pressed. "Logan is a genius with spells, and we're using the blood from a lot of wolves. It will work. It *has* to. But if the worst happens, we will deal with it after."

Derrick made a rough sound in his throat.

Meghan clutched his shirt with both hands. "We don't even know if our bond would be affected by my traveling. It's a chance I'm willing to take. More than that—I demand the right to take the risk, because I want to be yours now."

His eyes lightened to bright wolf yellow. "You already are, bond or not," he said, and she knew it was both Derrick and his wolf speaking to her at the same time.

Meghan smiled with tears in her eyes, spreading her hands over his chest. "Derrick and whatever else lives in Derrick—I want all of you, *now*. I won't wait another minute."

His chuckle sent a vibration through her. "All right."

Grinning like a fool, he backed out of the room. "But I better leave so you can change, because if I stay, we'll never get to the ceremony tonight, and there are enough kids out past their bedtime as it is."

"Good point," she giggled.

Saluting, he left her alone, picking up the velvet hat and tossing it on the bed on the way out.

Meghan hugged the dress and squealed. The future she had hoped for and despaired of never finding was suddenly here. And she was going to meet it wearing a dress that made her feel like a princess.

CHAPTER THIRTY-EIGHT

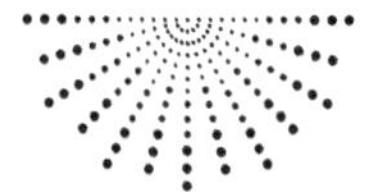

If Meghan had thought she'd been the cynosure of every eye before she changed, it was nothing compared to the reaction of the wolves when she appeared on Derrick's arm wearing the white gown and a goofy grin.

At least Derrick's face was equally silly, although his smile was touched with smugness as well. He'd surprised her with an outfit change as well—a suit someone had brought him from his house.

Logan took one look at them and the serious expression she'd been wearing melted away. She bounced over to hug them each in turn while Connell came over to slap Derrick on the back.

The Elemental hung off Derrick's arm while she bent backward at the waist to address Douglas, who was standing at the edge of the clearing speaking to a trio of men and women. "Hey Chief, I think you're up first."

The woman, who she recognized as the deli owner, handed him something small. Douglas clutched the object and turned, noticing their clothing. Unlike Connell, he didn't smile, but his face warmed visibly as he stepped into the center of the clearing to address the assembled gathering.

His tall and dark-haired form didn't seem all that physically imposing until it was compared to the other werewolves. Douglas possessed a palpable energy, something deep and clean, like a well of cold water.

His voice had the same depth as well. "Thank you all for coming," he said. "I know some of you know the reason for this gathering while others have only heard rumors and wild conjecture."

Douglas drew himself up a little straighter, hooking his thumb in the waistband of his jeans. "I'm here to tell you that the crazy rumors you've heard are true."

Meghan took a deep breath, edging closer to her wolf. Reading her anxiety with unerring accuracy, Derrick moved to stand at her back, wrapping his arm around her waist in a show of silent solidarity.

Douglas held out a hand, palm up, and pointed to her. "We have a new sister joining our ranks tonight. This is Meghan, and she is Derrick's," he announced. "As he is making plain."

A few titters and the crowd seemed to lean forward as one, hanging on their leader's every word.

"Like Logan, Meghan is gifted in stunning and unique ways," Douglas continued. "And she has helped our pack, expanding our numbers with her gifts."

A movement in the crowd caught her eye, and Meghan's breath caught when she spotted the Reddy-Young family. The two women had brought the cat cubs with them, both children now comfortable enough to be in human form around them.

Diya put a little girl on her shoulders. The toddler waved her still-chubby hands at them. Throat tight with joy, Meghan waved back while a serious boy of about seven years held onto the other woman's hand. After a slight hesitation, he also waved.

Douglas paused, his voice roughening. "Meghan has also returned one of our own to the fold, someone we long thought lost."

The murmur in the crowd increased to a low roar. Douglas let it go for a few beats before stopping it with that upraised hand no one dared disobey.

"What happened is miraculous, but it cost Meghan dearly. She is not safe as long as her magic goes unchecked. Neither are we. Thankfully for her—and all of us—she's more than willing to forsake this aspect of her ability. We're going to help her with that tonight."

He scanned the crowd, conveying with a glance that his word was final and true. Douglas didn't want any other wolves clamoring for the return of their lost. What happened with Lee couldn't happen again. Not without risking real damage to their world.

Please let it be my world too. Meghan clutched Derrick's arm with her hands, doing her damndest to will a future with him into being. A long one.

His wolf shared her impatience, making a clearing noise in his throat. "If we could speed this along," he asked, his tone respectful but tinged with urgency.

Douglas's mouth twitched.

"Thanks to Derrick's impatience, this meeting will serve double duty," he said as some in the crowd laughed. "Tonight, we will celebrate his union with our new friend."

The chief's face sobered, his voice deepening in resonance. "But first we will help Logan cast a spell that will bind Meghan to the pack so that she is no longer at the whim of capricious magicks or those who might seek to abuse her."

Douglas stepped back, gesturing for Logan to come forward.

"What we need from you is a single drop of blood," his daughter-in-law said.

The wolves liked this announcement a little less than all of Douglas's words, but no one shouted the Elemental down as she proceeded to explain how this would seal the binding spell.

"It's strictly voluntary of course," Logan said. "And we ask that only wolves who have come of age donate."

She smiled as more than one juvenile in the crowd protested in displeasure. "I know some of you younger pack members want to help, but it's my call, and I'm not going to budge. We need at least one dozen adults, but two dozen is better. So if the willing can form a line starting line here."

The crowd shifted and reformed, wolf after wolf stepping up to form a single file line where she was pointing.

The eager young men and women came first, but so did the middle-aged and the elders. Parents handed their smaller kids off to somewhat disgruntled preteens and older children.

Diya took the little girl off her shoulders and came forward holding her hand, right behind her wife, who'd whispered a few things to her new son, apparently instructing him to wait where he was.

Blinking, Meghan looked over her shoulder to look at Derrick. Unabashed at showing his true emotions, her wolf wiped at the moisture that had gathered in the corner of his eyes.

"Thank you, everyone," he said hoarsely.

Meghan echoed him in a small voice, waiting patiently as Logan pricked each donor's finger with a freshly unwrapped disposable syringe needle, collecting a drop of blood in a wooden bowl. Connell helpfully passed out bandages next to her.

When Logan finished with the line of wolves, she and Connell pricked their fingers. Douglas was the last—and he donated three times.

"This is from Edgar," he said, taking out two vials of blood, the kind she'd seen in the hospital. "And the other is from Kiera. Neither wanted to leave the hospital just now, but they wanted to participate, so they sent these with Jeannie."

He handed them to Logan. She dropped a single drop rose from each vial, suspended with magic so precise and perfectly controlled it made Meghan gasp in wonder.

Dear Lord. Derrick had described the things Logan could do—whip up tornadoes and fly through the air without her body. But seeing this small precision display was somehow more jarring than if she'd seen her strange new friend demolish a building with her power.

And isn't that the pot calling the kettle black?

Meghan recognized the irony, but she still watched in awe as the last two drops floated to join the rest in the pot. Then Logan spoke a few foreign phrases under her breath.

The bowl was handmade. Derrick had told her Connell had made it from one of the old pines, that his cousin had grown accustomed to fashioning instruments his mate used in her spell work. Logan had carved special symbols in the curved bottom, explaining that the bowl would be burned after the casting—a precaution against it being co-opted by a lesser witch.

Now Logan's words activated her spell, the blood its fuel. A cartoonishly red-tinted glow began to shine from the vessel's depths. But the red didn't last. Within a minute it transformed like an alchemic reaction into a bright pure yellow.

Heart beating a little too quick, she waited as Logan dipped a finger into the bowl. It came away stained with a transcendent gold that glittered, luminescent.

The assembled wolves had been quiet, but it was a silence pregnant with expectation and not a little reverence.

"She doesn't have to drink that, right?"

Logan scowled over her head at Derrick. "The consumption is symbolic."

She gave Meghan an impish grin. "Don't worry. You won't catch wolfiness from it."

Then the Elemental raised her head, managing to stand tall and imposing despite her diminutive height.

"What has been given here has been sacrificed with love," Logan said, raising her voice so that it projected over the entire clearing. "And it will be accepted with love."

Stepping closer, she lifted her glowing digit and used it to draw a symbol on Meghan's forehead. Two more decorated her cheeks.

"Mind, body, soul, and *heart*," she declared as a final symbol was sketched over the spot where that organ beat in her chest.

The golden design sparked bright, shining like the sun. A moment later it began to fade as the liquid was absorbed into her body. Meghan shuddered, but it wasn't in pain. The sensation was more like being covered in a heated blanket.

After a lifetime of cold, or temporarily borrowed heat, she was finally warm.

"I thought you said it was symbolic," Derrick muttered under his breath.

"It is." Logan grinned at him. "It's also literal."

She handed the bowl to Connell and took both of Meghan's hands. "This is your time and your place, Meghan."

Logan backed away, gesturing for Derrick to let her go. "Now close the doors."

"How?" Meghan asked, her chest so tight it was hard to breath.

"Picture it. Will it so. You have the strength. This is your magic. It belongs to *you*. You do not belong to it. Close the doors. Close *all* of them."

Giving her a shaky nod, Meghan closed her eyes. But try as she might her mind stayed blank. She couldn't even visualize it.

Then she felt him. Derrick had put his arms back around her. He'd sensed her difficulty. Logan must have as well, because she didn't scold the wolf for his interference.

Meghan kept her eyes closed, but Derrick's image bloomed in her mind, clear and vibrant. In her mind, he took her hand.

Visualization was easy after that. The doors had been hiding just beyond her in the dark, but they were clear now. And closing them proved simpler than she could have imagined—because any door that could separate her from Derrick wasn't allowed to exist.

So she shrank them. Meghan focused on the constellation around her. It was as if she were a child standing in a field of soap bubbles. They floated around her, shifting at the whim of entropy or other forces she couldn't see.

One by one each bubble grew smaller and smaller. Some popped, scaring the hell out of her, but when she told Logan what happened the Elemental said it was normal. The substance they were made of scattered and fell, a weightless, formless something sinking back into the atmosphere visible behind her eyes.

It felt like forever, but when Meghan opened her eyes again the fires were burning at nearly the same level, the piles of wood next to them almost as high as before.

Pivoting she turned to face Derrick—too fast. Dizzy, she staggered, falling into his arms. He gathered her up and pressed his mouth to the base of her neck.

Then he bit her.

It stung, but the melting sensation turning her body to mush over-rode the small discomfort.

Derrick pulled his head back then set her down on her feet amidst the sounds of cheers, claps, and one or two howls. "You were finished, right?" he asked a touch anxiously.

"Yes," she said, touching the tender spot on her neck. "It's really done? Are we mated?"

"Damn straight."

She let out a short bark of laughter, leaning on Derrick as the world spun giddily. She had never been drunk, but she suspected this was what it felt like.

The mystical mating bond she'd heard so much about was started with a single bite. And it had taken. She could feel it like a ribbon wrapped around the blanket.

Douglas cleared his throat. "Well, generally we say a few words first, but Derrick seems to have lost all the patience he was famous for."

Meghan's mouth dropped open. She turned to her mate. "He's being sarcastic, right?"

Derrick sniffed, looking nonplussed.

"*You* were known for your patience? When was this?"

Huffing, he pulled her into his arms, growling into her neck.

Douglas chuckled—the first time she had seen him laugh. But if he smiled, it was too quick. When she looked back at him, his face was wearing the same serious sober expression he always did.

He held out his hand. "Welcome to the pack."

She shook it with warm fingers. "Thank you," she said, trying not to sound breathless as the power he so skillfully hid surged beneath his skin.

It was probably an autonomic response to touching any witch, his natural impulse to take out the threat to his people. Douglas had to be highly evolved to ignore such a strong instinct. A flicker of amuse-ment appeared in his eye, but he turned to face the crowd so she couldn't be certain.

"Again, thank you all for coming and for your generosity. Those of you with little ones are free to take them home now. Those who want to stay but whose cubs need to sleep are free to take them into the house and put them down in whatever bed or couch is open."

He paused, gesturing for some wolves at the periphery to come forward. Two wolves materialized carrying kegs, another a case with the logo of a high-end whiskey. Still more appeared carrying trays that smelled of hot meats and savory loaves of bread.

Douglas clapped Derrick and Connell on the back, an infectious grin on his face. "Now let's celebrate."

CHAPTER THIRTY-NINE

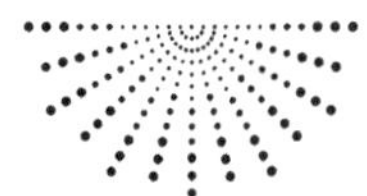

Meghan tried not to laugh as Logan stumbled out of Derrick's spare bedroom looking wrecked.

Connell and Logan had a house up in the hills overlooking the valley, but given how much both had drunk they hadn't been in any shape to make it up there.

Douglas had called it carousing. Meghan had never known the word, but she understood it well now.

Bleary-eyed, Logan staggered to the kitchen counter. *"Coffee."*

Biting back her amusement, Meghan poured her new friend a very large mugful in the shape of a cartoon wolf with bright blue eyes. "I never had coffee before I met Derrick," she shared. "Only tea."

"I love coffee." Logan disappeared with a gust of air, reappearing looking refreshed. She took the mug and sipped, then sighed in pleasure. "That's better."

"Can you make hangovers go away by doing that?" Meghan asked, fascinated.

The Elemental gave her an impish wink. "Alcohol can be left behind when I go non-corporeal."

Meghan chuckled, pouring herself a cup and adding some cinnamon creamer. "That's a nice trick."

Logan shrugged. "I just need to remember not to do it too soon, else I don't get to enjoy the buzz. I notice you didn't have a drop of alcohol last night."

"I was already euphoric. Having anything stimulating on top of that would be dangerous, although Derrick assured me you can't literally burst with happiness."

Logan laughed. "I bet the smug bastard loved hearing that."

Her mirth subsided. "But I sense you are less jubilant about stuff today. The wedding night go okay?"

"I, um, I wasn't—" She broke off, heat suffusing her cheeks. "Last night was wonderful. Both the public and the private. I felt so welcomed. But you're right. I do have a lot of...feelings."

Meghan came around the counter and sat down on the living room couch where Logan joined her.

"Don't get me wrong. I am so happy bursting is still a danger." She touched the bite mark on her neck. It was still sensitive but didn't sting to the touch. "I'm grateful that Derrick and I found each other and that we are mated. I feel different now. Settled and grounded in a way that I've never experienced, but also....bigger."

She put her hand over her heart. "I feel my wolf here now."

"Sounds like the spell and the mating bond are both doing what they should. That's good. It's healthy," Logan said, giving her a critical once over before settling back with her coffee mug. "I guess it's the other thing that is bothering you."

"The part where I'm not a real person." Pretense was useless around an Elemental, so Meghan didn't try to employ any. "More like a failed experiment."

Logan scowled. "You are *a* person. And as for the artificial nature of your conception—they do that here and now. Granted they're not at the place where they are splicing genes to the extent yours were, but trust me that it's not that far off."

This last was said with resignation. "As for the experiment that sent you back in time, all I can say is it's a good thing you were able to get away from the people trying to use you."

Meghan nodded, still too conflicted about her future past to put into words.

Logan let her mull, finishing her coffee. When she was done, she set the mug aside and leaned back, crossing her legs. "All that's left is deciding what kind of witch you want to be."

"What do you mean?"

"I mean, being a natural witch is fun, but you *can* study. You can develop your talent and focus on one or a few specialties. For example, my sister Gia's mate Salvador is a healer. My mom and aunt dabble quite a bit, but mom primarily uses her gift to research ancient history and find artifacts to inform her lectures. Other witches have an affinity for plants or animals."

"What if I choose to do nothing with it?"

Logan's lips pulled to the side, and she leaned a little closer. "I'm afraid with your strength it's not a good idea to let it lie fallow. Magic has a way of leaking out when you don't mean it to."

"That I believe." Meghan sighed, rubbing her face. "Do you think the shadow man will keep trying to break through?"

"Of course. Except from now on, it will be like beating his head against ultrathick glass. Unless you let him in, he can't get you here."

"But what if he just keeps beating against the glass and manages to crack it?"

"Then we kick his ass."

Meghan pursed her lips, studying the surface of her coffee. "And what if he's suffering?"

Logan drew herself up straight. "Are we talking about putting him out of his misery? Because I must be honest—I don't think he's fixable. Physically or morally."

"Yeah, you're right. I wouldn't even know where to start."

Lost in thought, she lapsed into silence. After a few minutes, Logan nudged her with her boot. "This isn't going to be a problem we solve in one conversation. I promise I'll keep brainstorming, and you can keep doing the same. We have time to figure this out."

She rose to her feet. "In the meantime, I hear your wolf stirring, so I'm going to go grab mine and clear out. Derrick and Connell are tight, but not the kind of close where it's kosher to crash a honeymoon."

A gust of air and Logan was at the sink, washing her mug. Another and she was at the top of the stairs. "I'm going to take Connell to see Lee and then we'll be at our place for a little while, barring any work-related emergencies. If you have any problems, just give me a shout. Derrick has our number."

With that, she was gone. A few minutes later Meghan felt the house was a little emptier.

Deciding to do what she did best—focus on the now—she poured a fresh cup of coffee into a large mug, adding sugar and a splash of cream the way Derrick liked it.

She and her wolf were alone in their own home.

No more surviving or just getting by. It was time to begin living. And she was going to start in the arms of her virile mate.

CHAPTER FORTY

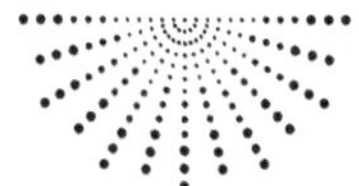

Connell watched Logan bustle around Leeland's unconscious form. She was listening to his breathing, checking his aura and all sorts of other diagnostics to explain his continued coma.

He wanted to help, but whenever he was in this room he could do little more than sit in the armchair by the bed, staring at the face of the man he had buried two years ago.

"Is he any better?"

Logan turned to look at him. Her expression said it all. Connell looked down at his hands, his throat tight.

She moved with a small gust, leaning against him. He pressed his head against her chest, her warm weight a comfort. "I called Gia. She's bringing Salvador here as soon as they wrap up that mess in Istanbul. He should remain stable until they get here."

"All right," he murmured, unable to take his eyes off Lee.

His mate waited patiently, one hand on his neck. It was a possessive hold, his favorite to use on her. He loved when she turned it on him, because she was rarely able to reciprocate. Logan might be one of the most powerful witches on record, so much that she wasn't even considered a witch, but she couldn't casually reach his neck unless he was sitting.

"If he does wake up, what the hell am I going to tell him?" Lee was one of his best friends. He had *died* for him.

"Well, I plan on starting with thank you." Her fingers stroked him, and there was a wealth of emotion in her voice.

"That's probably a good idea." He leaned more heavily into her side. "I should start writing a list. I expect it's going to be a long one."

They sat with Lee for a few minutes longer, talking to him to let him know that they were there for him.

Eventually, Kiera came in to take her patient's vitals, kicking them out with a gentle reminder that Edgar was on his way back. Lee's father had been coaxed downstairs for a shower and hot meal in the canteen by Jeannie.

Connell headed out of the back door, not eager to meet Edgar.

He wasn't a coward, but he didn't want to unbalance the old wolf any further. Edgar had been devastated losing Lee the first time. Now it seemed there was a very real possibility that he'd have to do it all over again. But Connell also didn't want his mate to poof him home. He needed a run.

Logan wasn't a wolf, but she was one of the few Supernaturals who could keep up with him—even on his hardest longest runs, thanks to her Elemental constitution. When they drew within a mile of the four-bedroom house he'd had built into the hillside for them, Connell shifted back to two feet, walking the last mile beside her in his birthday suit.

That was around the time he noticed her distraction. Wolves were rather blasé about nudity, but his mate was rather enamored of his body, gratifyingly so. When she didn't pat his butt, instead keeping her eyes on the path, he realized she too was preoccupied.

"Meghan will be all right. Derrick will take care of her."

She gave him a sidelong glance. "I'm sure he'll try. But that's not really what I'm concerned about."

"Are you worried that she's too powerful?" It was an Elemental's job to police witches gone bad. Those with Meghan's level of magic were automatically red flagged for close observation.

"Not too much. Without the time-traveling she's as powerful as some of the Seven," she said, referring to the power-hungry major witch clans that were constantly jockeying for supremacy. "But I'm not worried about her turning to the dark side. It's not likely given who she just mated and the ties she appears to be forming in the pack. That and your dad would never let that happen on his watch."

That last one was an excellent point. "Then what's your concern? Is it the shadow man?"

Was the spell to keep him out of their time in danger of failing?

Logan shook her head. "It's more to do with the experiment that made her."

"You're still sure she's a frankenbaby?"

"More than ever."

He winced. "How did she not know?" Not the circumstances of her birth. But in the time she'd been traveling Meghan must have seen many families. Did she never compare them to the way she started out and wonder?

His mate moved into the shadows, but he heard the intake of air that was let out slowly. "She saw her memories through the lens of a child's mind. Given her physical similarity to one of the researchers, it was only natural she thought that was her mother."

"Selective breeding isn't new in the witching world," he pointed out. "The Seven have essentially been conducting a massive eugenics experiment for centuries, way before they understood genes and DNA. The sister Salvador just discovered, the one born after his parents did all those power-enhancing rituals, is in pretty much the same boat as Meghan—down to the over-protective shifter mate."

Logan acknowledged that with a tilt of her head. "On paper they are similar. But Gia met Valeria, and she didn't mention anything unusual about her magic, other than that it was very strong, so I don't think she sensed what I do here with Meghan."

His mate stopped under the branches of a tall pine. "For all the strangeness of her abilities, her magic feels familiar. It has aspects that taste like my mom's and a bit like Noomi, the archivist at T'Kaieri."

Oh fuck. "She feels like an Elemental?"

Logan gave him a tiny nod. "Like a witch from an Elemental line to be precise. Hints of several of them, in fact."

"Huh." Connell wasn't a religious man. He'd never given much thought to the Mother, the all-powerful being that seeded life on Earth, not until the creature left, leaving the Elementals holding the bag.

More like she passed them the keys to the kingdom. Which was why the world hadn't descended into bloody chaos. Nothing about how it worked had changed. The Elementals were still the toughest kids on the block, and they still went after the bad guys—by mutual agreement.

But if Meghan "tasted" of Elemental magic, that meant sometime in the future things were going to change, in a fucking god-awful way.

"So the people who made Meghan were splicing their genes to concentrate Elemental-level magic?"

"Seems that way." Her voice was morose. "Which means the shadow man might have started as one of us, or near enough as to make no difference."

The idea that someone from an Elemental line would experiment on children was enough to send him into a red rage. Except the people he wanted to beat into a pulp, the ones who had let this happen to a child, weren't here.

"Meghan was born thousands of years in the future," he growled, starting to feel the same hint of existential despair. "There's nothing we can do."

"I'll talk that over with my sisters," Logan said. "But basically yes—I don't see a whole lot of options. We can make up rules and pass down warnings till the cows come home. It doesn't guarantee later generations will pay attention."

Connell smirked. "*Our* kids damn well better heed the warnings we leave them if they know what's good for them."

She snorted, the sound loud by virtue of its unexpectedness. "Right. Because mixing our gene pools is going to lead to beautifully obedient children."

"Maybe just beautiful," he acknowledged, before pulling her into his arms. Connell waggled his brows suggestively. "Speaking of kids, when do you think you're going to be ready to talk about making them?"

Logan snickered. "Give me another decade."

Considering he thought she'd give him a much larger figure, he decided to celebrate his victory. "I think I can wait that long…as long as we get lots of practice in the meantime."

His mate stopped and threw her arms around him. "That's what I love about you, Connell. I can always count on you to make the obvious sex joke."

He was about to point out that she was aroused. He could smell it. But there was no need. Between one blink and the next they were in their bedroom, and this time he wasn't the only one in a birthday suit.

CHAPTER FORTY-ONE

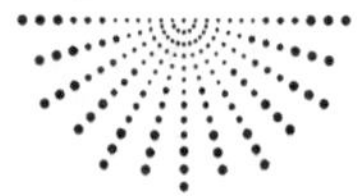

Kiera walked into the recovery suite and breathed a sigh of relief. Edgar wasn't sitting vigil at Leeland's bedside.

As the pack's only certified surgeon, Kiera was used to dealing with frightened and grieving parents. But nothing had prepared her for the special hell that was dealing with a Were poised to lose the same son twice.

Except...

"Hey, your color is better." Hustling over to the bed, she took out her stethoscope, rolling the bedclothes down so she could listen to Lee's heartbeat.

Strong, steady. Equal parts miraculous and terrifying. Kiera bit her lip, staring at the man who'd come back from the dead.

She didn't know Leeland that well. He was older than her by a good five years and was an upper-level dominant wolf to boot. Growing up, she had made it a point to avoid his crowd, avoid all the dominants.

Connell and Derrick had been safe, of course, but most of the other alpha types had either been dismissive or cruel to shy subs like her. Most of them outgrew that kind of behavior as adults, but some never did.

Granted Leeland had been, by all accounts, one of the decent ones. A handsome jock with a ready smile, Lee was known as a reliable wolf to have at your back, even as a teen. As a man, he'd been a good soldier and a dutiful son. His easy-going nature combined with his garrulous and sly sense of humor made him welcome wherever he went.

That was about the extent of her knowledge despite the fact Leeland had always been in the forefront, part of the pack within the pack. One of the elite. That was how she'd classified the popular boys earmarked as future leaders of their kind.

Not that she had first-hand knowledge of Leeland's manner and personality. He had never noticed her. Which had suited her just fine. Even now Kiera stayed away from the soldier dominants, keeping most of her interactions with them restricted to her medical duties.

Which you need to get back to. Giving herself a shake, she continued her exam, wanting to be done before Edgar returned.

She changed Leeland's bandages, satisfied to see that his healing was progressing apace. For a while there it had stalled, almost as if he were a normal human and not a werewolf.

Edgar and the rest of the pack wouldn't have cared if Leeland had come back as a normal human but knew Leeland would disagree.

No dominant would ever give up their strength and speed, would never choose to be *lesser*.

Kiera shook her head, refocusing on the bandages, including the one down his thigh. They had cut off the jeans and flannel shirt Leeland had been wearing in the woods that day.

Because Weres ran hot, they typically didn't put hospital gowns on them. That and most didn't mind running around naked. But there was something weird about having Leeland naked under the sheet. Maybe because the last time she had seen him dressed he'd been wearing a suit...at his funeral.

Edgar had eschewed the rustic funeral pyre in the woods for a more traditionally human service. But old timeline Leeland *had* been cremated.

Suddenly that was very comforting. Because the image of

Leeland's body decomposing in a coffin under the ground while this version walked *on* it was nightmare fuel.

The last bandage on his upper thigh was clean, so she decided to leave it. She was just covering him with the blanket when she felt eyes watching her.

Her patient's eyes were open...and they were pure black.

"Leeland?" she asked, a tremor running through her when he didn't speak.

Then he lunged for her, his growl filling the world. Black eyes flared with a spark of red as his hands wrapped around her neck and began to squeeze.

CHAPTER FORTY-TWO

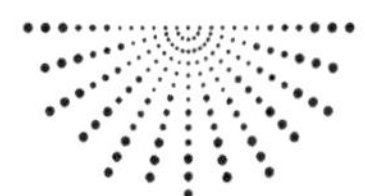

Nathan was whistling, carrying a pair of hot coffees from Jeannie's when he caught something he hadn't heard in two years—Leeland's growl. For a second he froze, marveling.

Then he realized that was not a friendly sound. The last time he'd heard it was when they had gotten pinned down behind enemy lines in Sudan.

He sprinted to the recovery room, which was standing open.

Lee was choking Kiera, a killing rage on his eyes.

Shouting over his shoulder for help, he tossed the coffees, running to help the small medic.

"Lee," he snapped as he grabbed the other man's hands, trying to pry them off Kiera's neck. "Fuck. *Stop it!*"

But it was more difficult than it should have been to break Leeland's hold—he was too strong for someone in a hospital recovery bed.

Lee snarled at Nathan, partially shifting so his teeth were wolf sharp. Kiera's face was bright red, almost purple under her dark skin.

"Lee, stop!" he gritted, pulling his fingers off one by one. "*You're killing her.*"

He was on the verge of breaking his friend's thumbs off when the chief appeared, Edgar at his side.

Douglas put his hand on Lee's forehead as Edgar grabbed his right arm, using all his weight to pin it to the bed.

"*Sleep*," Douglas ordered, his voice reverberating with preternatural command. It was an order from the most powerful werewolf in the Americas, something that could not be disregarded or ignored.

Lee fell back onto the bed, unconscious. Even Nathan flinched, swaying on his feet. But he fought to stay awake because Kiera had tumbled to the floor, breathing raggedly. His protective instincts for submissives kicked in, helping him overcome the peripheral effect of the command.

He crouched, nearly losing his balance. "Kiera?"

As a submissive, the pack medic had no chance of staying awake through that. She was lying on the floor next to Edgar, who had slumped against the side of the bed.

Nathan touched Kiera's neck, where a ring of bruises was blooming. He swore under his breath as the medic flinched in her sleep.

Douglas knelt next to him, placing his fingers on her neck. Heat suffused him and then left, drawn out like a thread. The chief was drawing on the pack magic. The pained, pinched expression on Kiera's face eased.

Douglas stood, picking the medic up in his arms.

Nathan got to his feet unsteadily. "Will she be okay?" he rasped. His head was spinning.

"Yes," Douglas confirmed. "There was some crushing damage, but it was surface level—she fought him."

But a small submissive female was nowhere near as strong as a dominant as big or as muscular as Lee, even bedbound.

Nathan frowned, his heart heavy as he looked at his friend. "What the hell happened? Did...did Lee come back wrong?"

The chief shook his head. "He still feels like pack and responded to my command, but I don't know what happened."

He stared at Lee, half-expecting him to jump up from the bed, claws out. "Maybe he still thought he was in battle, taking fire. His last memory would be of being in the middle of the ambush, right?"

Douglas lifted a shoulder, not saying what they both thought. Smell was a wolf's primary defensive weapon. Lee should have smelled Kiera and recognized her as pack. He should have known from the scents around him that he was in the hospital. Unless that part of his brain was off for some reason.

"A dying wolf's survival instinct is too strong. Unfortunately, Kiera was in the wrong place at the wrong time." He lifted the medic's body a bit higher, carrying her slight weight effortlessly. "However, we won't take any chances."

"Are we going to restrain him?" Steel chains with a high silver content were the best way to restrain a wolf of Lee's size and strength. But even if they used leather padding to protect his skin, being that close to that much silver would be draining. It would weaken Lee right when he needed his strength to heal.

But Douglas had something else in mind. "I'll stay with him for as long as I can. If he doesn't wake before I'm called away, I'll have two other strong wolves take my place. We won't be leaving any of the medical staff to handle him on their own."

Relaxing, he nodded. Douglas was the one wolf who wouldn't need backup to handle a maddened wolf. Next to him in dominance, his children Connell or Mara might also be able to watch over Lee without risk.

"I'll be happy to take one of those shifts," he offered.

Douglas murmured his agreement as Kiera began to stir in his arms.

"You're sure she's all right?" It was unwise to second guess the chief, but it slipped out in his concern. But under the circumstances, Douglas wasn't offended.

"She will be fine. But we should take her out of here before she regains consciousness completely," he said, handing her over.

Cradling Kiera in his arms, Nathan went out to find an empty hospital bed where the medic could recover.

CHAPTER FORTY-THREE

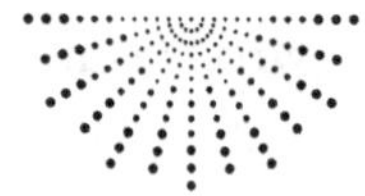

Two Months Later

What kind of witch do you want to be?

Meghan had asked herself that question at least one hundred times since her conversation with Logan. But she was no closer to finding the answer when Derrick convinced her to go for a long walk in the woods.

But he wouldn't leave until she allowed him to bundle her up in the thick new coat he'd bought her. "You know this is suitable for arctic temperatures," she teased as he fastened the zipper.

Meghan was also wearing new fleece-lined pants and boots lined in fur because according to her well-meaning mate, she was never allowed to feel cold again. No, her new fate was to be sweltering under her clothes whenever the thermometer dropped.

"Humor me." Derrick grinned and bent to retie the laces on her boot.

"I always do. But you know that's just going to make it harder to take them off me when you inevitably get lustful mid-hike."

Her werewolf's penchant for making love outdoors had taken a little bit of getting used to, but Meghan liked to think she had risen to the occasion. Derrick certainly had. Many, many times.

"Don't give me any ideas," her mate admonished. "It's gotten far too cold for outdoor naked time shenanigans."

"If you say so," she said, smiling at him suggestively as she took his offered hand.

But even she had to admit that there was a bite in the air when she stepped outside. It was late September, and fall had finally arrived, turning over so quickly there were already leaves on the ground.

"I can't believe it was in the nineties just a few weeks ago," she said, marveling at the trees near the Haunted Hollow, where they ended up. Many of the species around the lake were evergreens, pines and the like. But the ground in the Hollow was thick with aspens and a tree called a black tupelo that possessed leaves that were turning a spectacular purple or orange with hints of yellow.

"I sometimes think my grandfather planted these trees here just for the leaves."

"He planted them?"

"Yeah. He brought the seeds from Maine, where the pack settled briefly before continuing west."

Meghan's lips parted thoughtfully. "Then you have a special connection to this place?"

Derrick lifted a shoulder, examining his surroundings. "I suppose you could say that."

"Hmm." Meghan closed her eyes, spinning in a circle. She opened them, suddenly excited. "I can feel it, you know—the trees."

"What exactly do you sense?"

"Their energy. It's changing, going from a small flame to a fire that is banked."

His chin lifted. "You feel their life force, for lack of a better term. It's fainter now because the trees are preparing to go dormant for winter."

"Yes." She spun on her heel again, feeling the tree's waning energy swirling around her. It was almost visible to her naked eye if she squinted and twirled fast enough.

Meghan stopped short, as a major realization hit, along with a solution to the problem that had plagued her entire life.

"That's it! That's what I should do."

She ran up to Derrick and clutched his arm. "I'm going to be a green witch."

Her nonplussed mate stared down at her. "You mean green like these trees? You're not going into solar energy production, right?"

She pinched his butt. "No silly. I'm going to grow things."

"I hate to break it to you, but we already have a florist in town, and it's not big enough to sustain two such businesses."

"That's not what I mean. Logan asked me to think about what kind of witch I wanted to be. Plants have been responding to me all along—without spells. I never really thought about it much. The time-traveling tended to overshadow it."

She tapped her finger to her lip. "Do you remember when Logan's sister Gia came with her mate Salvador?"

The male witch was a healer. He'd done a few rituals to help speed Leeland McGill's healing. Salvador had confided those may have been redundant by that point. "His shifter healing is doing more to help him than anything I could do," he'd confided.

The healer hadn't had an explanation for Leeland's continued difficulty in staying conscious for long periods, other than to say coming back from the dead took time.

He never explained the comment.

"Salvador had a lot of interesting ingredients in his *curandero* bag," she said, managing not to mangle the word this time around—her tongue wasn't a flexible one. "Many were dried or fresh plants he used magic to preserve. He mentioned having difficulty sourcing some of the rarer plants and mosses."

"Ah," he said, catching on. "So, you are thinking of setting up a little farm, specifically for magical plants."

"Mushrooms too. And I don't want to restrict myself to spell ingredients. There are many medically beneficial plants and fungi.

Some tasty ones too," she said thinking of the dried candy cap mushrooms Gia had given her as a gift.

The interesting mushrooms smelled of maple syrup. Meghan planned on baking dessert bars with them.

Derrick was contemplative, then his enthusiasm warmed his expression. "That sounds cool actually. You could open a place on Main street. Part specialty grocer, part apothecary shop."

Meghan hugged him, pleased that he understood her so well. They stayed in that embrace for a few minutes, while the seed of an idea took shape in her mind.

"Derrick...I have a confession to make. I opened a window yesterday."

He grabbed her arm, jerking his head back. "You did what?"

"It wasn't a full bubble—just a small window."

"But why?" All mirth was gone. He held her shoulders, his grip just shy of tight.

"I just had a feeling that I should. But I didn't go through. I don't think I can. It was actually very difficult. Sluggish even. I felt rooted here. So I only looked." She bit her lip, deciding not to tell him the full truth, only what mattered most.

"I saw what happened to the cubs...their mother is dead."

Derrick sucked in a breath. "And their father?"

She walked into his arms. They closed around her unquestioningly.

"He wasn't around. But the mother, she had been part of this group. I think it started as a commune. But it changed, swiftly becoming more restrictive. Fundamentalist. There was a lot of talk of evil and sin."

He grew very still. "It wasn't a shifter community, was it?"

She shook her head. "Completely human. Except for the cubs."

"So the humans branded the cubs as evil because they could shift." His face darkened, but there was no question in his voice.

Derrick knew how groups like that functioned. Hate was their purpose and their fuel. It needed a target. Anything that was different from them would do.

"Why didn't their mother take them out of there?"

Meghan sighed. "I think she was afraid. She didn't appear to have anywhere else to go. And she wasn't a shifter herself. That much I saw. After she was dead one or more members of the sect must have taken the kids into the woods."

She also didn't know how the woman had died—if the community had killed her for bringing something they saw as evil in the world, or if it had been natural causes.

His face was hard. "I want a name."

"I would have to open another window to see. And I mentioned that it was difficult. More than it's ever been before. I think the ability will go dormant soon. Maybe permanently. Logan suggested that might be the case once I was anchored."

"Oh." He grew quiet, the conflict clear on his face. On the one hand, he wanted vengeance for those poor kids. They'd come so close to dying out there in the woods, abandoned and alone. But he would never risk her or want her harmed in any way.

Meghan wrapped her arms around his waist. "Before it does disappear, I think we need to open another one, but not to deal with those assholes. The cubs are safe now. Better than that, they are *loved*."

Derrick made a rumbling sound in his throat, but he didn't argue with her. She doubted that would be the end of this conversation, but for the time being there was something else she needed to discuss with him.

"I have been thinking of the shadow man," she began.

Derrick closed his eyes, his hold tightening reflexively. Meghan touched his face, forcing him to see her. "I know he can't get me here, but he's still out there doing damage to the fabric of the universe."

She stepped away from him to get a little space. It was easier to discuss this when Derrick wasn't touching her. "I think I should open another door while I still have the ability. I can't cross the threshold anymore, but he can."

"And you want to bring him *here?*" Derrick's skepticism and obvious aversion to the idea was enough to fill her with anxiety, but she felt strongly about this.

Meghan also realized that even though her wolf was a dominant and she wasn't, there were times when she had to stand her ground. "If we don't stop *his* traveling, he's going to keep killing people."

Derrick didn't like it, but when he heard her plan he reluctantly agreed. "Before you do anything I hope you consult Logan and her sisters—all of them."

"Don't worry. I plan on using every resource at my disposal."

He nodded once. Meghan waited until he turned away to let her worries about doing what she had to do surface on her face.

She knew Derrick had great faith in the Elemental's knowledge and power, but as Logan had explained to her more than once this was *her* magic. And the outcome of the plan would fall solely on her slim shoulders.

CHAPTER FORTY-FOUR

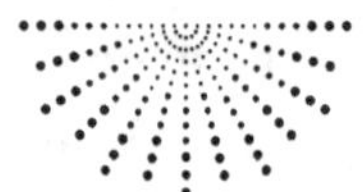

It took a week to finalize the plan to trap the shadow man. Not the actual trapping part. Logan and her sisters agreed that the ritual she had come up with had the best chance of success. The part that took weeks was deciding on what do to if it failed. They needed a way to boot the shadow man out of their world—perhaps banish him to an unpopulated dimension.

But that would be a last resort.

The day of the ritual began with a surprise snowfall. It only lasted a few hours, but it left a layer of fresh white powder several inches thick. Meghan was afraid they would have to cancel, but Logan said it wouldn't make any difference.

"It either works or it doesn't. As long as snow isn't falling and obscuring your vision, it shouldn't make a difference."

But that wasn't good enough for Derrick. He rounded up a group of wolves. Armed with snow shovels, they cleared the snow from the Haunted Hollow, their chosen spot to conduct the rite.

The wolves stayed for the ritual too, over her objections. She was worried they would be cannon fodder if she failed. But Douglas had insisted. They had needed his permission to conduct the rite in his territory. He had chosen the Hollow, saying she had left her mark on it already. According to him, one more grisly addition wouldn't hurt.

Douglas stayed as well, along with Connell, who would never let his deadly mate face danger alone despite her prowess and skill.

Meghan waited for the stars to start shining overhead. Her circle—a very large one covering a quarter of the clearing—was done, and her primary ingredient was primed.

It took a great deal of effort, but she opened a window, choosing the time and place by instinct. But Meghan didn't stop there. Working by feel she opened another window on the other side of the first one, leading to another place, and then another and another, a corridor of time and space contained in one tiny corner of the woods.

Then she began to chant the script Logan had helped her write. Meghan half-suspected the words were meaningless. All that mattered was letting her voice be heard, a lure cast into the darkness, echoing across multiple realities.

Less than an hour passed when she felt him, a tug on a fishing line made of magic and her will.

Silence claimed the clearing. Her audience, each one a deadly predator in their own right waited, their tension thickening the air. Most of the wolves had shifted, although a few remained human with clawed hands, their ever-present weapon ready to do battle.

Derrick was one of these. He wanted to make sure she could understand him if things went to hell and their mating bond didn't allow them to speak mind to mind. Only emotion was transmitted, but that was becoming clearer every day.

Right now, Derrick was feeling her apprehension, and it was putting him on edge. Fortunately, he was too disciplined to move or break the border of the circle—not even when the shadow man roared out of the doorway, a creature of sound and fury and death.

Meghan could hear Derrick snarl, but she kept her eyes on the shadow man. *"Stop."*

But he ignored her. *"Arrêt!"*

The French word came out of nowhere, but this time the creature hesitated. Lifting her arms, Meghan presented the dark-skinned seed cradled in her palms.

It was time.

She whispered and pushed energy into the seed, which sprouted immediately. The shiny black coat fell away as a delicate green shoot extended, growing longer and thicker until it branched several times.

There was no response from the shadow man, his roiling black cloud hovering a couple of yards away.

"Go," Meghan urged, sending the delicate tendrils into the cloud. They glowed a bright green that began to luminesce as she pushed the cells to divide and meld with the darkness.

Logan had said blood was the most powerful thing, making tree sap a poor substitute. But the magic she kindled now would work if the shadow man cooperated.

Meghan had bet everything that there was a kernel of awareness left, an echo of the brilliant man who, wrong or right, had created her. That man had never intended to *be* death, cursed to wander without rest for all eternity.

Her bet paid off.

The shadow opened himself up, embracing the magic-infused plant cells filled with her unique energy. He quieted as they absorbed him, becoming one.

The shoot sprouted small branches that thickened, as well as hair lengthening into a mass of brown fibrous strands at the base. These settled on the ground, penetrating, and taking root.

The face of the shadow man was the last to be absorbed, leaving an echo of his narrow visage imprinted on the trunk. But it was a ghost of an image that soon blended with bark.

And still, Meghan continued to send her energy running out of her like a thread. Her vision began to darken, but she kept pushing.

When it was over, a fifteen-foot tree stood in the middle of the clearing. It was a little twisted and gnarled, more like a bonsai version than a mid-sized tree of the species, but it looked healthy nonetheless, if a little warped.

Meghan shuddered, turning to tell everyone it was over. But her vision blurred, and she began to fall, her body nearly drained dry.

She never hit the ground. Derrick caught her, cradling her to him. "I was right," she told him.

His smile melted whatever was left of her stamina. "Won't be the last time."

Logan appeared at his side with Connell and the chief. "I'm going to call that a succ—what the hell is that?"

Meghan blinked, following her gaze.

A single bud had appeared at the end of a branch, directly over her head. White petals unfurled, lengthening. The flower bloomed for only a moment before the petals fell one by one. The base of the bed began to swell until it was a bulbous fruit, shiny and red.

"An apple?" The words were no sooner out of her mouth than the fruit finished ripening.

It fell.

She caught it reflexively and stared, almost mesmerized by its glossy surface.

A suspicion formed in her mind. Meghan lifted the apple, considering the strange, surprising gift.

"Meg—"

She lifted the apple and opened her mouth. Derrick would have had to drop it to stop her.

"No! *Don't.*" The admonishment came from several mouths. But it was too late. She had bitten into the flesh.

Connell, Logan, and Douglas all voiced their objections, but Meghan covered her ears as Derrick grabbed the remains of the apple and threw it far across the field.

Ignoring the shouts, Meghan swallowed the small piece whole. Image after image flooded her mind.

"What the hell are you doing?" Derrick yelled. "It could be poisoned! Haven't you read Snow White?"

"Snow what?" she asked, pushing away to get to her feet unsteadily. "But no—it wasn't poisoned."

However, the whole truth was too much for her exhausted brain. Hanging her head, she began to cry.

"Then what's wrong?" Derrick asked. "What did the damn thing do to you?"

"Knowledge," she whispered. "I'm crying because the apple was filled with knowledge."

You could hear a pin drop.

"This is all too fucking biblical for me," Connell muttered.

"That's probably why," Logan said. "Whatever spark of human intelligence that was left in the tree must have realized that story would be familiar, so it put whatever message it wanted to pass on into the fruit."

Stepping closer, she put her hand on Meghan's chin, turning it this way and that as she peered into her face. Meghan twitched when she pulled her lower eyelid down.

"You seem okay." Logan looked over Meghan's head to address her mate. "But keep an eye on her."

"Wait—don't skip ahead," Connell protested. "What did the tree say?"

"A lot." Meghan bit her lip, overwhelmed at the thought of sharing.

"The pack's not in danger, are they?" Derrick asked. "There's no more creatures like him waiting in the wings?"

"No, it was nothing like that." Meghan turned to the chief. "It was about my past—well, in your case the distant future. I don't think any threat was made. It was more of an explanation."

That was the most she could say until she processed that stream of memory.

"Is the tree sentient?" the chief asked, his face still dark with suspicion.

"No, I don't think so."

"I don't feel anything from it," Logan said when Douglas turned to her for confirmation.

The chief scowled, pointing at the tree. "Well, if it keeps sprouting psychedelic fruit or starts to eat people like an oversized Venus flytrap we're burning it down."

"I understand." But she didn't think that was going to be an issue.

True, she was exhausted, and her senses were dull, but right now all she felt was peace. *Finally.*

She didn't tell anyone what she learned until very late that night.

"He loved me," she told Derrick. "That's what he wanted me to know."

Her mate stilled. "Did he?"

"Not like you do. But he felt responsible for me. Felt pride too."

"So, the asshole felt fatherly towards you?"

"I wouldn't go that far. It was more like pride in *his* accomplishment. He saw me as a successful experiment, up until the end."

Derrick sidled closer, running a hand through her hair. "Some parents do see their kids that way—as extensions of themselves. Not the healthiest of relationships but unfortunately not uncommon either."

"That makes sense. Because what he called love was certainly not that. But his regret, that was real."

She inched closer. Derrick obligingly wrapped her in his arms, bolstering her so she could finish.

"The woman who I thought was my mother, her name was Selena. And she was on board with everything they did to me—up to a point. Then they started to argue about how far he should go. She wanted to take me out of there, to leave the city, but he had already started his grand experiment. Primed me, as it were. And he didn't inform her it was irreversible. I think he was ashamed. He couldn't bring himself to tell her there was no going back. She died not knowing the truth."

Derrick held her very close. "Then it began—my falling through time, leaving him unable to reverse what he'd done. The guilt ate him alive."

"That explains why he decided to follow you. It was to bring you back, not harvest the power in your cells," he said when her expression twisted. "Sorry I assumed the worst about him."

"That's understandable under the circumstances."

Meghan pressed her face against his chest. "I think he lost his mind after that. Whatever he did to himself to follow me never had a prayer of working. He wasn't made to accommodate that magic. Not like I was. And even I didn't do it as designed."

"Which is why he became the shadow man, his touch deadly…"

She nodded, rubbing her cheek over his heartbeat. "But it's over now. I can feel it. And yet, I can't believe it. I'm not sure I ever will."

Derrick rolled suddenly, landing "Give me a little time. Everything you've ever wanted to do, and a lot of things you don't *know* you want to do—I'm going to make them happen."

Meghan squeezed him. "What I want most is to stay in one place for a good long while. With you."

"No honeymoon out of town?"

"No trips out of bed if we can help it."

He laughed. "Well, I think I can talk Connell into covering for me for a while. How does a week in this house sound? We don't have to stir out of bed unless it's to accept grocery or take-out deliveries."

She pressed a kiss to his chest. "It sounds like heaven."

CHAPTER FORTY-FIVE

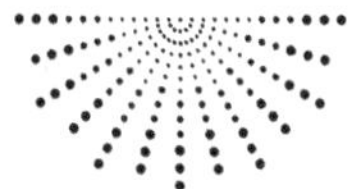

The locker room was quiet with all the nurses on the floor. Kiera pulled on her white coat in preparation for doing her rounds.

A couple of months had passed since Leeland McGill had opened his eyes and tried to choke the life out of her. Since then he'd been in and out of consciousness, rousing for a few minutes at a time.

The chief had ordered an around-the-clock rotation of alpha wolves to sit with him when he wasn't able to do it himself. It was very uncomfortable having so many dominants around her workplace and in her space, but not enough to complain. Kiera was grateful for their presence. She didn't want a repeat experience.

Sheldon, the clinic administrator had tried to assign another doctor to work with Leeland McGill exclusively, but Kiera nixed that in the bud despite the trauma and its lasting evidence.

Her throat was still a bit sensitive despite the chief's intervention. But the marks on her skin were gone. Only the memory of the bruises remained thanks to pack magic.

With the chief's help, she was a conduit of that magic. She used it to help speed the recovery of certain injuries. But the energy could do wondrous things beyond that.

It could give a wolf in trouble energy or a speed boost he or she could use in battle or to fight off the elements in a sudden snowstorm. The energy could bind wolves as well, informing them where other pack mates were during high-stress situations, another mechanism that gave them an edge when facing an adversary.

Compared to those things, it seemed selfish to ask for more to get rid of her last barely-there bruises. But the chief has insisted. He hadn't wanted her to look at them and remember the trauma. The residual tenderness was likely psychosomatic.

But she was prepared for this sort of thing. There were known drawbacks to being a submissive and a doctor. Larger, stronger wolves sometimes lost control when they were sick or injured. Her mentors had warned her to be careful repeatedly during her training. And with good reason.

Typically, being a submissive offered a thick layer of protection. Hurting a sub went against a dominant's strongest instincts. Only the maddest of rogues attacked one, their reasoning burned away by bloodlust. Most wolves were able to control their beast, but rogues had given themselves over to the wildest, most feral, aspect of their beasts.

Which made what happened with Leeland McGill truly frightening. She told herself that his reaction had been due to the fact he'd been brought back from an ambush where he'd been minutes from dying.

It wasn't because he'd come back without the capacity to reason.

But she couldn't help but think about that moment where he'd wrapped his hands around her neck. Kiera was strong for a woman her size, but only compared to a human. Leeland could have really hurt her...maybe even killed her.

Stop thinking about it.

Nathan had saved her. Well, he had with Douglas's help. As for today, the protection detail was here and they were doing their job. Everything was going to be fine. There was absolutely no reason for Kiera to get into her car and drive home right now, calling in sick.

She would never leave the medical team short-staffed.

But Kiera couldn't shake the feeling that something was going to happen. Her paranoia accompanied her on rounds. But Leeland was fine. She checked on him twice. Once in the morning and again after lunch.

So when four o'clock rolled around, she heaved a sigh of relief, chalking it up as a good day. She put her white coat in the laundry basket, grabbed her small purse out of her locker before closing it.

Kiera spun on her heel and screamed at the apparition blocking the door.

"*Lee*," she gasped, flattening herself against the lockers.

He stared at her, blinking bright clear eyes at her. *Wait.* Had his eyes always been that same icy shade of blue?

Swallowing hard, Kiera straightened up, but she didn't step any closer.

"Hi Leeland," she said brightly, her voice breaking despite her best efforts to sound normal. She cleared her throat with effort, painfully aware she sounded as if she were strangling. "H-how long have you been up? Do you need help getting back to bed?"

He just stood there. Then Lee looked down at his hands, staring at them as if they belonged to somebody else.

"I'm sorry." The deep voice vibrated in her ears, buzzing down her spine. It sounded like he'd been chewing gravel—as if he hadn't spoken in years.

He hadn't, but his body didn't know that. To his body only a few months had passed.

Remember your training. "What are you sorry for?" she squeaked. When in doubt it was best to engage a dangerous predator like him in conversation, to remind him that she was a person.

He held up his hands. "It's like I can still smell you on them," he said, the tendons of his neck standing out starkly.

Leeland took a step closer. Kiera flattened herself against the lockers, but he kept coming.

She tried not to panic, but her throat seemed to swell. So much she couldn't even scream.

Then Leeland reached out to touch her neck, a gossamer-light stroke. "I hurt you, and I'm sorry."

"*Oh*."

Kiera forced her features to relax but found it difficult to get her pulse to slow. Not with a dominant who'd nearly strangled her to death so close. "You had a rough awakening, b-but there's no harm done. It's okay."

"No, it's not," he barked with sudden sharpness.

Startled, Kiera gasped, flinching and putting up her hands to protect herself.

"No—I didn't mean that." Shame narrowed Leeland's full lips into a grim line, and he took one big step back. "I'm *sorry*. I was trying to say there is no excuse for what I did."

Kiera waited for her heart to stop racing before replying, else he would know any absolution she could give him was fake.

"You came to believing you were in the middle of a firefight. It's only natural that you would try to defend yourself. Do you want me to help you back to bed?"

Leeland's gaze grew unfocused. He stood there glassy-eyed, almost as if he was thinking too hard or listening to something else. He had made great progress thanks to continued visits from the chief, but he still had a long way to go before he was ready to be up and about like this.

Leeland didn't answer her question. After a long, sweaty moment, he refocused on her and frowned. "Your hair is longer."

Kiera's hand flew up to the thick black locks she'd pulled back in a no-nonsense ponytail. When it was loose, her hair came down a few inches past her shoulders. But when Leeland had died, she had worn it in a short and efficient bob. The difference was too much for a few months' growth.

Oh god. Kiera could feel her facial muscles slacken. Did Leeland not know? About Meghan and the trip through time?

"Don't be scared," he said in a strangely flat tone. A hint of mocking amusement crept into his expression. "You don't need to break the bad news. Douglas told me I died. I know it's years later."

Leeland had read her expression and had correctly deciphered the look on her face.

He drew himself up straight, even though she knew it must have pulled at his stitches.

"I know I'm not supposed to be here. I'm meant to be in the ground."

Kiera wracked her brain for the right words to say, but nothing came. They stood inches apart, his regret a thick perfume between them in complete silence.

Guilt began to nibble at her conscience. This was normally the point where she would hug a packmate in pain or offer physical comfort, but Kiera couldn't take the small step forward necessary to do it.

The door banged open with a crash, and someone large burst inside, running straight into the break room table.

Between one heartbeat and the next Kiera found herself pushed against the lockers once more, this time with Leeland's back pressed against her chest.

He was shielding her body with his own.

"Sorry," Nathan apologized, holding up a hand. He straightened, wincing. He'd run in pell-mell and lost control on the freshly waxed linoleum floor.

"Hey buddy," he said, holding up his hands, speaking to Lee as if he were a child. "I just got back from the bathroom, and you were gone."

He looked behind Lee to catch Kiera's eye. "Sorry, I thought Douglas was still with him. Lee woke up a few hours ago and stayed awake, long enough for the chief to talk with him."

Nathan refocused on Leeland when her patient remained silent, his arms behind him to touch her just above her waist.

"Connell is on his way. Why don't we go wait for him in your room? I can order some burgers from Jeannie's and have him pick them up on the way. I know you must be starving."

His tone was light but forced. It was obvious all Nathan wanted to do was get him away from her.

Leeland's pain was sudden and sharp. "I came to apologize," he rasped.

"He did." Kiera put her hand on Leeland's arm, peeking around his bulk to reassure Nathan. "He came to say he was sorry for what happened. We're good now."

Nathan's features visibly relaxed, but his posture was still that of a man facing off with a wild beast. Lee's scent changed again like quicksilver. He was still hurt, but there was a thread of anger in there now too.

"That's great…really great. So how do burgers sound?"

The answer was a long time coming. "Not as good as a steak sandwich."

Nathan grinned, his eyes glistening with tears that seemed to surprise him. "I'll put the order in now," he said.

Still smiling brilliantly, he turned to her. "Do you want to join us, Kiera?"

"No, thanks. I have plans." It wasn't a lie. She was supposed to have a video-chat dinner with her mother. "But I think I should give Leeland another once over before I go."

Nudging with gentle hands, she pushed Leeland into a chair while Nathan retreated to the hall to make his call. She could smell Nate's relief, but tellingly he left the door open.

Slipping into doctor mode took a little effort. She was still a little anxious to be so close to Leeland but determined not to let it show. Removing her stethoscope from her locker, she put it on and listened to his heart, before proceeding to check all his vitals.

Kiera kept her touch sure and determined, with no hint of reluctance or hesitation. Leeland sat still throughout the examination, his face nearly expressionless. But those icy blue irises were watchful and completely focused on her.

His eyes used to be brown.

And that wasn't the only difference. His silence felt off. It was quite a change from the garrulous and easy-going wolf everyone remembered.

She stayed with Leeland and Nathan until Connell arrived, holding two big paper bags that smelled so good her mouth watered.

It was the first time she'd seen any emotion from Leeland since waking.

Apprehension and confusion warred each other on his face, but in the end relief won. Then Connell dropped the bags on the table, and poignant tension broke as the two dominants embraced each other.

Aware she was witnessing a private moment among brothers in arms, Kiera ducked out of the room.

"Are you sure you don't want to join us?" Nathan asked, following her out. "Jeannie found out Lee was awake. She sent enough of his favorite steak sandwiches to feed the entire hospital."

But Kiera was done in, her emotions like a wet towel that had been wrung out too tight. "I need to get home. My mom is going to call in less than an hour. She'll be happy to hear that Lee is awake."

"All right," Nathan relented with a smile. "Tell your mom I said hi."

"Will do."

But Nathan didn't excuse himself. Giving Connell and Lee some private time, he offered to walk her out to her car, making small talk the entire way. Then he embraced her—a sneaky dominant wolf pretext to check her for injuries.

"That's enough, you," she chided, laughing.

Normally she would have been thrilled to get a hug from Nate. More than thrilled. But she was still a doctor, and extra coddling was a bad precedent to set. Especially when it was *this* dominant doing the touching, the danger of her arousal becoming noticeable too much of a threat.

That and Kiera didn't need the other dominants checking up on her ten times a day, especially not at the hospital. They would just get underfoot, making a muck of things.

She told Nathan as much, to his great amusement. "All right, I'll get out of your hair. But if you need to talk about anything, call me."

Kiera ducked her head to hide her blush. "Will do," she said lightly.

But she needn't have worried. Nathan was already jogging away.

Her eyes followed him to the door. Once he was inside, her gaze drifted up to the third-floor window.

Lee was standing there in the window of the recovery suite, staring down at her.

Kiera raised a tentative hand, waving to him. But after a very long minute he withdrew, moving away from the window.

He did not wave back.

EPILOGUE

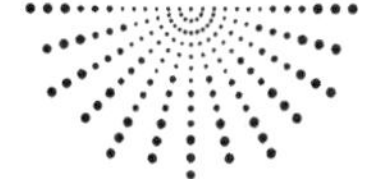

Five years later

The tell-tale meow was coming from under the picnic table. Crouching down Derrick fished out Molly. The leopard cub was over for lunch with her brother, ostensibly to help Meghan transfer her rare herb seedlings to bigger pots. But that was just an excuse to pick over the fruit bushes that produced fat berries year-round in his mate's complex of greenhouses.

Over the years he'd built three for her, one for flowers and herbs, one for fruit and vegetables, and a smaller one dedicated to rare cultivars, medicinal plants, and hybrid plants she was developing.

Meghan had become the go-to source for spell ingredients in the states. Her work was exclusive and very much in demand—and for that reason highly vetted. Neither Douglas nor Logan wanted her ingredients going to the wrong kind of witch. So, Derrick vetted her client roster religiously.

Meghan had a waitlist a mile long, but she preferred to keep her operation small so she could handle the bulk of the work on her own, with only a few volunteers.

Naturally, Derrick was one of these helping hands. They also corralled some of the middle-grade kids to help during peak harvest and drying times. The school gave them extra credit for that, so some of the biggest troublemakers ended up coming out multiple times a week. But Meghan didn't mind the rambunctious crowd.

Even the worst hard cases—teenagers struggling with their wolves—bent over backward to follow her sweetly-voiced requests. She read as a submissive to them, and even their hormone-bombarded wolves had the instinct to protect her. Not that it was an issue with Derrick around. None would dare cross him.

"Go find your brother and wash up so we can eat," he told the now nine-year-old.

Meghan had been busy in the greenhouse, working on a tricky moss cultivar, so he'd ordered sandwiches from Jeannie's for the lot.

"Do you seriously think we're going to finish all of these?" his mate asked, coming out of the greenhouse to find one of their picnic tables piled high with paper-wrapped bundles and drinks.

"I may have overdone it on the order," he admitted with a sheepish grin. "I should never order hungry. But don't worry. Most of these reheat well. I got a little bit of everything."

"Doesn't that include a steak and guacamole torta?" she asked hopefully.

"I got three to be safe." Derrick put his hands on her burgeoning stomach. "I know the twins make you twice as hungry. The third is for when you get a midnight craving."

Those were common now that she'd hit her sixth month of pregnancy. And the pair of wolves currently taking up residence atop her bladder *loved* their protein when it was slathered in avocado.

"Perfect." Meghan pulled him down for a kiss, setting the new blue hoodie he'd bought her on the picnic bench. She had at least ten at this point in different shades, but he had bought her this one recently because it reminded him of the one she'd been wearing when he'd first seen her.

Meghan lingered in his arms, soaking in his warmth and scent. "Mmm," she hummed before pushing away without obvious reluctance.

He cupped her cheek and neck. "When are the kids leaving?" he asked in a tone full of suggestion.

She tsked and wagged her finger at him. "Not till four o'clock when Diya comes to get them. So don't make them feel like they have to rush along."

"They're shifters with two moms hot for each other," he laughed. "They get it."

That got him a smile, but Meghan straightened suddenly, an odd look on her face.

"Is something wrong?"

Her eyes went from the table to the trees at the edge of the clearing and back. "No, my love. I just forgot something."

Clearing her throat, she excused herself, going inside the house. "Be right back," she called over her shoulder. "I should make sure the kids wash well since we're eating with our hands."

"Okay," he said, watching her go with a puckered brow. Meghan used many endearments but "my love" wasn't as common as some others.

Shrugging it off, he went to the kitchen to grab napkins and plates. He was setting the table when the skin on the back of his neck prickled.

Alert but not too concerned, he turned around, expecting one of the pack in wolf form had swung by while out on a run. Their house was a hub, the busiest one after the chief's.

But there was no one behind him. Given the way the wind was blowing, he would have caught a scent by now. Derrick shrugged it off. Then he caught a blur of movement.

Meghan stumbled onto the lawn.

He almost cried out, dismayed to see her traveling again. Belatedly, he noticed the Meghan in front of him was not pregnant. She was also rail-thin and appeared ten years younger than the woman in his house.

Teenage Meghan blinked, cupping her head as if it hurt.

The hot streak of anxiety and protectiveness nearly cut him down at the knees.

Derrick had to help her, but this girl didn't know him from Adam. He almost called out for the adult Meghan when he realized this was the moment *she* had met him.

You know what to do. Except he didn't. He had no clue.

On impulse, Derrick grabbed a sandwich and very quietly walked toward her. Teenage Meghan didn't notice him until he was six feet away.

When she did her eyes flared wide, the fear in them a tiny dagger to his heart. She took a step back, then another.

Derrick hurriedly put up his hands. "It's okay, Meghan. I know who you are."

Her lips parted, but she stopped edging away.

For a long moment, he just stared at her. Derrick's eyes stung, a wealth of emotion filling his chest.

"I know it's hard to believe, but everything is going to be all right."

A watchful silence was her only answer.

He took a deep breath, hoping he was doing the right thing. "That probably sounds like a lie or fake sympathy. Something you say to try and make someone feel better about their situation. But in this case, it *is* true. You are going to be okay. You're going to be safe. And you're going to be happy."

Meghan trembled, staring at him with crystalline eyes that began to fill with tears.

Chancing it, he walked forward, putting a hand on her upper arm. "I know it's hard and that you're very tired. But it's not going to be too much longer. A couple of years for you."

A thready whisper. "How do you know?"

He smiled down at her, trying to convey everything she would mean to him in a single glance. "How do you think?"

She sucked in a lungful of air and nodded.

Derrick hated what he had to do next. "I don't want you to go, but this isn't your stopping place. Not yet. But it exists. You need to come find me. I'll be a few years younger than I am now."

He pointed to his hair, which was a touch shorter than it had been when they met, describing the time and place Meghan had first seen him.

"You'll know me, but I won't know you. Don't let that scare you," he urged. "Because the first time I meet you, you'll know you are in the right place."

Meghan wiped her shaky hands on her long-sleeved shirt—a Henley she must have picked up at a secondhand store.

Her expression was half-disbelief, half-hope. It tore him to shreds, but he hid that, giving her a bracing smile.

"The first time I meet you will be the beginning of the end of your traveling. I *promise*. Look for me in Lake Veris."

"Lake Veris?" she echoed.

"Yes. We're a shifter town by the way. Wolves. Don't be afraid of that either. Most of the shifters you meet would rather slit their own throats than hurt someone like you. But stay away from lone wolves— just in case," he added, unable to stop himself. "But the pack is your haven."

The impulse to wrap her in blankets and take her inside was over-whelming, but he couldn't do that. To have the happy life she deserved, he had to let her go.

She seemed to understand that better than him. "I should leave," she said, looking around her as if sensing something.

It could have been a bubble or the shadow man currently losing his leaves in the Haunted Hollow.

"I know," he said, his voice scratchy. Eyes blurring, Derrick thrust the sandwich into her hand. "Here, take this. It's from Jeannie's Diner. You like it there."

Her head drew back, blinking at that information. "Okay," she said quietly, hugging the warm sandwich to her chest.

She began to turn away.

"*Wait.*" He hustled back to the picnic table, snatching the blue sweatshirt. Running back so fast he made her blink, he handed it to her. "I know it gets cold on the roads you travel."

That was when her tears escaped. She looked at him again, this time with real, unadulterated hope.

Then she gave him a tiny wave and walked away, disappearing before reaching the tree line.

Derrick staggered back to the picnic table. He sat there, silently getting his bearings.

The kids ran out with childish shouts, racing each other and rifling through their food choices till they found the sandwiches they wanted. Meghan followed shortly afterward, walking slowly. Tellingly, she was holding another sweater.

He looked up at her, trying to tell her with his eyes that he was so fucking grateful for her, because right then he couldn't speak.

She gave him a watery smile. "I didn't know it would be today," she whispered.

The children, occupied with their food, appeared to be ignoring the grown-up conversation. Or so he thought.

"I told them to give you a minute," Meghan explained. "That an old friend was visiting you."

"Thanks," Derrick managed hoarsely. He cleared his throat. "When did you know?"

"Just a few minutes ago."

The corner of her mouth lifted. "In my memories of today, I always believed you were having a really good day…living your life in your comfortable home with your happy family."

She looked around the yard, at her greenhouses and the trees. "There were so many times since that I thought 'it's finally here,' the day we first meet, only to be wrong."

Meghan grinned suddenly, with tears in her eyes. "I guess that's the drawback to having a wonderful life. There have been so many truly great and wonderful days."

Damn, she really got him with those words, like an arrow in the heart.

Blinking hard, he nodded, reaching out to grasp her hand. "Well, I did promise you everything would be okay."

Her thumb caressed the top of his hand. "And you wouldn't be you if you didn't go above and beyond. As for those great days, let's keep them coming."

He looked at her naked emotion, all defenses down, letting her see everything that was in his heart. "They will. I promise."

The End

ABOUT THE AUTHOR

A 7-time Readers' Favorite Medal Winner. USA Today Bestselling Author. Mom to a half-feral princess. WOC. Former scientist. Recovering geek.

L.B. Gilbert is another name for USA Today Bestselling Author Lucy Leroux. She is an award-winning novelist who spent years getting degrees from the most prestigious universities in America, including a Ph.D. that she is not using at all. She moved to France for work and found love. Her family moved back to California a few years ago after a decade abroad.

Lucy has always enjoyed reading books as far from her reality as possible but eventually the voices in her head told her to write her own. So far the voices are enjoying them.

If you like a little more steam with your Fire, check out the author's award-winning Lucy Leroux titles, FREE to read on Kindle Unlimited

www.elementalauthor.com

or

www.authorlucyleroux.com

amazon.com/stores/L.B.-Gilbert/author/B015T01IVU

facebook.com/lucythenovelist

instagram.com/lucythenovelist

tiktok.com/@candycappublishing

bookbub.com/authors/lucy-leroux

www.ingramcontent.com/pod-product-compliance
Lightning Source LLC
Chambersburg PA
CBHW070616170726
48291CB00003B/777